THE CELL BLOCK PRESENTS...

THE MOBFATHER

STRAIGHT OUTTA BOMPTON

Published by: The Cell Block™

The Cell Block
PO BOX 1025
RANCHO CODOVA, CA 95741

IG @mikeenemigo
Facebook /thecellblockofficial
Website: thecellblock.net

Copyright © King Guru, 2024

Send comments, reviews, interview and business
inquiries to: info@thecellblock.net

CHAPTER ONE

Friday nights in Compton are always lit. In the late 1980's, the Hub City was literally on fire. The crack epidemic was in full swing. Murders were at an all-time high and gang violence mirrored that of the Vietnam War.

At that point in time, Compton, which was also called Bompton by the Pirus and Bloods who resided in the trenches, was a full-fledged working ghetto. The jobs that once attracted throngs of working-class families from places like Louisiana, Arkansas, Mississippi and Alabama were now obsolete. On paper, the country seemed to believe the Reagan administration had turned the economy around.

But that couldn't have been further from the truth. The economic stability in the Hub City revolved around, and depended on, bloody drug money.

Just like any other ghetto in America, resources were low in a place where the population density was high. Which meant, if you were from Compton, or anyplace remotely like it, you had to work a lot harder to get what you wanted in life.

Youth who had dreams of reaching the NBA or NFL limelight had to play stronger and quicker than their peers in different zip codes. Small business owners had to haggle harder while watching their investments closer than others. What it boiled down, to was anyone growing up in Compton, California in the late 1980's had to have a jagged edge, or they wouldn't survive.

The city of Compton didn't even have its own police force. Lack of funds amalgamated with a surplus of corruption ensured that. This left the job of policing the city to the openly racist Los Angeles Sheriff's Department. The overly militarized sheriff's department, with their battering rams and aggressive tactics, gave the Hub City the feeling of a militarized zone. If you were Black or Brown, dealing with 12 was akin to a Jewish person dealing with the Gestapo in Nazi Germany.

Marion Hughes Knight Jr. was born and bred in this hellish environment.

Sugar Bear, as his friends and family called him, had grown up in the 70s and 80s watching the world turn upside down right before his very own eyes. Having been raised in the Lueders Park area of Compton, he had a front-row seat to the evolution of the gang and drug epidemic of the times.

The hood Suge (shortened from Sugar Bear) came up in was controlled by a street gang called Lueders Park Bompton Piru. But don't get the terminology twisted. The word "controlled" is a term that's used by gang task forces and other law enforcement agencies with political agendas. To soldiers in the trenches, the "set" was a family. And their only mission was to protect and provide for one another.

Anyone who has ever spent any amount of time in Compton will tell you the crab-in-a-bucket mentality is very much real. Yet, in real life, people don't use claws to drag you down in an attempt to climb over you. In the real world, automatic assault rifles are used to separate the head from the body of the opposition. At least, that's the modus operandi in the trenches of Compton, California.

Survival of the fittest can be the difference between life and death. In a reality like that, it takes a certain type of individual to survive. And Sugar Bear was one of those people.

On this particular Friday evening, Suge was at his set's Mad Pad, a house where the whole neighborhood hung out. It was located on Bullis Avenue next to the set's most active apartment complex. Even though the night was in its infancy, it was a dark Autumn evening.

From the street, the dark-colored house was a Beehive of activity. The curb in front of it was crowded with several shiny Chevys, Buicks, and other cars along with Suge's extra-large, all-black K-5 Blazer. A few ex-convicts in red were on the porch smoking trees and drinking 40's. NWA's song "Gangsta Gangsta" spilled into the street from the inside of the house.

The vibe was bright red. It was the beginning of the weekend, so the party was just starting. Inside the Beehive was a house full of gang bangers, all repping a subset of Lueders Park Bompton Piru. They called themselves "The Mob" or "Mob Piru." For the most part, the hierarchy of the subset stopped at Suge. He had already proven to be a worthy leader of his clique of sliders, hustlers, fighters and killers. The outcome was the loyalty of a crew of battle tested street marines.

The music, just like the weed, was loud. Though the majority of the people there were all in the backyard, a boombox stationed on a lawn chair played Ice-T's song "Colors" while several pitbulls tied to the back fence barked at one another. A group of thugs between the ages of 13 to 25 gathered around the situation that was unfolding in the center of the yard. Two teens with their shirts off were squaring off, ready to exchange blows with one another.

Suge was in the mix of things like usual. Although he was standing outside of the main circle, with his circle within the circle, his watchful eyes were very much alert to the main event. At 6ft, 3 inches, and 300 pounds, he stood a little taller than the average person. Yet, his presence glowed brighter than his size. In a way, his swagger made him seem bigger than he really was, and in a world where aggressiveness was an attribute, this worked in his favor.

His bald head shun in the dim light of the backyard. His scruffy beard made him look a little older than the 20-something years he had already spent on this earth. And this also worked in his favor.

Aaron "Heron" Palmer stood at his right side. His best friend Heron was just as tall as Suge, but his physique was more cut and his skin was two shades darker. After just being released from serving three years in California Youth Authority, Heron had the size of a bodybuilder, and the mentality of a menace to society.

"Y'all know what it is!" Suge bellowed over the crowd. "Niggaz got problems, they squabble up! So what's takin' y'all so fuckin' long?"

As if on cue, the young bangers locked up, exchanging blow after blow with one another. The skirmish resembled a dog fight. The crowd cheered the fighters on like a main event in Vegas. Bobbing and weaving barely happened in the Thunderdome. It was a knockout, drag-out fight between two members of the same gang. Even though they weren't there to kill one another, every blow thrown was meant to cause serious damage.

Suddenly, the shorter one of the two fighters slipped and fell. The other one didn't waste a second of his opportunity. He pounced on him like a hyena who hadn't eaten in weeks. Yet, after a few blows he backed up, letting his opponent get his footing back. If they had been enemies, the aggressiveness would have never stopped. But this fight was different. The combatants were homies reppin' the same set.

They went a few more rounds: Boom! Bang! Ping! Blows were exchanged, blood splattered, and an eye or two swole up. In the end, the crowd broke them up. After that, they took a moment before giving one another a thug's embrace. Someone handed them some 40s and the skirmish was over.

As the crowd went back inside, Suge found a spot at the kitchen table where he could hold court with his day-ones. Despite the backyard fisticuffs that had just went down, the overall mood was still glowing with festivities.

"What's on the agenda, relly?" Co-Co asked Suge.

Co-Co was Suge's closest female friend. She was a sexy fire pot. Her body was curvaceous and her voice was angelic. Yet, she was as dangerous as they came. She had made a name for herself in the set because her temper was short. Add that to the fact that she had fallen in love with the way guns bust, and you had yourself a beautiful beast.

"I'm waiting for the page right now," Suge replied. "Bobby Brown got a walkthrough at Eve After Dark! I'm waiting on his call, then we'll ride out there."

Heron and Buntry had taken the other two seats at the small table. That was their circle within the circle. Nine times outta ten, when you saw either of them, you find at least two others.

Buntry was another reputable from The Mob. He had a brown-skin tone with short hair and a goatee.

Heron caught Co-Co's attention and said, "Toss me a 40, blood." She took out four bottles, one for herself and three for the table.

Buntry started rolling a joint with some extremely strong Los Angeles weed. While breaking up the buds, he brought up a subject they had all been thinking about. To Suge he asked, "What's up with the work, blood? Niggaz getting hungry out here. There's a drought in these streets. Even the homies from the other side of the set is stuck with no work."

"I know. I'm on it," Suge replied. Then he leaned in a little closer to the table and lowered his voice. "This nigga I know from Watts got all the work we need. I'm 'posed to meet up wit' him in the morning to grab some. If everything goes as planned, we'll all be eating like Kings."

"You know," Heron said, "the YGs get restless when the work is low."

"I know," Suge replied. The last thing he wanted was for his young soldiers to go on robbing sprees that would make the set hotter than it needed to be. Not only that, but it also heightened the chances of losing homies to the system. "You can't blame them, tho'. Niggaz gotta get theirs one way or another."

Suge's attention then went to another homie who had just entered the kitchen and went straight to the stocked fridge. It was his homeboy China Dogg. China was one of Suge's best friends. His name held just as much weight as Suge and the others in the set.

"What's brackin', China?" Suge asked.

China Dogg had somehow walked in the room without paying attention to who was seated at the table. But as soon as he heard his homey's distinctive voice, he knew exactly who was at the table before he even turned around to face them.

With a bright smile, China took a 40 ounce out the fridge then went to the table and gave everyone dap. "What's brackin', P-Funk?"

"Piiiru!" they all replied in unison.

"Say, gangsta," Co-Co said. "What happened to them straps Wack and Bo Pete came up with the other day?" Co-Co always paid close attention when the homies came up on firepower. She was a certified gunner, so heavy metal was serious point of interest to her.

"Yeah, it's good," China Dogg replied. Then, to the rest of the table he said, "I got us two Mac-10s. The rest of them got passed out to the homies. They even sold a couple to some Tree Top niggaz."

They all appreciated the importance of having an arsenal. 'What good is an army with no guns?' was a common phrase amongst them.

Something about Suge that not many people knew was that he was a well-read individual. He had studied at UNLV and came home with a business degree. But most people only knew him from his football career. They didn't know he did a lot more with his time in college than run plays on the field. All of that mixed with the fact that he was born and bred in one of the worst ghettos in America gave him a dangerous edge over most of the people he came in contact with.

Then, right before the conversation continued, Suge's pager vibrated. He knew exactly who it was as soon as he saw the number. "Time to go, y'all!" Then he called out to the rest of the house, "Y'all ready to go clubbing?!"

"Blood, what-da-fuck we waitin' on?" Buntry said. "Let's go!"

That's when Suge announced, "Time to Mob up! Y'all coming, or what? I'm getting passes for the whole set. Whoever's coming better mount up, 'cause we leavin'!"

The energy in the house lifted even higher than it already was. It didn't take long for a group of Pirus to spill out of the house, into the front yard on their way to their rides. There were 13 people in all who were on their way out with Suge that evening. Several of them decided to stay there because they weren't into the club scene.

Some bangers preferred patrolling the hood. They were always on the lookout for an enemy to mirk. Some of them didn't go clubbing because they were hustlers. Everyone knew there was free money in the streets on Friday and Saturday nights. The game never stopped, and there were those who capitalized off the empty streets when everyone else went out.

Then, just as the majority of them made it to their cars, something happened that had the potential to change the trajectory of their whole evening: A dark-green Chevy Caprice slid onto their street sideways a few blocks away. The driver was speeding way too fast when she hit the corner. She barely missed a parked car. The whole tribe looked when they heard the screeching tires.

They all instinctively reached for their waistbands. In a split second, several firearms were cocked and ready to fire at the oncoming vehicle. Then, just as the Chevy rolled up, the passenger window lowered...

CHAPTER TWO

Earlier that same evening, Bolo, a YG from the Mob was riding around Lueders Park in a dope-fiend rental. It was a dark-green Chevy with a hot 350 under the hood. He had been smoking sherm all day and was looking for something to get into – something that would help rejuvenate his bank roll.

Bolo was a real hoodsta'. He rarely left Lueders park, so he knew everyone who was anyone. There was a house that caught his attention earlier in the week. It was on the outskirts of the Mob's territory, and it was getting a lot of traffic. That wouldn't have been a problem, but he didn't know the hustlers behind the closed drapes. Drug houses in the hood were normal. But not when they were set up by unknown sources.

As the day became darker, he started circling the area surrounding the drug house. His movements were not unlike a shark scoping out its prey. It was obvious business was being conducted from the spot he was stalking. He just couldn't figure out who was running it. And he couldn't move on it until he figured it out because it could have been one of his big homey's spots.

Finally, he caught two niggaz in gang attire coming out of the front door as he passed by. Bolo, a lifelong Bompton native, was trained in the art of recognizing an opp. It was a skill he had to master in order to survive. Even though neither one of them had blue bandanas hanging out of their left back pockets, his instincts told him they were Crips. There was no way they were from his neighborhood.

Lueders was a big neighborhood. Later on, the numbers would split based on the separation between the faction that followed Suge, and the others who would stay with the traditional neighborhood gang. But that's getting ahead of ourselves. The point was, Bolo knew everyone in his section, and he didn't recognize the two he had seen stepping out of the drug house he was watching.

Since he was confident whoever was running the spot was an alien, he now had several options. He could go to his dog and tell him he had a lick. Tommy Ru was always wit' the activities. Or, he could hit the house himself. Bolo was a young nigga, almost 20 years old. Yet, he had more than enough experience in home invasions to manage the lick alone. At least, that's what his recurring thoughts told him as he crept through the shadows.

The PCP in his system also had a say in the matter; the more he hotboxed the Chevy, the surer of himself he became. In the end, he decided to keep the jux to himself. But he would need the assistance of at least one other person, and he knew exactly who to go to.

He needed a closer look at what was happening inside the house. Technically, he didn't even know what was being sold from it. All he could tell was there was a lot of traffic coming and going. He naturally assumed they were selling rocks. Everybody else was.

The young thug took a few turns through the trenches and pulled up on a smoker named Dee. She was walking down the street by herself which was even better for him. "Perfect," he said to himself as he pulled up on her.

When the Chevy rolled up to the curb, Dee couldn't tell who was behind the wheel. The windows were tinted and she hadn't seen it around the neighborhood before. Then, suddenly the interior light came on and she could see inside of it. She immediately recognized Bolo. The first thought that shot across her mind was she was about to get high. Real high... She knew he always had product on him, and that was exactly what she needed in her life.

She opened the car door, leaned in, and said, "Hey, baby! Whatchu got going on?"

"Get in. I'm on a mission right now."

She naturally assumed the mission was sexual in nature so she gave him a seductive smile. "Is that right? What's in it for me?"

He pulled out a small clear baggy with stones in it. He didn't even have to say anything else. She hopped in and they were in motion seconds later.

As they were on the move, Bolo started giving her instructions.

The mission was simple. She was with the activities just as long as the boulders he promised her were up to par.

He dropped her off on the corner a few blocks away from the house. Then he drove past the spot and parked across the street, about two blocks away. From the position he chose he was able to see her and the front of the house in question from his rear-view mirror.

She was crafty. She didn't just walk straight up to the house because she had never been there before. Instead, she slowly walked past it and doubled back. It was completely dark outside. Even the street lights were dimmed, not offering much lumination at all. This worked in her favor since her mission was clandestine in nature.

Three cars drove past the house before the first one pulled up to its curb. When the passenger got out and scurried up to the door, Bolo whispered to himself in anticipation. "Work your magic, Dee."

The moment she saw her opening, she took it. She went up to the parked car, leaned in the passenger seat and struck up a conversation with its driver. She wasn't a bad-looking smoker. She could seduce a man whenever she wanted to. She still had sex appeal and knew how to utilize it, and she was obviously doing it then by the way she sashayed her hips in the wind. Bolo chuckled to himself, knowing the game that was being played.

Finally, after a few minutes, the passenger of the ride came back into view. From the distance it looked like he had started propositioning Dee. As Bolo watched from his car, he saw her give him a few giggles and a smile before backing away from the car.

Dee then made her way back to his car with everything she managed to pluck from the unsuspecting snitches. "They Crips, Bolo! They crabs from Park Village! They sellin' hard white!"

"Holdup, Dee! Slow the fuck down! You acting like you already high!"

"I am," she said with a smirk. "The nigga in the car gave me a hit."

"What?! I didn't see him give you shit. You know what, I don't even care. So what else did you find out?"

"Okay. So there's three people in there. One of them is older. The other two are probably 'round your age. They got big rocks, and it's good as fuck!"

"That's why they got so much traffic," he said while glancing in his rearview.

"So what's up? You got something for me?"

"What? We ain't done yet."

Dee did not like what she heard, "What?! You wanted me to get information and I did!"

"How many guns they got?"

"How the fuck am I 'posed to know all'at? I didn't go inside!"

"See what I mean, blood! You trippin'!"

"Fuck all'at! I don't need this shit!" She reached for the door handled but Bolo stopped her.

"We're not done!"

"Give me a hit then!"

"You can hit this dick, bitch!" he teased her, managing to lighten the mood a bit.

"Not without a rock in my pipe! Straight up! You gonna give me some shit, or what?"

He scoffed before reaching in his bag of stones and handing her a 20-piece. "Here! Don't smoke all of it, either. I still need you on point. Blow the smoke out the window, too! I don't wanna smell it."

Bolo took a half-smoked sherm stick out of the ashtray. After lighting it, he took a puff and held it in for as long as possible.

Sherm took him to a whole different place. It made him feel invincible.

And that's exactly what he wanted, because he was preparing to lay down a whole house. He wasn't going in with the intentions of killing anyone, but that option remained firmly planted on the table at all times.

After they both got their fixes, Bolo switched seats with Dee. Then he told her to circle the block. Meanwhile, he made sure his sawed-off shotgun was locked and loaded. After that he wrapped a burgundy bandana over the lower side of his face. When they pulled back around the block he had her park just past the house, on the far side of the garage.

"A'ight, this what you finna do. Stay here and leave the car running. I'm gonna go up there and knock on the door. The moment they crack that bitch, I'm on their helmets. Laying everythang down!"

"I don't think –"

"I got this, blood. Watch!"

She didn't say anything else. She didn't sign up for all this. But she was dead set on seeing it through. She had been up for a few days straight, so her judgment was just as cloudy as the smoke she was inhaling. On top of that, it didn't take a rocket scientist to understand if Bolo's plan worked, he would have enough crack to keep her high for days.

"I gotchu, Bolo!" she replied with a mischievous grin.

"That's all I wanna hear."

$$$$$

Not all of the neighborhoods in Compton had the same type of machines running. Where one side would excel in trapping, another would be known for flocking. Others would profit from extortion, where the next one might have a team of bank robbers operating out of it. That's where some of the territorial disputes would arise from. In this case, Lueders Park had a million-dollar spot when it came to crack sales. They had so much clientele coming and going on a daily basis that they rarely had enough product to supply the demand. Park Village, on the other hand, was a different story.

Jap, an OG from the Village had a sister who lived on the outskirts of Lueders. During the previous six months, she had been paging him when people would come through looking for rocks. It was a simple and safe set-up that allowed her to make a little extra spending money. And it was all good just as long as Jap came and went discreetly. But when his younger homies came up on a lick of several kilos of raw cocaine, he needed to amp up his operations in order to move all the drugs they had. That's when he decided to trap out of his little sister's house.

They always knew they had to lay low. They couldn't go outside. And none of their other homies could come over to hang out. Any unnecessary attention had the potential to turn deadly. But, just like the saying goes; everything that happens in the dark will eventually come to the light.

Damus aren't the only ones who like to party on the weekends.

In southern California, the glitter of the weekend was enticing. Jap and his locs, Frog and C-Rag, were wrapping things up, getting ready to start the weekend festivities.

"Cuz! Y'all ready, or what?" C-Rag asked. He was in a rush to close up shop and get back to his neck of the woods. There was a house party in their hood that was definitely gonna be cracking. He didn't wanna miss a second of it.

"Gina!" Jap called out. "We're leaving!"

"All right," she answered from the bathroom. "I'll meet y'all at Ni-Ni's house."

With Jap in the lead, the trio stepped outside. The house didn't have a porch light so the side of the garage was all shadows as they headed to the driveway.

Jap didn't make it halfway to the end of the side of the garage when he suddenly saw a lone gunman hit the corner heading in his direction. For a brief moment in time, no one moved. Not even Bolo who was just as shocked as they were to see them standing there outside of the house.

When the burgundy bandana on the face of a man holding a sawed-off shotgun registered in the minds of the Crips, all hell broke loose! Jap was the first to react. He quickly reached into his waistband for his revolver, but Bolo was already cocked. Nevertheless, three shots were simultaneously fired. One from the shotgun, one from Jap's revolver. The third came from Frog's 9-millimeter Beretta.

The Crips were hit with birdshot, but they didn't receive the full impact since their shots threw off Bolo's aim.

Bolo took off in a sprint heading back to the Chevy. He knew he was outgunned. Trying his luck in a point-blank range shootout against that many people was out!

The smoke didn't have enough time to clear before Jap asked his locs, "Y'all a'ight, cuz?"

"On Crip!"

"Let's get that nigga, cuz!"

They got to the end of the driveway just as Bolo was diving into his getaway vehicle. It was on! They jumped in Jap's Skylark and burned rubber into the street in reverse. After spinning into position, they took off in pursuit of the dark-green Chevy Caprice.

Dee was shook, yet still in control. When she heard the shots, her mind concocted the worst-case scenario. One where Bolo had been shot in the face. But, when she saw him racing around the corner of the garage, she got ahold of herself and took control of the situation.

"What happened?!" she asked while speeding away from the house.

"Take us to Bullis!" he said, after realizing the Crips were on their tail.

"Bladadah! Bladadah! Bladadah!"

The rear window shattered.

"Fuck, blood!" Bolo yelled angrily.

"Bladadah! Bladadah!"

"You gotta shake 'em, Dee!"

"I'm trying to!"

Bolo aimed his 12 guage over the backseat, and let off a shot. The echo of the blast reverberated throughout the interior of the Caprice, numbing both of their eardrums. All for nothing since it did nothing to thwart his pursuers. The chase was even closer now!

"Dee, get us to the Beehive, blood!"

"I am! I am!"

They fishtailed into corners throughout their neighborhood. The streets were dark and crowded with parked cars. Both vehicles missed obstacles by a hair's width. Finally, they hit the street the Mob's Mad Pad was on. The Skylark was right behind them when they hit the block sideways.

"Put your seatbelt on, Bolo!"

"What?!"

"Put yo' mothafuckin' seatbelt on!"

He did as he was told. He saw the Beehive up the street. They were almost there. And luck was on their side, too. He saw what looked like 15 to 20 of his homeboys all in the front yard. He immediately started rolling down his window as they quickly approached the gang.

$$$$$

Suge wasn't strapped, but two-thirds of his squadron was. His survival instincts were in full defense mode, and so was the rest of his crews'. The moment they heard the sideways arrival of the high-speeding vehicles heading up the block towards them, they all got locked and loaded. Nevertheless, he was seasoned, and growing up in the trenches gave him enough insight to know two things: One; never show fear or panic in the face of adversity. Two; an attack this deep in their territory wouldn't make it off the block. Therefore, he stood his ground while his goons took out their weapons and geared up to fire upon the unknown assailants.

The closer they got, the better everyone could see them. Even though all the street lights on the block had been shot out to keep the set dark, the moon was bright enough to illuminate the whole situation.

Suge watched as the Caprice drove towards them. A brown Skylark was on its tail with someone hanging out the passenger window taking pot shots at the car they were chasing. Then, as the window of the Chevy rolled down, everyone there recognized their homey, Bolo. His flag was tied around his neck and he was frantically pointing towards the car behind him.

Then, out of nowhere, the car in the lead slammed into an abrupt halt! The driver, who looked like a female to Suge, had purposely slammed on her brakes. The driver of the muscle car behind them wasn't ready. He was just as surprised as the rest of them and wasn't quick enough to dodge the Chevy.

"BLAAAMMM!"

The Skylark crashed into the Caprice with such force, both cars slid several yards. The man hanging out the window of the second car was thrown from the car like Superman. He stayed in the air for a long time until he landed face-first against another car that was parked on the curb. The Skylark was totaled. The driver didn't seem like he was in any better shape, either.

Bolo stumbled from the wreck. Blood was dripping down the side of his head. "Blood! These Crabs tryna kill us!"

"Awww, hell naw!" replied the crowd.

The Mob swarmed the car in the rear. Even though the two men inside the Skylark were in horrible shape, they showed no mercy. They dragged the passengers out the totaled vehicle and beat them into comas.

Throughout it all, Suge remained level-headed. "Somebody get Bolo. Get him and whoever was driving up outta here!"

Several people went to the Piru's aide.

Suge had the sense of mind to realize the whole scene was too messy to leave unattended. He had to get to the club where Bobby Brown and his entourage were waiting. But he couldn't bounce till the block was secured. If not, he risked the wrath of the gang task force and that was never good.

"They had enough!" he barked. "Put 'em back in they car and roll that bitch up the street!"

For the most part, the gang listened. But not before a few more kicks were let loose on the opposition.

"Get the car Bolo was in up outta here, too. Push one that way, and get rid of the other one that way. Hurry up before 5-O gets here!" Suge ordered.

"Get in the truck," Suge told Heron and Co-Co. "We gotta get outta here, blood."

They climbed into the K5 and sped off. Three other cars followed them in a caravan of Mob Pirus.

The wind was refreshing. Suge turned the music up, redirecting the whole vibe back to where it was before the crash.

"Damn!" Heron commented. "That shit was brazy!"

"I hope Bolo's bool," said Co-Co.

"They good. It's just another night in the hood," Suge laughed. "Somebody light some weed, Blood. I'm tryna get high!"

CHAPTER THREE

Lueders Park showed up and showed out when they arrived at the club. Eve After Dark was already a known hangout for Bompton represents, so the dress code was always bloody red. When The Mob showed up, all you could see was crimson all throughout the parking lot.

The outside of the club was crowded. The parking lot was popping so much, some people didn't even want to go inside. Lowriders in showroom condition were showcased like trophies. Beautiful women in next to nothing sashayed past reputable bangers. Everyone was electrified by the beginning of a Bompton weekend.

As soon as Suge's crew got out of their rides, he told them all to wait a minute. He didn't want them to get in line to go inside because they wouldn't have to once he pulled his juice card. Not only was he a club promoter, which meant he knew almost every club owner in Los Angeles, he was also on a job. He was there as a bodyguard for Bobby Brown. In a way, the whole Mob was there as a security force for the famous R&B artist.

After telling everyone to post up for a moment, Suge and Heron headed towards the back of the building. There, in the shadows, sat a luxurious tour bus where Bobby Brown and his entourage were waiting on him.

Since the tour bus was stationed in the darkest section of the alley behind the club, you couldn't really tell anyone was inside of it. Other than the two Italian looking fellas who were standing next to it, the alley was void of people.

"Hey... Suge! How you doing, my man?!" Eddie Lucerne said. He was Bobby's road manager.

Suge always smirked when he heard a New York accent. It reminded him of all the mafia movies he'd seen. Yet, for some reason, he didn't trust too many people with that dialect.

Nevertheless, with his set-you-at-ease grin, Suge greeted Tony with a handshake, then nodded at his sidekick. "Where's Bobby?"

"He's inside, big guy. C'mon, let's get 'im. He should be gettin' ready as we speak."

The inside of the tour bus was plushed out. TV screens were everywhere. Surround sound and all the amenities were within reach.

As soon as they stepped inside, it felt like they were entering an after-hours spot. The music was blasting. Several people, both men and women, were milling about drinking champagne. They all seemed to be in the midst of festivities.

"Where's Bobby?" Suge asked loud enough to be heard above the music.

"Sugar Bear! What's happenin', my nigga?!" Bobby said from the rear end of the bus. He greeted Suge with a bright gap-toothed smile.

Suge made his way down the aisle. When he reached him, Suge gave Bobby a thug's embrace. Bobby was looking sharp with his gold-rimmed specs and 24k gold chain. He even had a matching bracelet dangling from his wrist. It was all topped off with an obscenely expensive Rolex. His white cashmere sweater on top of the black jeans was all the way on point.

"Hey, Heron," Bobby said.

"What's brackin', homey?"

"You see it," Bobby replied as he motioned towards the two groupies who were slowly getting dressed.

Both Suge and Heron recognized the girls. They were local females who were known to party with the rich and famous. And since Suge was connected to the industry, they had met one another on several occasions. Still, they never really acknowledged each other when they found themselves in situations like the one they were in.

Suge and Heron were about to step into Bobby's private room when his road manager cut in. Both Suge and Heron were large individuals, so the doorway was already cramped. Eddie was positioned behind them. Yet, he could be heard when he said, "All right, Bobby. It's almost ten. We got to make this appearance, my man."

"Bobby," Suge said. "I got a little something you might want to see before we go in."

The R&B bad boy's face immediately lit up. He already knew what Suge was talking about. One thing about having a bodyguard who was connected to the streets as close as Suge Knight was, he always had a connect on anything a celebrity wanted.

The wicked offer didn't fly past Eddie. Warning lights started flashing in his mind the moment he heard the words leave Suge's mouth. Bobby had a penchant for partying too much, and his priorities were all fucked up when drugs were involved. As of late, he'd been flaking on club appearances more and more. This was bad for business. So Eddie had to be on him like a mother hen.

"Bobby," said his road manager before Suge cut him off.

"Say, B. I got about 20 homies out front, ready to get in the club. They wit' me. Let me get some passes, man."

"Done!" Bobby told him.

"But, Bobby," his manager tried again.

"We got this, Eddie," Suge told him as he turned around to face him. The cramped quarters really emphasized their size difference as Suge towered over the shorter man. "Heron."

"What's brackin'?"

"Get the passes he's going to give you. And go make sure the homies get in. We'll meet y'all inside in a few."

"A'ight," Heron replied. He wasn't new to the scenario playing out in front of him. He shot Eddie an aggressive scowl, daring him to protest. Then he followed the reluctant road manager back to the front of the bus where he was given free passes to get into the club, and they didn't take two steps away from the door before Suge shut it behind them. Then, almost as if on cue, Bobby pulled out a wad of rubber-banded dead presidents and dropped it on the bed.

"How much you got?"

Suge took out a Ziploc sandwich bag from his pants pocket that contained an ounce of Bobby's favorite intoxicant. The beige cream was hard and shaped like the inside of mayonnaise jar. He dropped it on the mattress next to the money then watched as Bobby's smile brightened even wider.

"That's my man right there!" Bobby exclaimed.

"Your girls might as well start getting undressed, B."

"You heard the man," Bobby told the ladies. "The party's just getting started."

The professional party princesses knew exactly what to do. With a giggle here and a giggle there, they quickly started undressing.

"So, how much you want, Suge?"

"Don't worry about it right now. I know you got me. I figure you gon' out with the ladies a little longer, so I'm goin' in till you ready to join us."

Bobby wasn't really paying Suge attention by then. He already had his smoker-kit out and was packing his pipe. "Yeah, I'll have Eddie go get you when I'm ready to meet up wit'chu."

"I need them VIP passes, B."

"What? Oh, yeah. I got you, Suge. Here you go." Bobby handed him a stack of VIP passes then went right back to what he was doing.

Eddie Lucerne stuck his head in the room just as they were making the handoff, "Hey, Bobby. You ready?"

"Yeah," Suge answered for him. "He'll be ready in a minute. I'm gonna go check on the layout. Make sure ain't no paparazzi lurking."

The frustrated Italian looked at the passes in his hand and already knew it was all bad. Suge then used his imposing stature to block his view and pushed him back. After shutting the door behind him, he stepped past the little guy and made his way off the tour bus.

Eddie followed Suge to the front and watched him leave. He reached for the cup holder next to the steering wheel and grabbed his cognac. He hoped the liquor would numb the frustration of knowing Bobby wasn't gonna do the walkthrough...

$$\$\$\$\$\$$

Sude didn't need the VIP passes to get into the club. He could've walked straight in since he knew the bouncer. What the passes did was guarantee him a table in the VIP section. The section where all the celebrities and big-money fish hung out.

Suge found Co-Co, Heron and Buntry waiting for him at the entrance. They were all full of smiles just like Suge figured they'd be.

After a few discreet words with the bouncers, Suge got his whole crew in for free. Once inside, Suge immediately saw his partna D.O.C. seated at the table with DJ Yella and some unknown groupies.

D.O.C. and Yella were at the peak of their careers. They were part of a rap group called N.W.A. N.W.A. was popping from coast to coast. Suge knew both of them very well, but he was a lot closer to D.O.C..

DJ Yella was from Compton too. But he didn't run in the same circles as Suge and his comrades. When D.O.C. moved to Compton, one of the first people he met was Suge. And Suge welcomed him like one of his childhood homies.

Eve After Dark was all the way live! The females were shaking their asses to all the latest music. The men sipped their drinks while grinding on the nearest shaking ass. All in all, the place was packed with partygoers. Everyone was having so much fun, it didn't even seem like anyone cared whether Bobby showed up or not. Still, the DJ had New Edition music on rotation which seemed to elevate the club's energy with every song.

When D.O.C. and Yella saw Suge heading in their direction, they eagerly stood up and greeted him and his crew.

"Sugar Bear!" D.O.C. exclaimed as he gave him a thug's embrace. "What's up wit' da Mob?!"

"Man, it's all good, homey!" Suge replied. Everyone took a seat on the soft leather couches. Drinks were ordered and they all settled in. "I figured y'all would still be on tour right now."

"Naw. We on a little hiatus," D.O.C. replied.

"What's up wit'chu, Suge?" Yella asked. "I haven't seen y'all pushing this deep in a minute."

"I'm actually at work right now."

"Bobby's out there, huh?"

That's when Co-Co cut in, "Yeah, Relly. Where's Bobby's fine-ass?"

"He's outside," Suge replied. "But I doubt he'll be coming in anytime soon." Suge exchanged a glance with Heron and they both chuckled at their private joke.

D.O.C. said, "You know he's supposed to be throwing an after-party, right?"

"Naw, he didn't tell me all'at," Suge replied over the loud music.

"Some Hollywood exec got a house out in Calabasas," added Yella. "We're all headed over there after the club."

Suge looked at his boys and nodded. "Man, we gonna definitely be up in that joint!"

The party never slowed down. Drinks were tilted upward before being chased by THC. The V.I.P.'s talked about all kinds of things throughout the night. Suge paid extra attention to the news of Ice Cube leaving N.W.A. He also made a mental note to talk to D.O.C. when Yella wasn't around.

At one point throughout the evening, Suge sent Buntry and Co-Co outside to go check on Bobby. He didn't expect him to leave the bus while he had all that dope in his possession. But he sent them anyway for good measure. And as for Co-Co, he knew she really had a thing for the star. That was his way of giving her an opportunity to shoot her shot. When they came back in, they had a good laugh at her frustration for not being able to see see her crush.

As the evening matured, the music got louder and the ladies got looser. Suge and his party had pushed their tables together and were officially partying as one. Even during the festivities, Suge kept a sense of mind to send some soldiers to keep an eye on Bobby. He wanted to make sure no one got the stupid idea to try and rob his bus.

The party remained lit. Suge had a fat Garcia Vega stuffed in his mouth while a skinny Mexican girl sat on his lap. The occasional grind on his Peter-bone was a welcomed pleasure. And so was the company he was in the midst of. The bouncers had to create a blockade at one point, just to keep the females from date-raping D.O.C. and DJ Yella.

Then one of the biggest club bangers of the year came on over the loud speakers. "Ice Ice Baby" by Vanilla Ice came on and the crowd went bonkers! All the women in the club rushed to the dance floor so they could grind their ass cheeks on the nearest penis.

"Can you believe that white boy stepped on the scene so hard?" D.O.C. commented.

Suge scoffed, "Blood's a piece of cotton! I don't really fuck with them white rappers like that anyway. But I've met Third Base and the Beastie Boys. You can see it in their eyes; they're cut from a certain cloth. That boy Vanilla Ice ain't living like that. He ain't got an ounce of gangsta in 'im."

"He rapping like it, tho'," Yella said.

"Bootsy-ass honky!" Heron scoffed.

"You know he didn't write that song, right?" Yella continued.

"It wouldn't surprise me," replied Suge. He then cut his eyes at D.O.C. because they both knew he wrote a lot of N.W.A.'s lyrics.

"Yeah. But did y'all know a brotha from Watts wrote it? I think his name is Chocolate or Mario or somethin'," Yella told them. "He actually stays in y'all set."

Suge glanced towards Heron and Co-Co. He didn't recognize the name. But the way Yella said it was as if he should've known him.

"You know Chocolate, Suge," Co-Co said. "He stays off Rosecrans with his girl. If you don't know him, you know Margy."

"Yeah," Yella agreed. "He does got a girl named Margy."

"How come I ain't heard of him like that?" Suge inquired. "If he wrote that song, there should be some money in the bity."

"Well... I can't tell you 'bout his finances," Yella said. "But I know he wrote that cut. That's where the gangsterism came from. It all leads back to L.A.."

"On Ru's!" Heron agreed.

"LAST CALL FOR LIQUOR!" The DJ called out over the loudspeaker. "LAST CALL FOR LIQUOR!"

Suge stood up and said, "I gotta go check on Bobby. Something tells me if I don't, there won't be no after-party."

"We'll meet y'all 'round back," D.O.C. told him. "We can all ride up there together."

"Bet dat!" Suge replied and they all got up.

Suge flagged down Buntry and told him to follow them out the back. His departure was strategized because he was only planning on taking his inner circle to the party. When they got to the tour bus, they met with the YG's Suge had sent outside to watch over the bus. Suge gave them some money and they left. But not before they let him know a little Italian guy was looking stressed about something. Suge figured as much, but he wasn't worried about it. He had sent a message to Alonzo, the club owner, letting him know no one was trippin' off Bobby. Since he had brought such a large crowd with him, it basically evened out any tension Bobby's actions could've created.

While all of this was going on, Suge kept having recurring thoughts revolving around Chocolate, someone who happened to live in his neighborhood writing the Ice Ice Baby song. He ended up remembering exactly who he was, except he knew him as Mario.

Mario wasn't a banger. He didn't run with a set. He wasn't from Lueders but his girl was. He made a mental note to reach out to him with a proposition to manage his affairs in the industry. It only made sense since they lived in the same section.

What a lot of people didn't realize about Suge at that time was, although he was young, he was well educated. Yes, he was a street nigga, but he was also book smart. His view of the world and its opportunities were framed in a much larger spectrum than the average bodyguard. On top of that, his drive to succeed pushed him outside the box every time.

One of his greatest attributes as a leader was the fact he knew he didn't know everything. This enabled him to delegate certain tasks to people who were better fit for certain positions than himself. It was a big part of why he felt more comfortable managing artist rather than being the star himself.

When he got to Bobby he found him in the back of the tour bus having the time of his life. After reminding him of the party in Calabasas, everything was set in motion. Within minutes, the luxurious tour bus was in motion with a caravan of late-night partygoers in tow...

CHAPTER FOUR

The morning after is never as productive as the evening before. Especially not for people who love the night. For men like Suge, the fast life filled with celebrities, nameless models and gangland politics was mandated. Therefore, getting up and moving around in the early hours of the morning wasn't one of his strong suits.

Suge had a few honeycombed hideouts where he could duck off to when he didn't wanna be bothered. But the place where he felt most comfortable was the two-bedroom apartment that he shared with Sharitha, his high school sweetheart. They had stayed there ever since they moved back to Compton after graduating from UNLV, a school they both went to together.

The apartment was in a complex on Bullis Avenue, smack-dab in the middle of the trenches. Although it was in the center of the ghetto, Suge felt most comfortable there. Lueders Park was where he experienced most of the lessons that made him into the man he grew to be. That's why, even though he played a short stint in the NFL after graduating and got married to the love of his life, he still went back to the hood.

The biggest difference between Suge and his other homeboys was he saw past his hood. His vision surpassed gangland boundaries. Being as articulate as he was attracted other like-minded individuals, and he made sure anyone who followed his lead ate just as well as he did.

If it weren't for Sharitha waking him up, he probably would've slept in. He rarely got out of the house before 12 in the afternoon on the weekends. Before climbing into his K5 he glanced at his watch and said, "Damn! It's early than a muthafucka!" It was just after ten a.m. when he started the engine. The purr of the 350 under the hood energized the extra-large gangster. He had a mission in mind and was on his way to tackle it.

Just as he was putting his ride in gear, he saw China Dogg walking up the sidewalk in his direction. China was a stocky dark-skinned brotha from the Mob. His murder game was at the top of the list when it came to gangland hunters.

"Suge!" China said when he saw him.

Suge waited for him and leaned across the seat to open the door when he reached the truck. "Get in, blood. You ridin' wit' me this morning."

China got in with no hesitation. "What's brackin', blood!"

"I'm 'bout to go holla at this nigga 'bout some industry business."

"Right, right," China said. Then he started shaking his head and said, "That shit was brazy last night, homey."

At first, Suge was a little confused because he knew China hadn't went to the club with them. For some reason he just naturally assumed he was talking about the after-party. But then he remembered the incident that took place before they left the set.

"Oh shit! Yeah... The homie was in some shit! On Ru's. I thought you was talking 'bout the after-party."

"Naw, I'm talking 'bout the hot shit. Niggaz on the lookout just in case some crabs try and slide. Bolo said them niggaz was selling dope in the set. But, man, fuck all'at! You talking 'bout after-parties an' shit! Tell me 'bout dat!" That last statement was filled with excitement. China Dogg was a quiet person, so when he was turned up, it brought smiles to his dog's faces.

"First of all, it was a bitch to get Bobby to remember how to get to the house in Calabasas."

"Hold up, what Bobby? Bobby Brown?"

"Yeah, nigga! I was security for him last night."

"Okay," China said with a chuckle.

"So, after the club, we all went to this big-ass house with a pool and all the good shit. Blood, the muthafucka had a ten-car garage with all foreign shit posted up in it!"

They passed another car with a few of their homies inside. They all greeted one another by chunking up B's with their twisted-finger gang signs. Then Suge continued, "D.O.C., DJ Yella and some more people was up in that bitch last night. On Ru's!"

"Blood! I should beat yo' ass for leaving me in the set last night!"

"Nigga, you wouldn't have went anyway. You act like you can't stop patrolling the set."

"Still, nigga! You should've said something. But anyways, what kind of bitches was there?"

"Ahhh," Suge laughed. "I knew that's what you'd wanna hear. Hold up, grab me a Vega out the glove compartment real quick."

"Gotchu," he replied while handing Suge the cigar. "So, what happened? You get some pussy, or what?

"You already know I got mines." He lit the cigar with K5's lighter.

"It's too easy. Them industry bitches be drippin' when they meet a real nigga. Not only that, them famous bitches go crazy when they know ain't no cameras around. Sucking up the whole party an' shit. And the groupies be on some shit too. When they can't get to a celebrity, they'll fuck the closest nigga to 'im. I guess they be thinking that'll open the door for them to get to the man."

"On Ru's."

"So last night I fucked with a dancer. On Bloods, I can't remember her name. But you seen her before. She has an East Coast accent. She dances on In Living Color."

"Rosie Perez?"

"Hell naw," Suge laughed. "Next time that shit comes on, I'll point her out. She short, 'bout five-five. I think she was Puerto Rican or something. Baby was sexy."

"What you tell her to get the draws?"

"I really didn't have to say shit. She was hella aggressive. Man, I was upstairs and I went to the bathroom to rinse my face 'cause a nigga was kind tipsy. I didn't know she was in there. When I opened the door, she was in there putting make-up on her face. I was like, 'My bad.' But she wasn't trippin'. She said she was done anyway and started putting her shit up."

He paused to take a deep puff of his cigar. He had gotten the directions to Mario's house from Co-Co the night before, and was trying to find it. "As she steps past me, she brushed her hip up against my dick. And, blood, I know I'm a big nigga, but she had more than enough room to step past me without touching me.

"I bet!"

"So, I'm like, fuck it. And I reached down and kinda grabbed her arm. I gave her that look, kinda like saying, 'What's brackin'?' Then she went to the door, shut it and turned around and told me to back up."

"For what?"

"Blood, she asked me, "What you like best? My ass or my tits?"

"That ass!" China exclaimed a little too loud. Making both men laugh.

"That's exactly what I told her! Next thing I know, she asked me if I wanted to hit it."

"Just like that?"

"On Ru's! Blood, I reached down, gripped that ass and pulled her closer to me. We started kissing. Baby tasted like champagne!

She backed up, turned around and lifted her skirt. Blood! All I saw was a fat-ass-booty with a wet pussy below it."

"That's what I'm talking 'bout!"

Suge blew out a large cloud of smoke before continuing. "Man, I slid my middle finger down the crack of that ass till I hit the pussy. She had a nappy little dug-out, too! Once I felt how wet she was, I pulled the anaconda out and tore that pussy up!"

"On Bloods!"

Suge saw the house he was looking for. It was an old green house with two beat-up looking cars in the driveway. One of them was on blocks. It didn't look like it had been driven in a long time. He was surprised to see the shape the house was in too. The front yard had dead grass. The paint on the house was chipping. Yet, even though the home was fucked up, it matched the surroundings. Every other house on the block was just as dilapidated.

Still, none of that seemed foreign to Suge. What seemed wrong was that Mario had written a platinum-selling song, and his house, if it was his house, looked like it belonged to someone living under the poverty line.

He pulled up to the curb, "C'mon, blood. I gotta holla at this nigga real quick."

"Who is it?"

"You know a nigga named Mario? He goes by Chocolate."

China thought for a moment then said, "Yeah. I know blood. He really don't come around, tho'."

"Yeah, that's him. He don't come around, but he's on his shit."

When they reached the front door, the security gate was closed, but the door behind it was wide open. There was a radio on somewhere in the house. They could hear a DJ saying something in the distance.

Suge knocked on the security door and said loudly, "Anybody home?"

From somewhere in the house, a female's voice answered, "Who is it?"

"It's Sugar Bear."

A brown-skinned sister came into view. When she saw who he was her whole demeanor changed. "Oh-uh... What's up, Suge?"

"Nothing much. Hey, you know China, right?"

"What's up?" China said.

"Yeah, I know China Dogg. Come inside, y'all." She let them in, but was obviously self-conscious about the shape her home was in. "Take a seat. I got some lemonade in the fridge. But what's up? What's going on?"

Suge scanned the room. The furniture was average. So was the entertainment center. No big-screen TV or surround-sound stereo system. Suge didn't see any signs of money in that house. There were pictures of Margy and a man on the walls. Suge vaguely recognized the man which he assumed to be Chocolate.

"Where's Mario?" he asked.

"He's at work," she replied cautiously.

"Where he work at?"

"Louie Burgers."

"What?!" Suge asked. He knew he couldn't have heard her correctly. But when she didn't reply, he really knew something was wrong. He gave China a quick glance, but his homey didn't catch it. "Margy, look, ma. I'm not tryna be all up ya mix, but I heard Mario wrote that song that be on the radio all the time."

"He did," she said plainly.

With a confused look on his face, Suge asked, "Where's the money? Why you living here like this?"

"I'm not gonna take that as disrespect, nigga –"

"It ain't like –"

"I already know, Sugar Bear. The fact is, he wrote that song. I was there when he was writing it. We lived in Texas for a little while, that's when he came up with it and a bunch of other music. That's what he does. But they didn't pay him for it. Straight up. They ain't paid 'im shit."

"You berious?"

She nodded.

"What song you talking 'bout?" China Dogg asked.

"'Ice Ice Baby'," Margy said as she took a seat on the love seat across from them. Then she looked at Suge. "I can't believe it either. Robert, that's Vanilla Ice's real name, used to come over to the house all the time! Mario wrote most of his music at our kitchen table."

Suge was getting mad. His anger was oozing from his pores at a slow simmer. He abruptly stood up from the couch, thinking, *This some straight bullshit!* Outloud, he said, "Take my pager number down and have blood give me a call."

"For what?"

"I'ma fuck wit' 'im. On Ru's, they not finna play him like that. Not on my watch! I already know how the music industry people be. They rob niggaz 'cause they can. Man, fuck all'at!"

After giving Margy his number, Suge and China left. Suge was quiet. He was thinking about all the gripes and complaints he had heard from other artists in the industry when he worked as a body guard in Las Vegas. They had all complained about getting swindled by shady music executives.

China noticed how mad Suge was by the way he was driving. The K5 was hitting corners way harder than necessary. "Blood, you good?"

"Naw, blood! I'm hot right now."

"Where you headed?"

"I'm going to Louie Burgers. I'm 'bout to holla' at blood. And if he's smart, he'll keep it real wit' me. If he really wrote that song, I'ma make sure he gets his bread!"

"Whatchu finna get out of it?"

"Blood, I play chess! On Ru's, if Mario wrote that song and I'm managing him, I'ma hit a whole 'nother level! I'm talkin' 'bout, platinum level. Six-figure level..."

CHAPTER FIVE

Mario was heading out the back of Louie Burgers with a bag of trash in each hand when his co-worker called out to him, "Chocolate! You got a phone call!"

"Who is it?" he asked just as he stepped outside.

"Margy."

He put the bags down and went back inside. He figured she'd want him to pick something up from the store on his way home. That was the only time she called him at work. What she ended up telling him surprised the young nigga.

When she told Chocolate that Suge said he wanted to help him get his money from Vanilla Ice, he was hit with an overdose of skepticism. "What can Sugar Bear do? Robert ain't in the streets," he had told her before they hung up.

On his way outside after the phone call, "Ice Ice Baby" came on over the small radio in the break room. He clenched his jaw muscles when he heard it. More and more, hearing that song pissed him off in ways he couldn't explain. He had written hundreds of songs. Then, finally one of them became a hit, and he wasn't seeing any of its profits!

He had just tossed the trash bags in the bin when he saw a Blazer parking on the side of the burger shack. He recognized the tall brown-skinned man who hopped out the driver seat, but he didn't know who his friend was.

Suge saw him too.

"Mario!" he called out to him after getting out. "Let me holla at you real quick, homey."

Suge had told China to wait for him inside the truck before he made it across the parking lot. Chocolate was medium build. He had a step-style high-top fade that a lot of East Coast guys were rocking at the time. Suge realized he knew Chocolate from the neighborhood. He had passed him in traffic more than a few times. Even seen him in the clubs. But he never sat down and had a conversation with him.

"Man, how you doing, Mario?" Suge asked with his palm extended.

Chocolate took his hand, and just like anyone else from Compton, was cordial. Yet, he stayed on his toes. He didn't really know what Suge's angle was. But he halfway expected one, so his guard was most definitely up.

"I've been trying to catch up with you, homey."

Here we go, he thought. "What's going on?"

"Look, man. I'm not gonna beat around the bush about why I'm here. I was at the club with Yella and D.O.C., and when that Vanilla Ice song came on, they told me you wrote it. Is that true?"

"Yeah. Why? What's up?" he replied defensively.

This subject obviously bothered the man. Suge sensed it. And he fully understood why.

"I'm not coming at you with ill intent, Mario. When I heard about you, I decided to come at you because I'm in the industry and I'm starting a management company. I don't know what you had going on wit' them folks when it came to that song. But, what I do know is the industry is shady. As a manager, my job is to protect my guys and make sure they get what's coming to them."

Mario scoffed, "You ain't never lied! The industry shady as fuck!"

"Tell me something. How much you get paid for that song?"

Anger quickly flashed across Chocolate's face. "Peanuts! When I wrote it, I submitted it to the record company. They told me I'd get royalties from it. But they also gave me a fifteen-hundred-dollar check. That's all I got. I never seen a penny from the royalties."

"Then what? You never tried reaching out to them?"

"Of course, Suge. Once I started hearing it all over the radio, I called the record company, and nothing! They stopped answering my calls."

"What company? What's the name of the record company you deal with?"

"Ichabod Records."

"How long ago?"

"I wrote it about a year ago."

"And you ain't seen no bread since that fifteen?"

"Nothing!"

Suge's jaw muscles clenched. He shook his head as he gazed off into the distance. Chocolate was another artist on a list of many that had been duped by the record companies over the years. He was hot. But he also had an instinct that told him this was an opportunity of a lifetime. He just had to reach out and grab it.

Then, just as he was going to say something, both of them heard some bass thumping from the trunk of a car that pulled into the gas station across the street from the burger shack. Suge looked at the car and saw the driver hop out with a blue bandana hanging out of his left back pocket.

The Mob, technically, wasn't at war with any particular set at that specific moment, so it wasn't as if they were in danger of getting in a shootout. Nevertheless, Bompton was a powder keg. Any little thing could trigger a firefight. So, he used that as a sign to secure the deal and move on to the next phase.

Suge looked at Mario and said, "I can help you, homie."

"How?"

"Did you sign any contracts?"

"Naw."

Suge thought for a moment before continuing, "Okay. Check game. I'm gonna have a talk with my folks who is a lawyer. Then I'm gonna let you know what he says. But, trust and believe I'm gonna get you paid."

"I don't know how you gonna do that."

"Don't worry 'bout all'at. I'm gonna make it happen, tho'. Sometimes all you gotta do is make some noise. And I ain't got no problem doing that."

Chocolate studied the eyes in front of him. Somehow, they looked surprisingly sincere. That's when he realized he could trust them. "A'ight then. But, Suge."

"Yeah."

"Why you doing all this?"

He smiled. "'Cause I'm your manager."

$$$$$

After dropping China Dogg off in the hood, Suge headed west. He was still on his mission. The next phase of his plan was securing some legal assistance. He figured that part of the plan would be the easiest.

When he was in college, he made the best of it. He used it as a time to network as much as possible. One of the ways he was able to do that was by keeping things people liked.

Since he was able to go back and forth between Vegas and Compton, he kept a supply of the latest candies in his possession. This helped him meet and cultivate working relationships with a number of trust-fund babies who had goals of having careers in the Hollywood Hills.

Victor Lazono was on of those college buddies who Suge had stayed in contact with over the years since his graduation. Vic was originally from Rhode Island, but his family owned a law firm that had an office on the West Coast. He majored in entertainment law with a specific goal of taking the reins of his family's West Coast operations.

At UNLV, Vic was a smooth-talking ladies man. He was both handsome and rich. He wasn't shy with women like so many others who Suge had met there. But he did have a taste for two things that Suge had special access to: white powder and Black women.

Their relationship ended up growing past that of two individuals exchanging goods. It grew organically.

It was a friendship based on a mutual respect for one another because they both saw each other in one another.

Chess players.

Vic was of a new breed that came from old money. He was a man of the times. He listened to the current music and paid attention to the latest trends. In a way, he identified with the underdogs of society. So when he received the call from his receptionist at the front desk telling him his college buddy Simon was there, he didn't hesitate to tell her to send him in. He had a scheduled appointment coming up, but that didn't matter. He was dying to see what his old friend was up to.

Suge was met with a big smile the moment he stepped into Vic's spacious corner office. The energy was contagious. They gave each other heavy handshakes and Suge took a moment to take in the view.

"Yeah... I told you I'd have an office overlooking the city of angels," Vic said as he watched Suge staring out at the expanse.

"This what the fuck I'm talking 'bout, Vic! I gotta get me a view like this too."

They both took a moment to admire the Los Angeles skyline.

"It's even prettier at night, big guy. So what brings you my way, Simon? They still calling you Simon these days?"

Suge chuckled. "Not everyone. But they soon will."

"I bet they will. I'm sure you've got yourself a master plan. But before we get to any of that – 'cause

I know there is one in the making – I gotta show you something. You're gonna love this."

Victor stepped away from the window and went to the bookshelf on the opposite wall. He took a hold of a camouflaged door handle and opened a hidden room.

"What da fuck!" Suge exclaimed with the excitement of a fifteen-year-old boy. He quickly made his way to the door and looked inside. "A fuckin' secret bathroom!"

"I've done everything in there from shit to shower to fuckin' a few sistahs," he laughed. He was at the bar pouring them drinks by then. Moments later, they were both at the mahogany desk.

"So, what's up, Simon. What's going on these days?"

"I got a situation I'm hoping you can help me with. I got a guy who wrote that song Vanilla Ice has all over the radio. It's a platinum –"

"'Ice Ice Baby'?"

"Yeah."

"Let me guess... the record company is stiff-arming him."

"How did you –"

"Happens all the time, bro. It's common."

"They won't even answer his calls. That song is at the top of the charts. And my guy, the guy who wrote it, works at hamburger place in the middle of Compton."

"Sounds about right. Points on a song like that can be worth millions. Record companies don't like giving up that much money unless they have to."

"That much, huh?"

"Yeah. "So, what do you need help with?"

"I'm not a lawyer. I just started managing this guy. And I already figured the situation is worth a lot of money. So naturally, I'm trying to get my client his money."

Vic leaned back in his thick leather seat thinking for a moment. He wanted to help Suge as much as possible. "Okay, so I don't do music law. I'm into the Television drama these days. So I can't say I can represent you in this case. However, I can tell you a case like this can takes years in litigation. The record companies bank on these types of cases because they have the money to wait out the litigant. But, on another note; you said you're managing him. Do you have him under contract?

"Verbal."

"Is your company all the way legit?"

"Not yet. I don't have the paperwork –"

"Don't worry about it. I'll get all the paperwork done for you. All you gotta do is sign a few things and your management company will be all the legitimate. You're gonna need everything you do to be legal from this point on. If you're gonna play with the big dogs, everything you do needs to be in black and white."

"I get it. You're dead right."

"Something else... You're definitely onto something. But, are you positive this guy really wrote the music?"

"I'm sure of it. The streets been talking. That's how I heard about it. Some people I know in the industry told me about it so I went to go see him in person. I had a good conversation with him, and I believe he really wrote the lyrics to it."

"Then fight for it. Don't let up. Make the sons of bitches pay!"

"I hear ya, man."

"As a matter of fact, I'm going to get the paperwork filed today. I'll just need a few signatures and my assistant will do the rest."

Suge was visibly disappointed. It wasn't the end of the world, but he knew he had a fight ahead of him. And without proper legal representation that would be even harder. Something he had learned while he was a bodyguard was how important it was for artist to have a good lawyer on their side. Lawyers spoke, read and understood a language normal people didn't understand.

Vic saw the disappointment in his friend's eyes. He wanted to help as much as he could. "Simon, look, man. I'll talk to some people and see if I can find you someone who can help you. Whatever Simon says, always gets done!"

It was an inside joke they both smiled at. It helped lighten the mood. But Suge was still in the same position he was in when he first walked through Victor's door...

CHAPTER SIX

Suge left Victor's office with a lot to think about. He analyzed everything that was said and he was dead set on capitalizing off the situation. There was no way in hell he was going to ease up on the Chocolate and Vanilla Ice situation. With all the information he learned about the industry while protecting different artists, he knew when he was looking at a million-dollar lick.

As he maneuvered through traffic the wind whipped at his face. The sun was shining, giving the Los Angeles afternoon the perfect setting for business.

The next stop on Suge's itinerary was Nickerson Gardens Housing Projects. In his eyes, he wasn't a drug dealer. He never stood on a street corner with a pocket full of stones. Yet, there he was, on his way to meet with a heavy hitter named Dave.

Suge had a gift when it came to recognizing profitable opportunities.

Even though selling dope wasn't his main hustle, he saw the need for supplying the demand in his section of the city. He had an army of Street Marines who needed work. Someone had to feed them. Since he knew where to get enough work to make that happen, there was no reason why he wouldn't.

Especially at that time in his life. Suge knew how deep the music industry was tied to the underworld. If he was going to penetrate it on some hostile takeover shit, he'd have to have the loyalty of his team.

The closer he got to the Nickersons the more the scenery changed from opulence to poverty. On his way to Victor's office, the traffic was filled with foreign whips driven by white people. South Central was a contrast to all of that. He was no longer driving through the utopian mirage set in Hollywood.

Even though his K5 sat up higher than the average car on the road, he didn't stick out as much in Watts as he did in Hollywood. Suge was gangsta. He was part of the underworld which not only meant he didn't stick out in the trenches, but that he also felt comfortable in war torn environments.

It didn't take long after pulling into the green and white housing projects before he started seeing gang signs chunked up by young niggaz laced in red. Suge was known throughout almost every hood in the county. He was respected and well connected through his interactions with high-ranking criminals.

Not just anyone could move in the circles he travelled in. He could, only because of all the work he put in for reputable individuals over the years. If a baller needed help getting money from a delinquent hustler, Suge was someone who could be counted on to collect such funds. To him, it was all business. He handled everything professionally. Applying just the right amount of muscle necessary. That alone earned him passes throughout several different gang zones.

Dave, Suge's coke connect, had a very secure setup. He had an unlimited amount of bodies looking out for him all throughout the projects. If anyone would have ever even imagined a plan to rob him while he was in the projects, they would have had to be crazy. Pulling into the Bounty Hunter strong-hold with ill intent never worked in favor of the opposition. The Nickersons was the biggest projects in the State of California. And they were controlled by one of the strongest Blood gangs in the country.

Suge pulled in next to Dave's Five-Point-O. Even though he'd been invited to the kingpin's place of business, he still took the time to scan his surroundings. A person could never be too careful when pushing through the trenches.

A group of young men were congregated in the parking lot watching everything just as closely as he was. They were soldiers on post, patrolling their territory in their black and red uniforms.

He made eye contact with one of the Bounty Hunters. The dark-skinned soldier with a gheri-curl was wearing a red t-shirt with tan Dickie shorts. Suge chunked up the universal Blood sign with his right hand and was met with the same twisted up fingers.

"Fiiive Liiine!" announced a younger Blood in cornrows who was standing next to the guy Suge was looking at.

Suge nodded then replied, "Mob Piiiru!"

Getting hit up by the locals didn't bother him. It was expected. Still, he kept a mug on his face. It didn't matter how much work sat waiting for him behind the door he was heading towards. A person just didn't smile too much in those types of situations.

Suge was about to reach the front doorstep of the unit he was heading to when the door came open and

Dave greeted him. He was just as tall as Suge and just as imposing. The biggest difference was their skin tones. Dave was a lot darker than Suge.

"Suge! What's brackin', my man?!" Dave said with a smile. He looked like money in his black silk shirt and matching slacks. Both his neck and wrist was dipped in 24k gold.

Suge gave him a smile with a dap. It was all love between the bosses. "Man! I'm good, Champ!"

"C'mon," he told him, motioning for Suge to step inside. "I've been waiting on you. I got somewhere to be after this."

Dave led Suge to a couch in the small living room. From the moment he stepped inside, he felt a whole different vibe. The unit was air conditioned and smelled clean. The walls had decorative portraits and masks that created an African theme.

They sat on couches across from an extra-large television screen. Everything seemed slightly too big for the small living room. Yet still, it was cozy, inviting and rich. A complete contrast from what surrounded them outside the apartment.

"Man, what's good, Dave?" Suge started. "I'm tryna make some moves in these streets. But shit be hard when you can't find a secure line on what's needed."

"I feel you," Dave chuckled. "There was a time when me and my brother had to spend with three and four different plugs just to have enough to make it through a week of hustling."

A female with short hair and a lot of curves had came from the kitchen with two glasses of dark liquor in her hands. She placed them on the coffee table in the center of the room before leaving them to each other.

"Not only is it hard to find enough work," Suge said. "But you gotta add in politics, too. Certain niggaz know if they keep work out a specific hood, the business will eventually migrate towards the next set."

"Been there too! But the good news is you ain't gotta worry 'bout that with me. I wanna see you eat, blood. Onda set, I got it for you. All you gotta do is say the word."

Suge respected Dave. He was a millionaire who never left the set. He was still in projects with the grimiest niggaz in L.A. even though he didn't have to be.

"On Piru, I'll take whatever you can put in my hand. My niggaz is ready and the set is dry. So the return is damn-near guaranteed."

"What about three chickens for fifty? How dat sound?"

"Like a blessing! Fifty, huh? I can work with that for real!" Suge chuckled. He started rubbing the palms of his hands together in anticipation of the moves about to be made."

Dave lifted his glass and motioned for Suge to do the same. "Enjoy the drank, homey. Savor the moment."

Suge smirked before taking a sip of the rich, dark liquid. Then he sat back to watch the boxing match playing on the big screen. It was a Tyson fight on VHS. He knew who was gonna win the 'bout. But that didn't matter. Tyson was the sickest fighter of all time. Watching him annihilate his opponents never got old.

Then, after a while, a thought hit Suge prompting him to ask, "Didn't you have somewhere to go?"

"Huh?"

"When I got here, you said you was waiting on me so you could go somewhere afterwards."

"Oh yeah," Dave replied. "I'm gonna take the boat out tonight. I gotta go early to make sure everything's running right. Since my brother's been gone it's been on me to wine and dine people in the industry."

"Music industry?"

"Naw," he replied. "Harry was into everything but music. Blood was doing plays an' shit. Dealing with actors and Hollywood execs."

"Plays? Damn..."

"Yeah. That shit makes money, too. You get the right script with good actors and it's an easy flip. Damn near as easy as the dope game. Not as fast, but at least it's legal. You ever put your money into clean investments?"

"I got a little management company I'm working on right now. Managing different artist an' shit. It really doesn't need a lot of money –"

"Money makes money, Suge."

"I get it. Onda set, I get it."

Suge sat on that notion for a minute. He'd never been too loose with his money. Even when it looked like he was spending, everything was calculated. He was educated, had a degree in business. But, he was also laced up in the streets so he specialized in building things from the dirt.

The seed had been planted, though. Using dirty money to fund clean ventures was quickly becoming a viable option. He wasn't sure when or how he'd have to invest in something legal. But he knew he eventually would because illegal endeavors didn't have the longevity he was searching for. He was only using the dope game as a stepping stone for bigger and better things.

Just like any other Tyson fight of that era, the one they were watching didn't last long. He KO'd his opponent in record time. After the fight both men got ready to leave. Then somewhere between shaking hands and walking to the door, Suge asked, "So, when you want me to –"

Dave smiled, anticipating Suge's question. "It's already in ya ride, Champ. Check out that new speaker box in the back of yo' shit. The bass in the box is guaranteed to beat up the block!"

It took Suge a whole second and a half to process what he'd just heard. Then his grin widened. He was most definitely impressed. Dave was putting him on and he couldn't wait to press play! His whole hood was gonna eat off this bag and he couldn't wait to get back and kick things into gear.

When Suge stepped outside, he held his chin up a little higher than before. He was on the verge of turning the temperature up to whole different level.

The afternoon had gotten late. Meaning, Suge caught the brunt of Los Angeles traffic. But on that day he didn't mind. He welcomed the slow-moving traffic. It gave him time to plot, plan and strategize his next move...

CHAPTER SEVEN

The next day Suge was with his niggaz. The trap was a Beehive of activity as he dispersed the work he'd picked up from his plug in the projects.

To his surprise, not only had he been fronted three bricks of coke, there were also a few pounds of extremely sticky green buds placed in the speaker box as well. Even though the weed wasn't discussed, it wasn't a problem. He knew exactly what to do with it.

There was steady flow of in and out traffic to the trap that day. Suge was posted up with Buntry, Heron and Co-Co the whole time. Off the top, he'd given them each a quarter Ki' apiece. Of course, they had to put money back in the pot. Suge wouldn't profit off them though.

They were his circle within a circle. It was never about making money off them. It was more about eating with them. Sharing the plate had never been a problem with the young hustler.

Co-Co was at the kitchen table bagging up ounces of trees. She had to put a pair of late gloves on so the weed wouldn't stain her fingers with its sticky residue. The aroma was intoxicating. It could be smelled all throughout the house. Moving it wasn't going to be a problem. It was the best weed Cali had to offer.

Co-Co had jumped at the chance to separate the ounces from the pounds. She was a heavy weed smoker who couldn't wait to bust the bags open.

"Suge! This shit sticky as fuck! Check it out!" Co-Co squeezed one of the buds between her fingers as they both watched it slowly smash together. "You can't do that with that dry-ass bammer shit, blood. On Piru, dem Bounty Huntas came through with this shit!"

"That's how niggaz gonna be talkin' 'bout us now! We got that shit!" Suge replied absent mindedly. He was at the counter next to the sink with the cordless house phone in his hand. The phone book in front of him was being studied like one of UNLV's text books the night before an exam. Suge was looking for the number of Ichiban Records.

It didn't matter how much work he had, Suge wasn't going to ease up on the Chocolate and Vanilla Ice situation. The dope would feed his wolves for the time being. But he wasn't a drug dealer. He was a business man dead set on breaking into and taking over the music industry. After tracking down the number to the studio where Vanilla Ice recorded his music, he started making calls.

"...Yes. This Marion Knight. I'm calling on behalf of Mario Johnson. I understand... He's the author of a song that was sold to Vanilla Ice... OK... Yeah..."

Suge's crew knew how important those calls were. He'd been talking about it for a minute. So whenever one of their dogs came in the kitchen talking loud they were told to shut da fuck up while he handled his business. It didn't stop them from lighting up some greenery, though. Suge's business calls were part of the trapping process. It was all connected to the grind.

"It ... That doesn't matter... I'm trying to set up a meeting with either one of them. Him or his manager. Both of them, if that's what it takes... Alright, I'll wait."

He shook his head after being put on hold. A move he anticipated way before calling the record company. There was no point in getting frustrated, he told himself. This was business.

He was trying to collect some money from some people who didn't want to pay up. He had no doubt whatsoever that it wasn't going to come easy. But he wasn't worried about it because he knew the payoff would be worth it.

Suge leaned against the counter with the phone to his ear, watching all the activity around him. The homies were all working. Bagging up the cookies straight out the Pyrex pots. Cutting down ounces into stones for the packs they'd sell to the block bleeders.

They were also counting money as it came, then stacking it to the side.

Buntry and Heron were coming and going, fielding all the traffic.

A scene he had seen way too many times to count. He was glad to see his clique feasting. The Mob had been growing restless in the previous weeks with no work to eat off of. But now they had it. The energy was both positive and focused. Getting money was the mission of the day.

"So, what's up wit' Bolo?" Suge asked Co-Co. "Blood a'ight?"

"Blood boolin'. He somewhere round here recuperating from that sick one he was on. You know, blood get on water and don't know what he be doing."

"We gotta keep the set clean, blood. Especially now that we got this work. There ain't no reason to have pigs in the hood on some dumb shit."

Buntry stepped in the kitchen and took a forty ounce of Old E from the refrigerator. Heron came in behind him and took a seat at the table. The traffic had slowed down for the moment, giving them time to exchange notes while Suge sat on hold.

"I just got word they hit Q.Q.'s house with the battering ram this morning," Heron said.

"What?" exclaimed Suge. "Don't he –"

Buntry cut in, "Live with his mamma and all they kids. Yeah, blood. And you know them kids be huddled up in the living room watching their only TV."

"Yeah, blood," Heron continued. "On Piru, they bulldozed through the front of the house! The whole front wall gone!"

"On Piru, dat's some bitch shit!" Suge growled. "L.A.P.D. be on some Third Richt-type shit!"

Both Co-Co and Buntry stopped in their tracks and said, "Huh?"

Heron shook his head Suge was always coming with something high-powered. "Go on and school the homies, blood. Tell 'em what the Third Richt was."

"It's some German shit," Suge explained. "The German government was terrorizing the Jews under Hitler's rule. They moved all the Jewish people to certain parts of cities and called 'em ghettos. Then they started looking for reasons to lock 'em up."

"Just like they doin' us," Heron agreed.

"On Bloods," Suge commented. "They'd run up in people's houses at five in the morning when families were in bed asleep. Kick in their doors and take them to concentration camps. It's the same concept they using on us."

Just as he finished his statement, Suge heard the receptionist on the phone come on and say, "... Ummm... Mr –"

"Knight. Mr. Marion Knight. I'm right here."

"Yes... Mr. Knight, Mr. Van Winkle isn't in the office right now. He won't be back for several weeks –"

"But, you just told me you'd ask him –"

"I didn't say that, sir –"

"What?!" Suge snapped before getting ahold of himself. You just sat there and told me to hold on while you talked to him. Now, you telling me he's on vacation?"

"Mr. Van Winkle is not in the office. I will have him call you when comes back from his vacation."

The line went dead.

Suge stood there in disbelief as he sat the phone on the counter.

Co-Co, who had been listening to the exchange, said, "I know that bitch didn't! She didn't just hang up on you, right?"

"These mothafuckas is brazy," Suge replied.

"I ain't got no problem whoopin' a bitch ass!" Co-Co assured him. "We can go up there right now!"

"Hold up," Suge said. He had the phone back up to his ear. When the call was answered he said, "This is Marion Knight. I'm calling 'cause you hung up on me."

This time the receptionist was obviously feeling herself because she raised her voice when she replied,"Mr. Knight, I will have Mr. Van Winkle call you when he comes back from –"

"Check this out, bitch! I was very respectful when I was talking to you earlier. Even when you started lying to me. I came at you correct 'cause this is business and you're just doin' your job. But now, you getting besides yourself without knowing who da fuck you're talking to.

"I'm actually calling your dumb-ass back to give your incompetent ass my mothafuckin' number. The fact that you didn't take it down before hanging up on me let me know you're playing games. And what you don't seem to understand, or take into inconsideration is I got your number out the phone book. Your office's address is right here, too. I can push up there anytime I choose. The smartest thing you can do is shut da fuck up and take my number down!"

Suge let that sink in for a moment. He didn't want to show that side of him, but he wasn't against it. He was a gangsta no matter what industry he was in. If the music executives thought they were gonna play with his intelligence, they had another thing coming.

After a moment, the receptionist asked him for his contact information. Suge made eye contact with Co-Co, smiled then nodded his head.

"Yeah... my number is..."

CHAPTER EIGHT

Suge was Stanley Steaming, but he didn't let a small bump in the road derail him from the larger mission at hand. Another person would've felt played for being forced to show their ghetto face. He welcomed it. Suge was dead set on taking his ism anywhere he went, whether it was called for or not.

Business in the Beehive resumed. Lueders Park hustlers came and went, picking up work to get off on the block. Then, about an hour after the call, Suge's pager vibrated with a familiar number.

D.O.C. was tapping in, looking for something to smoke on. To Suge, his friend D.O.C. was a major piece in a whole different mission. So he didn't have a problem taking a trip to the other side of the tracks for him. Plus, Suge enjoyed hanging out with the nigga. He looked forward to the vibe he'd enter when he got to his partna's house.

One of the biggest reasons Suge respected D.O.C. was his realness. They had known one another since D.O.C. came to Compton and he never changed. Even after N.W.A. blew up, he stayed the same person he was at first. Being from Texas gave him a swagger with sharp edges which is probably what drew them together in the first place.

D.O.C. had a big white house with four bedrooms and a pool in the back. It wasn't as big as Eazy's mansion, but it was raw. Suge liked going over there because it gave him a live glimpse at how he would be living before it was all said and done.

Even before he reached the mansion, Suge saw all the foreign cars lined up in front of it. He smiled to himself already knowing they most likely belonged to a bunch of different White women. *Blood love him some White bitches*, he said to himself as he pulled up behind a two door Beemer.

Suge hopped out the K5 with his backpack slung over his shoulder. Something caught his attention across the street, just in time to see a front-room curtain quickly move back into place.

It brought a smile to his face. Suge always felt a sense of satisfaction when he saw the reactions while white people had when they saw young, rich, Black men living just as well as them. Most of the time, he'd see it at high end restaurants, downtown high-rises, and neighborhoods such as the one he was in at that very moment.

Suge already knew that no matter how much a Black man obtained, the white establishment would never accept him. And that didn't bother him. He didn't want a part of the White man's world. He wanted his own world, with his own people surrounding him.

A beautiful sistah in a small bikini answered the door with a drink in her hand. She smiled when she saw Suge, "Sugar Bear?"

"Yeah, baby, it's me," he replied while taking in her freshly oiled skin.

"We been waiting on you. D.O.C. is in the backyard."

He didn't need an escort, but he didn't mind watching them ass cheeks lead the way. He was well acquainted with the layout of the house. Suge helped D.O.C. move into the home.

For a second, he was taken back to the first night they hung out there. Suge helped D.O.C. bring in what little furniture he had.

It was nowhere near enough to fill up all the rooms, making the home feel even bigger than it really was. The rapper had just cashed his first big check and the first purchase he made was that house. After a whole day of moving, they ended up sitting next to the pool with some Chinese takeout. It was a bright evening. The moon illuminated their dreams. Just thinking of that night was nostalgic.

In Suge's eyes, that was the beginning of it all. It was his glimpse into the future. Two gangstaz on the precipice of greatness.

His sexy host gave him a lusty stare just before they stepped into the backyard. And just like the inside of the kingpin's spot in Watts, the scene he stepped into was like night and day from what was outside the home. The quiet, upper-class neighborhood he had just driven through did not match the scene taking place in D.O.C.'s backyard.

The party was lit! Music was blasting. A bar was set up, where a woman was passing out free drinks. And the men-to-women ratio was three to one.

It was an all-out gangsta party at its finest.

D.O.C. was seated at the table under a gazebo on the far end of the yard. When he saw Suge he lit up and called out, "Simon Says! What's brackin', blood!"

"Sup, blood!" Suge replied just as energetically. D.O.C. wasn't a banger, but he was family.

They greeted each other with dap and hugs. All smiles and good vibes echoed from their exchange. Life was good and getting better by the moment.

They hadn't settled in for thirty seconds before D.O.C. announced, "I can smell that shit from here! You really got dat bomb shit, huh, Suge!"

Suge smiled. He knew he had some of the best weed in Los Angeles. He reached into his backpack, took out a freezer bag with a quarter pound of the stickiest Christmas-tree looking buds he ever saw and dropped it on the table in front of his friend.

"When my nigga says he wants something to smoke, I'm fo' sho' finna come through wit' da' best! On Piru, this that one-hitter-quitter!"

D.O.C. put the bag to his nose and took a long whiff of the high-grade buds. "Mmm-mmm! Now, this is what I'm talkin' 'bout!" To one of his partnaz walking by he tossed the bag towards him and directed his attention back towards Suge. "So, whatchu been up to, relly?"

Suge leaned back on his seat and let out a long breath. He was frustrated about something. "You know me, D.O.C. I'm sniffin' out this money. But this industry is a mothafucka. Some of these folks don't know who they playin' wit'. And they not gonna like the way I move when I'm forced to show 'em it's not a game."

A skinny White girl jumped in the pool, making a loud splashing sound just as Suge finished his statement. The party was at full swing. Still, it didn't disrupt their conversation. They were used to having talks in that type of setting.

"Somebody owe you some money, or somethin'?" D.O.C. asked.

"Somethin' like that. Remember what we talked about at the club when Yella told me someone else wrote that "'Ice Ice Baby' song?" Well, I tracked down the author. It's a nigga named Mario. And get this, he hasn't been paid for it. So I'm managing him now, which means, that money is now owed to me."

"You gonna need a serious mouthpiece for that one. I don't see them people givin' up anything on anything."

"I already know. I'm on it. But I'm tryna do this without havin' to go to trial and all that."

"So, what's happening?"

"I keep calling Ichiban Records. They already started started playing games. The receptionist —"

"Let me guess... She said Ice and his manager on the road. That they gonna be gone for a minute."

Suge scoffed "Yeah. I had to cuss the dumb bitch out!"

D.O.C. caught the attention of a woman walking by and told her to bring them some drinks. Then, to Suge he asked, "So, how that work out for you?"

Suge chuckled, "She got wit' the program real quick. I just can't stand having to take it there. I know they just not used to dealing with a nigga of my caliber, tho'. I'm not the type of fool who's gonna start talkin' white when I approach 'em. I've been sittin' on the sidelines long enough to know them crackaz only respect niggaz who show they fangs."

"You dead right! They're snakes, Suge. You can't let up, not for one second. You give these folks any little leeway and they gonna run over you."

Gator, D.O.C.'s partna sat down at the table with a tray holding some weed and rolling papers. "Here you go, mane," he said as he handed him an extra thick 'J.'

D.O.C. lit the tip. The strong herb immediately made his eyelids droop like an Asian's. He looked at Suge and found his friend lost in thought. No one had to tell him what he was doing. He'd seen that look on Suge's face many times before. And, every time he saw it, he could count on him coming out of his zone with a mapped-out million-dollar plan.

D.O.C. continued giving time to come to whatever conclusion he was mulling over. "These industry people hide behind those glass high-rises like they in some sort of protected environment. They sit behind their desks thinking they can't be touched. And, what's really twisted is how the average person actually believes the hype. Niggaz be acting like they're untouchable when they really not."

"Here you go, guys," cut in the pretty White girl. She handed them their drinks. "You need anything else, D.O.C.?"

"Naw, baby. It's all good."

"Let me know if you need anything."

"Bet," D.O.C. replied. After she left he turned to Suge and said, "See baby right there? Her dad is the District Attorney."

"Yeah?" Suge said, suddenly interested in the conversation.

"Check game... Her mother and father both showed up last night. Her pops left with Jerry, and ain't no tellin' what they got into. But her momma stayed all night. She got ran through by the homies. "And, that's not even the point. What I'm getting' at is when they in they offices, in their suits an shit, niggaz look at 'em like they gods. But in real life, they normal people. Twisted and warped. Feel me?"

Suge didn't say anything. He was obviously in his own head formulating a thought or two. Then, as if he was hit with a sudden realization, he took his glass and downed it's contents in one gulp.

"I gotta go!" he announced while picking up his backpack and standing up.

"Huh?" D.O.C. said. "You just got here! What's up?"

"I gotta go! Gotta beat the Beverly Hills traffic! I'll meet up wit you later. I got some business to take care of."

Suge rushed back to his truck and slid straight into traffic. He was on a mission, operating through tunnel vision, and time was of the essence.

CHAPTER NINE

Suge pulled up to the Ichiban Recording studio approximately forty minutes after leaving D.O.C.'s house. The traffic had been rough but that was regular. It didn't even bother him since it gave him time to prepare himself for what he was about to do.

Before he left the house that morning, he had put on his hood-wear. A red and white Polo shirt, black jeans, and a pair of size thirteen red and white Nike Cortez's. It was what he wore to D.O.C.'s house and what he had on as he approached the glass doors he was heading into.

A gangland Chief was about to enter the White man's world.

All eyes were on the flamed-up gangsta the moment he stepped in the building. You would think the employees who worked in the same building where Vanilla Ice called his base of operations would've been used to seeing thugs on the premises. But by the looks on several faces he passed by, one could tell that wasn't the case. Suge didn't give a fuck, though. He went straight to the elevator and headed up to the fourth floor where he was determined to meet with the bitch he had spoken to earlier that day.

Jennifer Landers was an aspiring singer in her late twenties. In an effort to penetrate the music industry, she had gotten the job as the receptionist for a recording studio. She was used to seeing stars dressed in comfortable attire enter the office. That's why Suge's outfit didn't raise red flags when he first entered the office and approached her desk.

At first, he was greeted by a toothy grin. Upon her first glance, she caught herself immediately attracted to Suge's light skin and tall stature. The spark came fast and deep. But the moment she heard him speak, everything changed. She instantaneously recognized his voice. He was the man she had spoken to earlier in the day.

"I'm here to meet with Robert Van Winkle."

She turned white. She stuttered nervously when she asked a question she already knew the answer to. "Do you have a –"

"No, I don't," he hissed as condescendingly as possible.

Her shaky hand knocked the phone's receiver of its cradle in her attempt to call Vanilla Ice's manager. Then, instead of putting the phone to her ear she nervously glanced towards a door a few feet away. "Mr. Knight, I can assure you Mr. Van Winkle isn't in today. Neither him or –"

"You sure about that?" Suge asked, most definitely not believing her. He glanced at the door she cut her eyes towards a moment earlier.

"Yes, sir."

He wasn't stupid. He knew the games they played. He had been a fly on the wall during hundreds of conversations with their kind. None of the average runaround bullshit he witnessed them try on others was going to work on him. Not if he had any say in the matter.

Without as much as another word, he shot across the room towards the door in question. He wasn't gonna give an inch to the leaches on his mission to get Mario's money.

In in aggressive swoop, he snatched the door open and barged into the room. Inside, he found no one. It was empty!

The bitch wasn't lying, he thought to himself before backing out the room.

Still, he didn't allow that fact to soften his approach. Something told him this would not be the last time he'd have to deal with her, so he was intent on establishing his ism right then and there.

"A'ight... He ain't in right now. That's bool. Now that I know you're not lying, we can have an honest conversation, right?"

"Yes, sir."

"Call me Mr. Knight. Marion Knight."

"Yes, Mr. Knight."

"You got my number, right?"

"Yes. It's right here," she stated nervously.

"Make sure Robert calls me the moment he comes in. If you don't see him, then have his manager get at me. Let them know I'm calling about unpaid funds due to Mario Johnson." Suge paused, letting his words sink in. Then he continued, "Understood?"

"Yes, sir..."

CHAPTER TEN

When Suge got back to the trap house on Bullis, he saw black Trans Am parked out front. He didn't recognize the car, but the Nevada plates narrowed the suspect list. He could count on one hand how many people with Nevada plates knew how to find him in the trenches. The good thing about that was, all of those individuals were people who could put smiles on his face without even trying.

He was halfway up the steps when the front door opened and his partna stepped out the house to greet him.

"What's up, nigga!" Ricky said energetically. Suge smiled brightly as he rushed towards his friend for a thug's embrace.

"Damn, homey! I forgot you was on your way out here."

"Shiiit! I'm all about crossing State lines on a cheddar chase. You got me twisted if you didn't think I was coming home for some work."

"C'mon, " Suge told him. "Let's go inside. I got all kinds of shit I need to talk to you 'bout. Where's your brother? Did Wes come with you?"

Suge was stepping inside the house as he asked the question. Before Ricky could reply, his brother who was seated on the couch in the living room answered for him.

"Simons Says! Man! What it do, bro?"

Another hearty embrace took place.

Suge was ecstatic when he saw them. Ricky and Wes were old friends who stayed in Las Vegas while he was going to UNLV. They were all big enough to be NFL linebackers. Wes was more clean-cut than his brother. Ricky had a gheri curl and he was more street savvy than his brother. But Suge loved them both the same. Wes had gotten him his first gig as a bodyguard. It was how met Bobby Brown.

Buntry and Co-Co were still there with several others. It wasn't the first time they had met the brothers. Their crews had entwined on more than a few occasions. Especially when there was money to be made.

Suge led his company to the kitchen where they all took a seat at the table. Somewhere in the house there was a radio on. An Al B. Sure song was playing over the airwaves.

"Y'all staying overnight?" he asked.

"Naw," replied Ricky. "Not this time. Shit, we getting this work and heading straight back."

"That's bool. It's probably for the best anyway. 'Cause I'm not really in the mood to hangout tonight."

"What?!" exclaimed Wes. "Not Simon Says! You ain't never turned down a night to get wicked! What's wrong?"

"Yeah," Ricky agreed. "What's wrong? You tired? Oh no!" Ricky looked at his brother and said, "Sharitha! Sharitha got Suge on curfew!"

Even Suge had to laugh at that one.

"Naw. It ain't the wifey at all. It's these mothafuckaz I'm tryna catch up wit'. I got a client I'm managing. He's a songwriter. He wrote a cut called "Ice Ice Baby" and the record company is refusing to pay him. They playing hardball."

"That's not surprising," Wes replied. He had been around just as many famous musicians as Suge had. He was well versed in the bullshit song writers and other performers had to deal with when it came time to collect their dividends.

Then Ricky said, "Oh shit, you're talking about Vanilla Ice's song, 'Ice Ice Baby'!" Suge nodded, Ricky whistled. "That's a prize, ain't it? That mothafucka had to have gone platinum. If not, at least gold. It's gotta be worth –"

"Millions!" Suge said for him. "They know it, too. That's why they stonewalling us. Then when I went to my lawyer –"

"Who? Victor?" Wes asked.

"Yeah. He got a job at his parent's law firm in Hollywood. I just talked to him. Bro got an office with a million-dollar view on top of a hideaway bathroom!"

"I bet!" Wes replied. "He come from old money."

"Y'all talkin' 'bout the rich white boy who likes sistahs?" Ricky asked.

"Yeah," Suge replied. "That's him. I thought he'd be able to help, but he couldn't. Says he does TV and movie deals, or some shit like that. That's why I'm hot. I gotta figure out a way to get paid off this shit."

They all got quiet for a second. A dice game had gotten started somewhere in the house. The sound of slick talking and dice shaking became their background noise.

Then Wes sat up as if a thought jolted him up. "What about Griffey? Dick Griffey?"

Suge looked at Wes. The name sounded familiar but he couldn't place it.

Wes saw the confusion in his eyes. "Suge, c'mon, man. You know about Dick Griffey. He's the founder of Solar Records."

He had to think for a moment before he remembered exactly who Wes was talking about.

"I'm telling you," Wes continued. "He can help with whatever issues you having. He's like a mob boss in the music industry."

"Where's he at? I know he's stationed out here. Ain't his studio, Solar, in Hollywood or something?"

"I don't know the exact address. But I can call 'im and set up a meeting for you. He's down to earth, Suge. I'm sure he'll hear you out. If you need a lawyer, he'll point you in the right direction, too. He's established in a real way."

Set it up, homey. Let me know when and where, and I'll meet up with 'im if he'll see me."

"Bet."

"Now that that's over with," Ricky said, "it's time for us to talk business..."

CHAPTER ELEVEN

Later on that evening, after all his business had been put to rest and he climbed into bed, Suge laid there restless as ever. His bedroom was dark, yet cozy. Illuminated by the flickering light from the TV screen he wasn't watching. He was comfortably propped up against a pillow while Sharitha rested her head on his chest. The familiar setting usually set him at ease. But that night, work seemed to overpower his peace.

Sharitha could sense the tenseness in her man's body. She had known him long enough to recognize the subtle clues that exposed his thoughts and emotions. It didn't matter how hard he'd try to hide his emotions (whether good or bad), she could always see past his defensive lines.

Suge had been preoccupied with his thoughts all evening. His loving smile was there when he came home. He was even talkative during dinner. An outsider, even some close friends wouldn't have been able to see the stress in his life. It was there, though. She knew it. She could sense it.

It was close to twelve midnight when Sharitha sat up, looked into his eyes and asked, "What's wrong?"

Suge looked at her and was about to hit her with a sidestep right before she cut him off with an even more concerned inquiry.

"And don't give me no 'Everything's good, baby,' Marion! What's on your mind?"

Suge glanced at the television. A commercial selling something he didn't give a fuck about was on. He hadn't been paying attention to anything all night. He really didn't wanna stress Sharitha 'bout it, but she was his better half. She was his partner in crime through it all. So if he'd confide in anyone – it would been her.

"Suge... What's wrong, babe?"

"It's this shit with Vanilla Ice and Chocolate. I'm just trying to figure it out. I need a game plan. This deal is worth millions but they stonewalling us."

"How?"

"Baby, this nigga wrote one of the hottest songs in the country! He actually wrote most of the music on that dude's album. They haven't paid him shit, either. What's so cold about it is, just a few points on its earnings is worth millions. Millions! Not hundreds of thousands, ya hear me?"

"Yeah. I get it."

"Since I'm managing him, I can basically get any sort of percentage I draw up. Anything will be better than what he's getting now."

"That doesn't mean you're gonna get over on him, right? You promised me you'd always do right by your clients."

"Onda set, I'm not gonna rob blood. I'm not like that. Sharitha, I wouldn't even have to. Legally, this song's residue is enough to move us to a whole different tax bracket. That's why I gotta come up with something that works. I can't let these folks tie us up in a legal battle. I can't let them buy us off with crumbs. This is it. It's the chance of a lifetime. I gotta make things shake right now. If I ever plan on making it in the industry, I need to make my move *now*."

She picked up the remote from the nightstand and turned the television all the way down. A distant police siren along with some stray dogs barking filled the night. It wasn't enough to distract them, though. It was the soundtrack of their lives.

Her eyes were deep. Understanding as well as nurturing. She looked at Suge and asked him, "You love me?"

"Damn right! I fell in love with you from the moment I first saw you."

"You trust me?"

"On Piru."

"Then listen to me. Do you remember that first night we met? At that house party where we wasn't allowed to use the bathroom? And all my homegirls needed to pee, but we couldn't?"

Suge smiled. "Yeah. I remember it like it was this morning. You wasn't fuckin' wit' me back then. I was gettin' at you hard, too."

"Yeah. You was trippin'," she teased. "You didn't give me a chance to talk to anyone that night. But something I remember the most is how my homegirls told me to talk to you 'bout getting us access to that bathroom. Danielle's auntie was hella mean. She wasn't budging for nobody! But we all knew you could make things happen. Even back then."

"You trippin', baby."

"I'm serious. And what did you do? You went back there, said something, and made that happen. Now you might think that's funny. But, it's the first night I ever met you. And not only did you get us bathroom service," she chuckled, "you also bulldozed your way into my life. You changed my perception of you. It went from me not liking you –"

"You can't say you wasn't just a little bit into a nigga."

"Hell naw!" she laughed. "I thought you was a player. Trying to lie to me about your name. There was no way in the world I was gonna believe your parents named you Suge!"

A smile crept across his face. He remembered that night clearly. From the moment he saw her enter the party, he had fallen in love. He even told China Dogg under his breath, "You see her... I'm gonna marry her one day." Something he never told her.

"Anyways," she continued. "The point I'm getting at is you never changed. Always remained the same. Anytime you ever came up with a plan, you always saw it through. I remember you coming to me when we was in Vegas talking 'bout you was gonna be a bodyguard for famous people. What did you do?"

"I became a bodyguard."

"And when you came up with a plan to be a manager for musicians –?"

"I did that!"

"You even played in the NFL! Baby, you can and will do anything and everything you put your mind to. You're too smart; too strong; too smooth not to. That's why so many people trust and believe in you. Shoot, my little brother idolizes you. He'll go to the end of the earth if you told him to. Suge smiled. "I fucks with Silk. That's my young nigga right there."

"He's not the only one who sees you like that, baby. You're special. You're going places. Remember that!"

He stared into her eyes. She was the one person in his life who he could trust with his life. She had no ulterior motives. She knew his weaknesses just as well as his strengths. Even when he didn't. That's what made her words even more meaningful as well as motivating.

"Come'ere, baby! I love you!" he told her before taking her into his arms and planting a passionate kiss on her lips.

They spent the rest of the night making love. At times it was soft and slow. Other moments it became rough and rugged. Even a little nasty... The elixir of lust was enough to set him at ease. Giving him a clear mind full of confidence to tackle his mission.

When they finally fell asleep, Suge was able to fully rest at ease...

CHAPTER TWELVE

"Baby... Baby! Wake up!" Sharitha that purred from the comfort of her man's chest.

"Huh?" Suge said from his sleepy haze. It hadn't been but a few hours since he collapsed on her torso after busting the fattest nut in history.

"Baby, your pager is blowing up! You don't hear it?"

With one eyelid barely cracked open he reached towards the nightstand for his beeper. There were nine messages from the same number.

It was a Big Wes' code. *Fuck dat!* he thought to himself. *I'll get back to that later.* He was about to toss the pager back where he took it from until he remembered the conversation, they had the day before. That jolted him out of his slumber. He sat up suddenly, grabbed the phone from the nightstand and quickly dialed the number.

Big Wes answered on the first ring, "Hey!"

"Wes!"

"Man, you need to wake yo' ass up, bro! I just got off the phone with Dick. I told him a little about your situation and he agreed to meet wit'chu."

"Yeah?" asked Suge out loud. But on his end, he hit the air with a fist pump.

Sharitha wiped the sleep from her eyes. She felt the energy change in her man. She knew whatever news he was receiving on that call had to be connected to his current mission. By the sounds of it, the tides were turning in his favor.

"When does he wanna meet?"

"Today! He's at Solar studio –"

"I'll find it!"

"He said he'll be there all day. But you need to hit 'im up ASAP! Ain't no tellin what might come up and we won't be able to reach him for months."

"You think I should call –"

"No! Don't call him. Go up there. Take that nigga who wrote that song and go up there and talk to Dick in person. He can work wonders for you if you get him on your side. And this might be your only chance to make that happen."

Suge was already sliding on a pair of jeans. He knew Wes was right. He had to jump on this opportunity. It was the type of door that only came open once in a lifetime.

"Gotchu! Let me clean up real quick and head down there. Wes, call blood and let 'im know I'll be down there in the next hour –"

"Depending on traffic."

"Onda set!"

Suge ended the call, then rushed to the adjoining bathroom to wash his face and take a piss.

Sharitha was up and moving too. "What was that about, Marion?"

He was splashing water on his face. Between splashes and putting his toothbrush in his mouth he said, "I got a meeting with Dick Griffey from Solar Records."

"Solar?! How?!"

"Big Wes connected some dots for me. I gotta go, baby. Do me a favor and go in my sock drawer and take out my black book. Find Chocolate's number."

"Who?"

"Mario Johnson."

Sharitha stepped into the bathroom while Suge was brushing his teeth. She sat on the toilet and started peeing. "What you want me to do? Call 'im?"

He spit out some toothpaste and said, "Yeah. Call him and make sure he's ready to go somewhere with me. If he's not there, tell his girl to track him down and have him there when I get there. We're gonna go meet Griffey together."

Suge wiped his mouth, dried off his face, then bent down to kiss Sharitha goodbye. "I'll keep you posted, baby. Gotta go!"

CHAPTER THIRTEEN

Suge and Mario arrived at Solar studios in less than the hour he thought it would take them. The multiple-level building was iconic. It was the Motown of the 80's. As Suge stepped through the doors he knew things were about to blow up. He could feel it in his bones.

Dicky Griffey had them buzzed in immediately. His receptionist led them to his office where they found Dick and another man waiting for them.

Dick's office was just as plush as Victor's office was. Suge couldn't help but quietly search for a secret door leading to a private restroom. The most notable difference between the two offices were the plaques on Griffey's walls. Awards he had been presented over his years in the music industry adorned the walls. Giving his lair the vibe of a man who created superstars.

The older, light-skinned man with a thick mustache stuck his hand out to shake Suge's then Chocolate's. "How you doing, Marion?"

Suge smiled, "I'm good, Mr. Griffey. This is Mario Johnson."

"How you doing, Mr. Johnson?" After greeting them, Dick introduced the fourth man in the room. "This is Virgil Roberts, fellas. The best contract lawyer in the country."

"Now, c'mon, Dick," Virgil said humbly. "You know damn well I'm the best in the whole Western Hemisphere."

They all laughed at the statement, two of them hoping it was true, the other two confident that it was.

"Come on, fellas, let's take a seat," Griffey told them. Then to Suge he said, "Big Wes told me a little about your situation. I'm not sure I can help you. But you can go ahead and tell us what's going on."

"Well, it's like this," Suge began. "I was hearing about how Mario had written 'Ice Ice Baby' and hadn't gotten paid for it.

"The song is all over the place, on TV and all that. The song is making money. Vanilla Ice's whole career is based on the music Mario wrote for him. And they haven't paid him shit."

After Suge stopped speaking, they all looked at Chocolate. It was his turn to talk, but before he could say anything Virgil asked him, "How did that happen? How did you write a platinum-selling song without seeing a cent of the profits? Walk me through it."

"Well... it didn't go big at first. I was living in Texas with my girl. We had a one bedroom in Houston. Anyways, I'd write songs and Rob would –"

"Rob? Who's that?" Dick Griffey asked.

"Vanilla Ice's name is Robert Van Winkle," Suge clarified.

Mario continued, "He'd come over to my apartment and practice 'em. It was our regular program. I'd write music and he'd rap it. We'd go to a studio out there and he'd record the tracks. After the album dropped, we kinda just lost track of one another.

I'd call him, but he'd be gone so I just lost contact with him."

"What's the name of the album?" Virgil asked.

"It was originally called 'Hooked.' I wrote about four tracks on that album. So, one day I saw a video for 'Ice Ice Baby' on BET. I had moved back home by then. Rob had moved out here too. I made some calls and found out who his lawyer was and I went by his office to talk to him about it. That's when I found out how big the album really was."

"What do you mean?" Virgil asked. "What did you find out?"

"His lawyer didn't seem to believe me. That, or he didn't think I'd be able to fight it. But, he was sitting there reading some spreadsheet and said some shit like, "So, you're telling me you wrote almost half the songs on an album that has two million pre-orders before it's even been properly released?"

Virgil whistled in amazement. He shot a glance in Griffey's direction.

"I told him I didn't know anything about all that. All I did and do know is I wrote them songs. And I haven't been paid my proper dues. It didn't really matter anyway. He wasn't trying to hear me out. The honky basically dismissed me. I never heard back from them people after that."

The room went silent after he stopped talking. Suge studied the older, more experienced Griffey. He watched him and Virgil exchange silent stares. Then Griffey spoke.

First, he looked at Suge. Then he looked at Mario before going back to Suge. "This is all very interesting. It doesn't sound farfetched. It actually happens more than people think. Artists get songs and become overnight sensations; travelling the country, performing and doing interviews. It all goes to their heads, making them feel untouchable. All while the unseen artist, the true savant gets left with nothing but crumbs. I've seen it happen too many times.

"Then there's the other side of the hustle," Virgil began. "A guy hums a tune one day. May even write a few lines that resemble the chorus of a song, and he starts claiming he wrote said music. Starts claiming it to the point where he either believes he created the piece himself, or at least tries to get others to believe it. But all along, he never wrote anything worth arguing over."

"I ain't lying," Chocolate stated defensively.

"At this point, what you say means nothing. You've got two million pre-ordered reasons to lie about this. But, don't get me wrong. I'm not telling you I don't believe you. No one in this room is calling you a liar at this time. But, I'm a lawyer. My job is to prove things in a courtroom. The only way I'm going to be able to do that is if you come with some proof that you wrote this song." Virgil then addressed Suge. "It's like this, brother; this is a big claim. We're talking at least several hundred thousand dollars is at stake. Money that Vanilla Ice's people obviously don't wanna pay. The way the courts work is you're gonna have to prove your man wrote this music. They aren't going to make him prove you're lying. They're gonna make you prove you're telling the truth. Do you understand this concept?"

"Yeah," Suge replied.

That's when Griffey cut back in, "So, how do we know you really wrote this song, Mario? What kind of proof do you have?"

Suge knew the next few minutes would dictate whether Griffey and Roberts would back their play. It was on Chocolate.

"It's like this, man. My girl was right there when I wrote these songs. I actually got all my notes of when I was writing them. I also got some tapes I had recorded myself when I was coming up with the melody. I got another witness too. My nigga Quake did the beats for these songs. He was there too. He heard the songs before Ice did. And he was there when he was practicing his delivery for them. I helped him catch the flow for every song."

Dick and Virgil exchanged some deeper looks. Suge watched it all play out. Things seemed to look better. Chocolate had a good case once he laid it all out.

Griffey addressed Chocolate, "Do you still have these tapes? What about the people you're mentioning, do you still talk to this guy Quake?"

"Yeah. Hell yeah!"

Griffey looked at his lawyer, "What do you think?"

Virgil nodded. "I think we got a strong case that'll stand up in court. But, that can take years in litigation. I've got to see all the evidence myself. Then I'll make some phone calls and set up some meetings with their legal team. Maybe we can get them to settle out of court."

"That's more along the lines I'm thinking," Suge interjected. "How can we make that happen?"

"If you can somehow get that Ice character to agree to concede some points on the music Mario wrote, we won't have to spend years in court. There's a chance he'll do it if you can show him all the evidence. But I doubt it. That's not how these people move."

Suge didn't say anything else. He looked around the room knowing he would do anything it took to make this go through. But first, he had to know something. "So, are you guys with us? Can you help us?"

Everyone looked at Griffey. He was good. His poker face was immaculate.

If he would've shown his true emotions, they would have all seen how much he liked Suge. Suge reminded him of the Hip-Hop version of himself. After a long moment of silence he said, "I'm in.

For a percentage, of course."

They all laughed. It was an all-around victory for them all.

"I'll make some phone calls. But, keep in mind, cases like these can take years."

That last statement lingered like rotten wine. It was almost interpreted as a challenge that rested on Suge's shoulders. There was court. And there was a settlement. The latter was the one Suge was banking on...

CHAPTER FOURTEEN

The coldest nights in Bompton are usually in the summer. It's the time of year when gangland demons come out of hibernation.

Every section of the city is activated and ready for war. Conversations between killers can mean the difference between whether someone lives, or someone dies. Needless to say, in certain situations a person may have to die in order for someone else to live. The trenches were like that at times.

Stars take the main stage when the moon disappears. On this particular evening the sky was bright even though its main attraction was nowhere to be found. Suge, Buntry, and Heron were outside of Buntry's house, on his porch drinking 40's.

Buntry lived in a small two-bedroom house in the heart of Lueders Park. The fenced in yard kept his two pitbulls from running into the street. While the front porch gave the Pirus a familiar spot to plot, scheme and strategize.

Suge had just cracked open his bottle of Old English when he heard Heron ask him what was on his mind. "All kinds of shit, Ru. I gotta come up wit' something 'cause these mothafuckaz is playing with me about this song."

"You already knew that was gonna happen," Buntry commented. "Them devils stay on some bullshit!"

"Blood," Suge began. "I've been callin' that studio for over a week. I'm tryin' to give them fools a chance to fix this shit before we involve the courts."

"How many times you call 'em?" Heron asked after lighting a Newport and tossing the pack back to Buntry.

"On Piru, I've been calling that studio like two or three times a day."

"You ain't been up there?" Heron asked.

"I rode up there a few times. The bitch keeps tellin' me they gone and she ain't talk to the white boy or his manager. But, that's bullshit."

"For real?" Buntry asked.

"Onda Mob! I know she in contact with them. Every secretary has direct access to their boss at all times of the day, and or night. And the type of pressure I've been applying isn't supposed to get ignored."

"On Bloods," agreed Heron.

As if on que, both of Buntry's dogs started barking at a hooded figure riding by on a bicycle. Neither of the men on the porch moved. They all recognized their young homey in the red sweater.

"Blood," Buntry said suddenly sporting a smile.

Heron replied, "Yeah."

"You remember when Lil Kenny tried paying me and Suge to jump you?"

The change of subject didn't catch him off-guard since they were all used to their conversations bouncing from subject to subject. It was like that with friends who shared a past as far back as theirs.

"Yeah," Heron replied. "What made you think about that?"

"The lil homey on the bike. It made me think about Kenny 'cause blood was always on his Mongoose pushin' through the set."

Suge laughed. "He did, huh? Blood never walked anywhere."

Heron smiled at the memory of their younger days. "Blood was trippin' 'cause I took his bike one night when I was walking home from practice. Blood left that shit in his yard and I was tired as fuck from all them up-downs coach had a nigga doing that afternoon."

"Naw, blood!" Buntry argued. "On Piru, Kenny wasn't trippin' off the bike. You gave it back."

"I remember that shit," Suge said. "He was trippin' off you and Shondelle. That nigga said he rode by the alley behind yo' granny house and saw you kissin' on his bitch."

Buntry let out a loud laugh from deep within his chest. He remembered it just as clearly as Suge had.

Shondelle wasn't blood's bitch, tho'!" Heron chuckled. "At least she didn't act like it when she was sucking this pipe!"

After another round of laughter, they took some more drinks from their bottles enjoying the nostalgia. Once the chuckles subsided, they got right back to business.

Buntry asked Suge, "So, other than stalking Vanilla's studio, what you been doin'?"

"Whatchumean?" Suge asked.

"What da fuck you think he mean?" Heron cut in. "You been M.I.A. ever since you dropped off the work."

"You been in the Nickerson's this whole time?" Buntry inquired. "Fuckin' wit' da Hunta'?"

Suge took a moment to think before he replied. Something was on his mind, but he was trying to formulate the right words. Especially since the whole subject was causing him so much frustration.

"Naw," Heron said. "Blood got a bitch tucked off somewhere. This nigga been creeping on the unda."

"It ain't dat," Suge assured them. "Sharitha would kill me in my sleep if she caught me wit' another bitch. It's not that. It's this whole Mario situation." Suge's face became sullen.

The tone of his voice changed, and so did his crew's vibe. "I'm tryna get this check. Mario is my artist now. So, whatever he gets from that music he wrote is gonna get split between us. I'm tellin' y'all, the points he 'posed to get off that song is worth millions." He let that sink in for a minute before continuing.

Even the dogs noticed the change in the men. They both came onto the porch and squatted down next to Buntry's feet.

"My lawyer talkin' 'bout how long the court case gonna take. It'll be worth it, but it can take decades. I don't got that type of time."

"Onda Mob!" they agreed.

"My time is now!" he stated. "I'm not about to wait that long. Not for this kinda ticket."

"Onda set," Heron agreed. "So what you need?"

They all knew it was a loaded question. Heron, just like everyone else in Suge's inner circle, was a cold-blooded killer. He would've topped any federal serial killer list if gang-related murders would have been a federal priority.

Suge took a long look at his friend. Murder was always an option, never to be taken off the table. Yet, in this case, it would've only complicated matters even more. Killing Vanilla Ice would have brought in even more vultures trying to cash in on his estate. *No.* Suge thought to himself. He couldn't kill the white boy.

Not yet, at least.

"The mouthpiece told me we need some proof; some real proof that Mario wrote the music on the white boy's album."

"What kinda proof?" Buntry asked.

"Handwritten notes, witnesses. Any sort of letters from the studio – shit like that."

"Does he got any of –" Heron started to ask before the pits stood up and started growling.

They all looked towards the gate and saw Jody, a neighborhood crackhead standing on the sidewalk. She was on the other side of the fence looking anxious. Although the night was ridiculously dark, she was still recognizable. Her wild hair and trademark loose t-shirt gave them a familiar silhouette to work with.

"Buntry," she called out, barely able to see their faces either. She knew he was one of the figures on the porch. And it wasn't too hard to guess who the other two men were. Men of that caliber only pushed with familiar faces.

"What's brackin'?" Buntry responded.

"I got thirty," she said while fidgeting on her toes from side to side.

Buntry got up to serve her.

Suge kept talking to Heron. "Chocolate gave me his notes from the song. Blood saved that shit and he don't even know how lucky he is. Them tapes and scraps of paper he got are worth the whole case. I took 'em to
Virgil —"

"Who's that?"

"My lawyer."

"On Ru's."

"He said the notes from the song along with Mario's girl as a witness is enough to take them to court and win."

Buntry came back and sat down.

Heron said, "So, you got the proof. Which means you can beat 'em in court. But that takes us back to you not wanting to wait for all'at."

"Onda set," Suge replied.

"So, what's really on your mind?" Heron continued inquiring.

Suge took a swig from his 40 then set it down before saying, "D.O.C. said some real shit the other day that keeps playing in my head. Blood was talking 'bout how mothafuckaz be intimidated by industry people. But industry people ain't nobody to be scared of, 'cause they're just normal mothafuckaz. They not untouchable. He said some real shit, blood. The only difference between them and everyone else is their money. Other than that, they bleed just like anyone else bleeds."

"On Ru's," they agreed matter of factly.

"You know what," Suge continued, "let me take that back. There is a difference between us and them. We're dangerous. We're Apex creatures. Pirahnas. Where they're guppies. The more I think about it, the more I wanna handle this the Mob way. I'm on the verge of showing that honky how Bompton really do shit. It's just getting on my nerves that I can't seem to catch his bitch-ass."

Neither one of them said anything when Suge finished. The porch went silent. The only sounds came from the night. A dog howling to the serenade of an ambulance speeding by. The beat from speakers in someone's trunk. An argument over a disputed debt. All of it was regular. The soundtrack to their lives played on and never stopped.

Buntry was the first one to break the silence. "Blood! The white boy be in L.A., right? He's actually living out here, right?"

"I think so," Suge replied.

"Mothafuckaz see famous people all the time. All we gotta do is put out an APB on his bitch-ass. Think about it; if we really tried, we can catch 'im in traffic. He's gotta go out to eat, or go to a club on the weekends."

"Onda Mob!" Heron agreed. "All we gotta do is put the word out. Let everyone know we're lookin' for him. Somebody's gonna see 'im, blood. L.A. ain't that big where a mothafucka won't be seen."

Suge's mental was in motion. What they were saying was realistic. He knew damn near every club owner, bar owner, and bouncer in the county. He could definitely use his connections to put out an APB on Vanilla Ice.

"We can catch the white boy in traffic if you berious, blood," Buntry assured him.

"On Ru's," Heron agreed.

Suge was already visualizing the process in his head. The plan they formulated could realistically be orchestrated. He slowly started nodding his head. A smile crept across his face. He then looked at them and said, "Onda Mob! Let's press play!"

CHAPTER FIFTEEN

Anyone who lived in L.A. their whole life will tell you that somehow, someway everyone is connected in one way or another. You might have a cousin that grew up in Watts. Or a childhood friend who moved away one summer and ended up spending his adolescent years in South Central. You might even go to Fox Hill Mall and meet a couple females from a whole different section. Linking with them can make you familiar with another set too.

The walls in the trenches will tell you where you're located at all times. Learning how to read graffiti is necessary for survival in Los Angeles. They serve as street signs that let you know who controls the zone you're sliding through. Nevertheless, even though gangland boundaries are definitely set in stone, a person who really grew up in L.A. County will always know at least one person from every section.

The same goes for Hollywood. Hollywood and its surrounding areas are a playground for the rich and famous. That's why it's considered normal for "regular" people to see the stars amongst them. From L.A.X. to Rodeo Drive, famous people are everywhere.

Suge immediately put his plan into play. It started from Buntry's porch. Early the next morning there was a meeting at the Beehive. From there, word spread through word of mouth. The Mob was looking for Vanilla Ice like he was an opp.

Pirus told bloods. Dealers told smokers. Relatives told friends. Valets told bouncers who then told bartenders, who then conveyed the message to dancers. When it was all said and done, there was nowhere Robert Van Winkle could've went without being seen.

Suge knew how far his reach went. It wasn't the first time he tapped in with the streets for this type of assistance.

An underworld APB was more accurate than L.A.P.D.'s tactics.

And this way before social media. It was only a matter of time before he was given a line on the white boy.

It was Saturday night and Bompton was brackin'! Suge was posted up at Louie Burgers with a group of his dogs. The whole parking lot was filled with thugs in red, black and burgundy uniforms. Shiny lowriders with big speakers in the trunk making the pavement vibrate set the backdrop for the evening.

Suge was next to China Dogg's candy apple red Cadillac Seville. He was puffing on a Tampa while scanning the busy street. Co-Co was next to him, talking to Buntry and Silk. Sharitha's little brother had said something that had them laughing non-stop. The vibe was smooth until sirens sounded in the distance.

"Y'all hear that?" someone announced.

"Pigs on the prowl," yelled someone else.

The sirens kept getting louder until a cop car sped past, almost getting sideways as it took a sharp turn in the opposite direction of the group.

There was a run-down gas station across the street from where the Mob was congregated. They had front-row seats to what took place next.

The black and white with red and blue lights sped past the decrepit gas station. Then, half a block past the corner, the cruiser slammed into a screeching halt! At the same time, a dark figure came bolting from the shadows, running into the parking lot from the direction the cop car had been heading in. It was clear, he was who they were chasing after.

At night, after the sun went down, the run-down gas station turned into a homeless encampment. Local bums and drug addicts with shopping carts and tents would set up shop for the rest of the night.

Everyone across the street at Louie Burgers saw the whole debacle play out. The black-and-white was having problems making a U-turn, which gave the track runner a head start. One that he desperately needed.

As soon as he hit the corner, he ran past a few tents, then slid up under a blanket next to an old woman who'd been living there for a few years.

Seconds later, the cop car came back into view going straight into the parking lot with its spotlight directed towards the homeless campers. By the sounds of the night, a whole squadren was on its way.

Then someone in the encampment yelled out, "Get his ass! He went that way!"

This triggered others to do the same. Soon, the whole crowd was yelling, "He went that way!" All while pointing away from the lot.

"He's getting away!" someone yelled.

And the pigs listened. The black and whites took off in pursuit of their man. A few seconds later, three more cars raced past in the same direction.

"That's right! Hell naw! Dumb-ass pigs!" Suge laughed. "The hood's brazy!"

"Onda Mob!" Co-Co agreed.

"Who was dat?" China asked.

"I don't even know, blood," Suge replied. Then, just when he was gonna turn and say something to Co-Co, his pager started beeping. Suge didn't recognize the number on the screen, but he did understand the code that came with it.

The smile left his face as he left his group and headed straight for the payphone. *If this code is accurate*, he thought, *it's finna go down!*

"Somebody page me?" Suge asked when the number he dialed was answered.

"Yeah," replied an excited female's voice. "Sugar Bear? This you?"

"On Piru! Who dis? Janet?"

"Yeah, it's me! He's here! The white boy's here! He just got a table! Ni-Ni's 'bout to take his order right now!"

"We got 'im!" Suge exclaimed. "You still work at —"

"The Palm! Yeah! We here! He's here!"

"Don't let 'im leave, Janet! On Piiiru, don't let him go nowhere till we get there!"

"Alright! I got this! I'ma make sure they order takes a minute. And I'll send 'em some extra dranks!"

"Check dis out! Check dis out!" Suge announced once he made it back to his crew. There were close to thirty of his dogs with him. He had their attention within seconds."

"Wazzup, blood!?!" a few of them asked.

"Y'all know I been looking for Vanilla Ice's bitch-ass. I just got the call! Blood's at the Palm Restaurant in West Hollywood. Y'all ready to Mob up there?"

"On Piiiru! Onda Mob! Let's ride!" they said.

Suge turned to Co-Co and China, "Ready?"

"Fo' sho'!" Co-Co replied then they all hopped in their rides.

Suge's K5 led the caravan of lowriders as the sped from Compton to Hollywood. It was the first time he was gonna speak to Vanilla Ice in person about Mario's points. He couldn't wait to pull up on him...

CHAPTER SIXTEEN

Robert Van Winkle aka Vanilla Ice was at the peek of his career.

He was gliding on superstar status everywhere he went. His tramp traffic was at an all-time high. Paparazzi hit him with their flashing lights anytime he was seen in public. He had it made and loved every moment of it.

On this night, he was dripping in superstar perks. A-list actors seated across the Palm Restaurant dining area sent him their salutations in free drinks. And the three women (one White, two Black) he was with couldn't wait to get to a private location where they could all join in on sucking his balls dry.

The plan was set. After dinner and drinks, Ice would hop in the limo he arrived in with his groupies. Then they'd spend the rest of the evening in the V.I.P popping bottles and dancing the night away. After all that, they'd pull up to a high-rise and fuck till they passed out.

Regular program...

"Ice," the blond nineteen-year-old at Vanilla Ice's table said while sliding a hand on his thigh to get his attention.

"What's up, baby?"

"This place is rad! The food is great! And I can't believe this, but is that Tom Cruise over there?"

That made the other women look in the direction she had pointed.

"Yeah," Ice replied. "If you look to their right, a few tables over, you'll recognize some more people – "

"Oh-my-god!" one of the sistahs exclaimed. "Is that Judd Nelson and Molly Ringwald?"

Again, Ice chuckled, "Y'all girls wanna meet 'em?"

"For reals? Yeah! Hell yeah!" they replied.

Tom's cool. But Judd likes to party and he keeps some coke, he thought to himself before addressing the women. "Let's get some more drinks in us. Then I'll go see if Judd and Molly wanna ride with us tonight."

"You for real?" the lighter of the two Black girls asked.

"Baby, I run this town. I gets respect everywhere I go. From the hood to the Hollywood Hills, everybody knows me and they salute when they see me 'cause I'm real!"

The starstruck trio took it all in. The dark-skinned beauty gave him a seductive grin while the other two giggled. He beamed with pride while hitting them all with his brightest smile.

As he was reveling in the attention he was receiving, something in the distance caught his eye. There was a large crowd entering the restaurant all at once. All the tables were taken so it didn't make sense. And what made even less sense was the fact the group was made up of all Black people, mostly dressed in red.

Pretty soon everyone in the Palms was watching the mob of people dressed in gangland attire overtake the restaurant. The tension was building quickly. Their presence alone was enough to spook most of the patrons. Add that in with their demeanors and you had several people pissing in their pants.

Vanilla Ice knew what was going on from the moment he saw several fingers pointing towards his table. He could've sworn he heard someone say: "The white boy's over there!" right before the mob steered towards his side of the restaurant.

For a few fleeting moments, he looked around for an easy exit. He was ready to break out in a full sprint. Even if it meant not only leaving the girls at his table, but also knocking over whoever was in his way. The doorway to the kitchen area was almost twenty yards away from his table. Robert Van Winkle was three seconds away from making the dash when his attention was taken by an extra-large, bald-headed brotha in a red and black plaid button-up shirt approaching him with a smile.

The girls that were seated at his table moments earlier were gone. He couldn't tell if they had been physically moved, or had risen on their own. They were all standing together a few feet away looking scared and confused. Which really didn't matter since he wasn't paying them any attention. His concentration was fully directed towards the big Blood taking the seat next to his at the table.

Suge was loving every minute of the quiet storm he had created. His soldiers surrounded the table like they were the Fruit of Islam, blocking any sort of outside interference. All while he and his much anticipated one on one with Robert Van Winkle.

"Wazzup, Ice?" Suge said as he held out a firm paw for a shake. Ice obliged with a sweaty palm, trying to calm a case of the shakes. "I'm Marion Suge Knight. Mario Johnson's manager. You know, the guy who wrote 'Ice Ice Baby'." Suge saw the flicker in Ice's eyes. Robert knew exactly who he was. "I've been to your studio a few times. I'm sure Ms. Landers has informed you of my visits."

"Uh-uh-no... I wasn't told anything."

Lie, Suge thought. *Okay. Now I know he'll lie to my face without flinching.*

"That's fine, Mr. Van Winkle –"

"Vanilla –"

"Van Winkle," Suge stated a little louder than he had been speaking before. By the look in Vanilla's eyes, he could tell it had its desired effect. "I represent Mario Johnson. I see you're enjoying yourself right now so I'll get straight to the point. My artist has done some work for you. He was promised compensation in the form of some points of the profits that came from that song along with several others that he wrote on your album *Hooked*."

"I'm not sure –" Ice started.

"Oh – you sure! You know what da fuck the homey is talkin' 'bout, blood! Cut in Co-Co."

Suddenly, the crowd moved. The movement was slight but purposeful. Vanilla Ice's eyes grew a half - size larger thinking it was cookies for himself. But they didn't attack. Nevertheless, he was terrified of the Black men and women in red clothing who surrounded his table blocking his view of the rest of the establishment.

"So, I don't understand why the homey is having so many problems getting ahold of you when y'all worked together in Texas."

Again, Suge saw a flicker in the white boy's eyes. Vanilla was recalling all the nights he spent in Houston when Chocolate was helping him come up with the right delivery for his music. He did know Mario. He knew him very well. They had actually become close friends until money and fame catapulted Ice's career.

"Now that I got your ear, there really shouldn't be a problem for my client to get his money. I'm sure you're just a little busy these days. And, your receptionist probably isn't giving you all your messages..."

Suge paused for a moment, giving his prey a moment to speak.

In a perfect world, Vanilla Ice would've taken out a check book right then and there. But, in the real world of grimy industry hyenas, he got a fumbling white rapper who said, "Uh... I don't deal with that part of the business, Mr... Uh –"

"Mr. Knight. Call me Suge Knight."

"Okay. I don't deal –"

"Yeah. I heard you," Suge said, all the while maintaining a smile. He didn't have to frown or scrunch up his face. They were literally seated in the middle of a circle of his niggaz. If Suge would've told them to "feed," they would've eaten the studio gangsta up like an appetizer.

Suge stared at Vanilla Ice for a while. Just looked at him allowing the silence to do the talking. Then, just as he saw him getting antsy, he leaned forward, lowered his voice to a whisper and said, "Chocolate's family. I'm representing him now. So, from now on, you'll be dealing directly through me." Suge leaned back, confident he got his point across. Then he said, "When's a good time for me to meet with the powers that be?"

Ice was sweating. He would've said anything to end the conversation he was caught up in. "Tomorrow!"

"Tomorrow, huh?"

"Yeah! Come by the studio in the morning and my manager will straighten out whatever situation you bring to the table."

Vanilla Ice knew he fucked up the moment he heard the words leave his jaws. He had heard about the irate giant coming around talking about the song Mario wrote. The last thing he wanted or needed was having any of the people in that restaurant showing up at the studio. Still, he was glad when Suge stuck his palm out for a shake. Ice shook his hand and invited him to the studio two more times before Suge left with his mob in tow.

As he watched the gang disperse, he saw the girls he came with leave with them. They weren't close enough for him to hear their conversations, but anyone could see they were enamored by the ism of thugs.

He even saw when Judd Nelson made eye contact with Suge. He saw them nod towards one another as if they knew one another. Suge Knight was somebody. He was obviously known throughout the industry. But he was different than normal people in the business. Ice had never met anyone like that before.

The Palm's energy changed from when Ice first arrived that evening. The tables were still filled, yet the once jovial conversations had changed into hushed tones. When he looked around, he was met with eyes that looked away instantly.

He barely gave his legs enough time to steady themselves before he got up from his table. Something was wrong. His instincts told him a storm was coming. There was an issue in the air. He knew exactly what it was, too. He'd been able to put it off for some time, but now it was coming to a head.

As soon as he got into the back of his limousine, he picked up the phone and called his manager...

CHAPTER SEVENTEEN

Robert tried lying to himself about the stress he was going through. Suge and his gang had pressed him severely. It wouldn't have surprised him if paparazzi had taken a roll of film of the incident at the Palms.

At first, he ordered the limo driver to stay with the night's itinerary and head to the club. He popped open a bottle of champagne and drank from the top. He spent the whole trip trying to call his manager. But no one answered. So he drank and drank some more.

He was plastered by the time he hit the club, too smashed to go in. Luckily, he had the sense of mind to head back to his house in the Malibu Hills. In the end, he forgot all about Suge as he stumbled into his home and passed out on the couch.

$$$$$

The sun was bright that next morning. A loud, persistent knock on the door woke Vanilla Ice up, right as the rays of sunlight began to peak into his living room.

His head started spinning the moment he sat up. "Bam! Bam! Bam!" sounded the front door. He had to make it stop. Every pound felt as if he was getting kicked in the head!

"Hold on!" he called out as he got up and trudged towards the front door. Then, the moment he opened the door he was hit with a whirlwind of energy that he wasn't ready for.

Tommy Quon, his manager, along with Marco, his publicist, barged in right passed him as if they lived at the house with him.

"God damn, Ice!" Tommy remarked. You smell like shit! What-da-fuck you do last night?"

"Sheesh!" Marco added. "Somebody run a bath! Robert! You knew we had a whole day ahead of us! What da hell are you still doing asleep?"

Ice followed the duo into his kitchen where his manager immediately started some coffee. A moment or two later, he was handed a glass of water along with a palm full of aspirins. "Thanks," he muttered.

Marco disappeared, calling out from the hallway, "I'm gonna start the bath. We don't gotta worry about an outfit because they'll dress you at the studio. But we gotta hurry, Rob!"

"Alright. Alright," he replied. He looked at his manager knowing there was something important to talk about. He couldn't remember exactly what it was though. He could barely recall the evening before. And it didn't help that everyone around him was operating at 150 miles per hour while he was still riding at a school-zone speed.

Tommy looked at him in his disheveled state and said, "You need to wake up, Rob. You got that cameo on Saved By The Bell. After that, we gotta shoot across town for a photo shoot for Guess apparel. Then we're flying to Houston."

"Fuck!" Ice exclaimed. "I haven't even packed yet."

Shaking his head while filling a coffee mug, Tommy continued, "Don't worry about that. We'll just buy you brand-new shit when we get to Texas. You would've had to buy all new stuff anyway since we'll be away for a couple of weeks."

Ice nodded. It was all starting to come back to him. He was doing a Late-Night talk show circuit. He had forgotten all about it.

"Robert! C'mon, man! The bath is ready," his publicist said when he came back to the kitchen. "Seriously, man. You gotta hurry. We got a lot to do before we get to L.A.X. We gotta go!"

Vanilla Ice got in and out of that bath in record time. His hair was still wet when he was rushed into the awaiting Lincoln Towncar. With all the rushing to handle business he forgot all about Suge and his band of not-so-merry men. The incident was never brought up to his manager. Nor was it mentioned to his publicist.

Life didn't slow down for the superstar. Everything was business as usual...

$$$$$

While Robert Van Winkle was hopping in and out of Luxury town cars and private planes, Suge was going back and forth from his trap in Bompton to Ichiban Studios. He made the trip three times in four days. Not one time did he get the meeting he was promised. On the fourth trip he wasn't even allowed in the building. They had officially froze him out. Cut off all communications before they ever even started.

He was seething on the inside. The Piru in him wanted to burn the whole building down in broad daylight. Yet, the college-educated business man in him stalled out the violence. Knowing the fight wouldn't be won easily from the beginning of it all is what really kept him from taking the street route.

Suge also had other things to consider. As far as the streets were concerned, his whole team was at the peak of things. The work he was getting from Watts was A-1! The illegal money was coming in so fast he almost got sidetracked from his main mission.

Still, the old adage is always true! With more money comes problems.

Suge and his day ones were from Lueders Park. Their neighborhood had several factions in it, yet they mostly operated as one.

Suge's clique, Mob Piru, was one of the subsets in that neighborhood.

Since they all pushed under one banner, the subsets didn't feud with one another.

Things started changing when the drug money started circulating unevenly. Factors, individuals with murder reps that rivalled most serial killers felt like the pie coming from Watts wasn't being distributed correctly once it left the Mob's hands.

In all actuality, their assumptions were pretty much on point.

It wasn't done out of malice as much as from loyalty. Suge always took care of his inner circle. It was a given that Heron, Buntry, China Dogg and Co-

Co got the best deals. On top of first dibs to extras like high-powered fireworks, Suge's cipher always got a bigger cut than anyone else.

Suge was sharp. He knew how hood politics were manipulated by thugs with sour tastes in their mouths. He couldn't help it, he was grown from the same dirty soil as the rest of the snakes he ran with. He already knew there'd be a target on his back once the cash started flowing. It was part of the terrain.

That was precisely why he fed his demons so well. He fed them just enough to keep them dangerous. It was a tactic he would continue to utilize years later, in the music industry.

Although nothing of substance had came up, Suge knew he had to keep his ear to the pavement. No matter how big he became, he once told himself he'd never leave the set. The problem with that mentality was the bigger he became, the more of a target he'd become. Knowing this kept him several steps ahead of the friends and foes who would eventually come for the crown he would obtain.

Suge was spending more and more time at Solar Studios with Dick Griffey. It got to the point where he started pulling up for no other reason other than to hang out with the older man.

Griffey didn't mind. He actually admired the young hustler. In a way, he had taken Suge under his wing. He became Suge's mentor in the industry. Not only had he adopted Suge as one of his own, he also became invested in the Mario and Vanilla Ice situation. From behind the scenes, he was working on securing a publishing deal for Suge and his client.

Suge felt at home at Solar Studios. Walking through the same hallways that so many famous artist stepped through on their way to, from, or during the recordings of their multiplatinum hits. He actually used his surroundings to motivate his team as well. Chocolate was usually the main person with him when he took his trips to the studio. That environment motivated him to keep writing, knowing what he was doing would one day get him a bag.

On this particular afternoon, Suge had taken Co-Co to Solar to hang out and they caught up with Dick in the corner office on the top floor of the building. Like any other time they linked, Dick was full of insight and game.

"... I like your drive Marion. I saw it in you from the moment I met you," Dick said as he took out a Cuban cigar and offered it to Suge.

Suge smiled and said, "I hope so." Suge then saw the gold lighter Griffey was using and commented, "That mothafucka's nice."

"It is," Co-Co agreed. "Probably real, too. Huh, Mr. Griffey?"

"Yeah, eighteen carat Rose gold. It was a gift from Marvin Gaye."

Griffey stared at the lighter for a moment before putting it back in his desk.

The room went silent for a moment before Co-Co asked Suge, "So, Ice's people still dodging you?"

He took a puff from his cigar, let out a plume of smoke then chuckled before replying, "Yeah. He thinks it's a game. He's outta town, though. I know that fo' sho'."

"How you know?" Griffey asked.

"He's been on TV. I've seen him on a couple late-night talk shows."

"He's riding his wave," Griffey commented.

"You mean, Chocolate's wave," Co-Co said.

"On Bloods," agreed Suge. He took another puff from his 'gar. "I got something for his bitch-ass, tho'."

Co-Co let out a chuckle. Suge was one of the smartest individuals she ever met. There was no doubt in her mind on whether or not he had a plan. And, there was even lesser of a doubt on whether he would accomplish said plan. Suge had always been the type to make things happen.

Suge continued; "This is the Land. We run this shit and it's time mothafucka's wake to up to the fact they in our territory. I'ma turn up the heat. Make it real uncomfortable for 'im."

Griffey looked at Suge in awe. He loved his energy. He knew right then and there that Suge would one day see millions of dollars from the music industry. He understood its unseen dynamics way too well.

"On Piiiru!" Co-Co exclaimed. "Check this out, Suge. I've been talkin' to some homegirls about all this. You know how Sassy and Layla be strippin'? They do private parties and all the shit. Anyways, they actually met the white boy before. They said he's got a type. He likes sistahs. Not them light-skinned, half-breed bitches, either. Suge, blood likes 'em dark. Dark and skinny as fuck!"

"Is that right?" he replied. He cut his eyes towards Griffey for a moment then went back to Co-Co.

"When I heard that," she continued, "I thought about Pee-Wee's cousin, Sharon. You know... the one y'all used to tease for being so skinny and black."

Suge chuckled, "Shiiit! Pee-Wee's black-as-night, too!"

"I know you ain't talkin', nigga! Didn't you fuck his cousin Monica behind the pool across the street from Louie Burgers?"

"Never!" Suge lied.

"Bang dat! Put dat on da Mob!"

Griffey watched them in amusement. *They really are ghetto*, he thought to himself. *These two really are from Compton.*

Suge didn't say anything. He stone-faced his homegirl. They both knew there was no point in continuing on that topic. Suge wasn't gonna budge on his stance. Lying on one's dick was only acceptable when denying a body.

Changing the subject back to business, Griffey addressed Co-Co. "So, what're you thinking? Puttin' the ebony princess on Van Winkle?"

"That ain't a bad idea," Suge said. "But that means we gonna have to put them both at the same place at the same time."

"Not a problem," Co-Co said. "Bitches talk, homey. They say he's a trick. He stays in strip clubs. This can happen, for reals!"

Suge looked at Griffey. Griffey gave him the slightest nod possible.

Then Suge chunked up the blood B and said, "On Piiiru, press play!"

Co-Co smiled and replied, "Done!"

CHAPTER EIGHTEEN

Robert Van Winkle got back to California on a Monday afternoon. He couldn't wait to get off the plane he was on so he could get back to his normal life. As soon as they hit the runway, it was as if a weight was lifted off his shoulders. The jet-life was coming to an end, at least for the time being.

To the rest of the world, being on television shows and doing interviews looked fun. Even for him, at one point before the fame, he egged it on as if he would love it all. But things weren't always as pretty as they seemed for the person in front of the camera.

It was work. Everything was work. His manager and publicist acted like they worked off commission. For every stress-filled day that took hours off of his natural life expectancy, they seemed to get a bonus. The public didn't see the sixteen-hour work days.

They didn't realize the two or three minutes they'd see him on the television screen was recorded at four a.m., which meant he had to be up by two. Nor did they see all the red-eye flights he took, crisscrossing the country for weeks at a time. Not to mention the months he spent on buses when he was on tour, performing his music in packed arenas. That shit was hectic.

All of that was why he was salivating at the thought of getting off that plane and getting back to his normal life. The life of the rich and famous.

"I bet you couldn't wait for those doors to open, huh?" his manager asked him when they stepped into the terminal.

Ice sighed with relief before replying, "I need some R & R after all that work. I can finally go to sleep and not have to worry about being rushed into a stylist's chair at two a.m.

Tommy laughed hard. "I get it. But, what's the difference between making TV appearances and this shit?" He motioned towards the group of paparazzi who were on their way towards the superstar with their cameras and tape recorders in hand.

"Ice! Vanilla Ice! How does it feel to have the number one song in the country? Ice, is it true you'll be doing a movie with Micheal Douglas? What about a clothing line?" The reporters yelled out a barrage of questions as soon as he exited the glass doors and stepped onto the sidewalk.

"We got the answers to all of your questions!" Ice replied to the crowd. "Just ask my manager!" With a slight push, he fed Tommy to the masses, then cut in the opposite direction. His driver was waiting next to the limo the whole time. Ice let out a laugh at the prank he played on his manager. It tickled him to know Tommy would be stuck answering questions for the next thirty minutes.

It was already looking like a good day in L.A. Until he bumped into a woman, almost knocking her over.

"Ahhh – oh shit," she chirped in surprise.

He instinctively reached out to steady her, "Sorry 'bout that. My fault," he said with his best famous-person smile. After getting a closer look, he couldn't believe his luck. The petite Sistah was beautiful. "You alright?"

"Yeah," she replied coyly. "I should've been watching where I was going. I was just being nosy. Trying to see who was in the middle of them reporters over there."

Ice took a good look at her. The moment couldn't have lasted for more than a second, but there was a lot said. First of all, there was a connection between the two in the instant they made eye contact. There was a spark. Secondly, Ice immediately recognized the fact that she had no idea who he was. He had been in the presence of enough star struck fans to know one when he saw one.

She wasn't one. She had no idea who he was and he liked that.

Then, just as fast as she came, she suddenly departed. They exchanged a vibe... just a vibe. Then she was gone.

He got into his limo, hoping he could ditch his manager. But he wasn't so lucky. Tommy tossed his bags on the seat next to his and hopped in right before the limo took off.

"God!" Tommy sighed. "You see how bad they want you? They can't get enough of you, Rob!"

"I see that. But, man, I need a break—"

"Doesn't look like you'll get any downtime this summer —"

"What? I don't even go on tour till fall."

"You should be thankful you got all this work. My pager has been going off nonstop with messages from the office! Ever since you've done these late-night talk shows, we've been getting bookings like crazy! You've got all kinds of shit going on, Rob..."

Ice logged out of that conversation real quick. Tommy kept talking, but he wans't listening. The money was great. The fame was even better. The lack of downtime is what fucked with him the most, though. It was as if he barely had enough time to appreciate the benefits of all his hard work.

He couldn't wait to pull up to his house. He needed to get the fuck away from his manager. It was all work with that man, and Ice was at wits end with him at that very moment.

Ice lived in a house that overlooked the Pacific Ocean. It sat on a cliff above a private beach. The stairway that led from his back patio to the sand was damn near a straight drop like an apartment fire escape. Everything about his neighborhood screamed "secluded," even though it wasn't a gated community.

When he finally got home and out of the limo, his manager stuck his head out the window and told him, "You got a few days at the most, Rob. Then it's back to work..."

"Alright!" he replied loud enough to be heard as the limo drove away. He was glad he was finally alone. He could finally get some rest.

Ice was heading up his driveway, towards the house when he heard a car coming up the street. When he turned to see what he assumed would be one of his reclusive neighbors, he was caught off guard. Two Black men in baseball caps were in a four door Chevy

Caprice. One of them had short hair, the other had a gheri curl. Both had scowls on their faces.

Ice was suddenly taken back to the night at the Palms Restaurant. The night before he left California. He managed to somehow block it out of his mind, but the two thugs in the Box Chevy brought it all back to the forefront of his mind. It wasn't as if he recognized them. But their red and black hats and shirts matched the attire of the mob who confronted him that night.

They didn't linger, yet they didn't drive away quickly either.

The whole vibe was ominous. He didn't know what to do. Should he rush inside and lock the door? For a moment he thought about acting as if he didn't live at that particular house. As if he had been dropped off in front of the wrong home. *That's stupid,* he thought to himself. *They obviously know where I live or they wouldn't be here.*

He turned around and locked the door as soon as he stepped inside. The interior of his home wasn't dark at all. The back windows facing the ocean were all shadeless, allowing natural light to illuminate his home.

Nothing looked tampered with. It didn't seem as if anyone had broken in while he was gone. But that didn't stop his mind from going there. For the first time since he bought the property, he found himself regretting the fact that he hadn't had a security system installed. From the way the Suge Knight character had pushed up on him at the restaurant, it wouldn't have surprised him if the thug was having coffee at his kitchen table when he stepped inside.

Ice walked down the hallway into his empty living room, taking a quick scan of the house. Everything was intact. Exactly how he left it. Probably even cleaner, since he was sure his housekeeper had came there and cleaned while he was gone.

After dropping his bag on the floor and plopping down on the soft leather couch, Ice laughed at himself. "Next thing I know, I'll be sitting in a barricaded office with Tony Montana cameras everywhere."

CHAPTER NINETEEN

Prison was an inevitable part of life for gang bangers in Bompton. Some would even say elementary school yards were the first level of training for it. Others look at prison as if it's a rite of passage for seasoned gangsters.

You can tell where a man stood in his hood by the amount of love he received when he got out of prison. A high ranking, extremely respected boss will get mail and money from his gang while he's upstate. If he's truly connected; as long as his hood is eating, he will be too.

Most of the time, when a soldier is out of sight, he becomes out of mind. Especially if he was a mediocre member. Every-so-often a real hunter will go to prison on a short term and no one forgets his aura. Stories are told about him and rap songs are written about the drills he slid on. If he was really dangerous, even his opps will keep track of his time. They'll count the days, weeks and months he has to do before he hits the turf again.

When G-Boy came home from a five-year term in California Youth Authority, everyone from Lueders Park showed up at his welcome-home party. He was one of those guys who showed nothing but love to his niggaz. Yet, he was also as cold as leather in the winter when it came to an outsider. At five-nine, one hundred and seventy pounds, he wasn't as physically imposing as Buntry, Heron or Suge. But he was just as much as a factor, though. He was an all-around gangster. Both a hustler and banger.

G-Boy was one of them ones...

The sun was gone on his first night out. He was at the apartment complex on Bullis with the rest of his gang. The Mob was having a full-fledged block party and G-Boy was their guest of honor.

The whole parking lot was lit up. Barbeque pits were smoking. Trunks were rattling. Everyone affiliated was there smoking and drinking to the occasion.

"Suga Bear!" G-Boy exclaimed when he saw his dog for the first time in half a decade. "What's brackin', P-Funk?"

"Da Mob!" Suge replied with love. They both gave each other a bear hug. "Damn, blood! You got big as a house!"

"On Piiiru!" China Dogg agreed as he stepped in on the welcome wagon.

G-Boy flexed his chest muscles. His red Nike shirt squeezed around the chest area. "Non-stop heavy metal lifting! Y'all know the program! Bustin' down for five calendars straight, blood! They not there for sho', either."

"I already know!" Suge replied. "Word been circulating 'bout dem hands, Ru!" Suge slapped China on the shoulder, "Blood been knocking shit out, huh!"

"Yeah, Ru," China interjected. "We heard 'bout all that work you've been putting in."

"Puttin' in work is all I know how to do, blood."

Suge took a long, hard look at his homey. They had known one another since elementary school. They played high school ball together and were damn near inseparable. But, life took them in separate directions. Suge went to UNLV. Got a degree in business even played in the NFL. G-Boy took to the streets... fumbled and ended up in CYA.

It's ironic how a person of the shadows can be viewed in different paradigms. To some, a person from the trenches, a shadowy figure, can be labeled America's nightmare. But that same person, by his family and loved ones, can be seen as a savoir. Someone who feeds and clothes the people he's devoted to.

Suge, as well as everyone – man or woman – he ran with were bred in the war-torn streets of Compton, California. They were cultivated in a land so harsh that a percentage of them didn't live to see twenty-one.

In a world with no foundation, the gang gave them a family. Not only did it furnish them with a cipher of kindred souls to run with, it also gave them a community, even an army. In a universe like that, one learned to love just as hard as they are taught to hate. They were trained to protect just as dangerously as they attacked. It was a culture that kept funeral home owners driving in luxury sedans.

Marion had an obvious head start on his partna G-Boy. He was up, so it was on him and their team to make sure one of their real niggaz hit the bricks running.

"C'mon, G," Suge said with a smile. "Let me show you something."

Buntry had just walked up and gave all three of them dap. The red cup in his hand told them he had been there longer than them. "What's brackin'?"

"I'm 'bout to take G-Boy to the bandy lady house."

Buntry smiled when he looked at G-boy. "You remember Ms. Davis mean-ass?"

"She still around?" G-Boy asked. "Damn right, I remember the bocolate bandy bars she'd have for fifty cents back in the day."

"She still stay in the same apartment," Suge informed him.

"Naw!"

"On Piru," Suge added. They all took a stroll through the complex. China teased G-Boy for not having sex in half a decade, which got them all started. They all joked around with one another like they did in the old days. It was a stroll they had taken together hundreds of times over the years.

When they reached her unit, Suge took out his keys and opened the iron security door. They all entered the apartment finding Ms. Davis in the living knitting a blanket.

"Hey, Ms. Davis," Suge greeted her.

"Sugar Bear, what you up to? Hope you ain't out there putting that poison in ya' system."

"No, ma'am."

"You know how y'all get when you're all liquored up."

"I know. But we aint on all'at, Ms. Davis. Look who we brought with us."

Ms. Davis looked over her reading glasses at the man in the middle.

"Lord, is that G-Boy?" Ms. Davis got up and went towards him. "Boy! They finally let you come home! I bet ya' mamma is happy as can be!"

"She sure is, Ms. Davis," he replied.

"Your mamma been in that church house praying for you ever since you went away! Boy, you betta stay away from them law-dogs!"

That statement caused all four men to start laughing. Old folks' antics always amused them. The straight-forwardness of their elders was authentic at all times.

"We gonna keep 'im out of trouble, Ms. Davis," Suge told her. Then he led the crowd into the hallway towards the rear of the apartment. On the same key chain where the key to her front door was hung another key that unlocked the door all the way at the end of that hallway.

Suge opened the door, hit the light switch, and all four of them entered the room. Inside, there wasn't a dresser or a bed. The only furniture in it was a table set against the back wall. It held a phone, scale, money counter, and a few stacks of different-size bags. There were several stools against the wall that was used when they needed to bag and weigh some product on the table.

G-Boy studied the set-up, immediately putting two and two together. "So, the bandy lady done turned into the safe house?"

"On Piru," China replied.

"You ain't seen shit yet, G," Buntry added.

Suge went into the closet and took out three Vietnam-era duffle bags. He set them each on the floor next to the table and said, "We got straps, weed, and coke. And, when I say "we," that means you too!"

G-Boy looked on in amazement. The game wasn't new to him. Selling dope and squeezing triggers was part of the lifestyle he was born into. That part was regular. What really impressed him was seeing his childhood friends so comfortable at the level they were at. *My niggaz is real thugs!* he thought to himself as he looked on.

Buntry started taking guns out of one of the bags and setting them on the table. He laid an AK, a couple sawed-off shotguns and an array of pistols as well as an Uzi on the table. For the most part, they were all used. It really didn't matter, though.

All that really mattered to the gang was whether they worked or not. And, every single one of those weapons had proven themselves on the battlefield already. It was an arsenal made of dirty weaponry.

"Look, blood," Suge started. "We got a machine established. The whole hood is on right now."

"I heard," replied G-Boy.

"On some real shit," Suge continued, "I need you out here. I've been making sure the set eats. But niggaz lookin' at the Mob like we're a threat, or something."

"Onda set!" China added. "Niggaz ain't said shit. But, we know it's boming, blood."

"G-Boy nodded. He knew what was being asked of him. Over the previous five years there had been an unofficial split between Lueders and The Mob. Even though, technically they were all the same set, Suge, Buntry, Heron and China had inadvertently created a subset. At that point, it was still lovely. But money had gotten involved. Everyone knew once revenue was interjected, the dynamics of the game changed.

Since G-Boy had a strong allegiance with the "other side" of the set, there were certain expectations of him. They were counting on him to be the mediator who would thwart a possible civil war.

"Things understood need not be said. On Piru, I'm on deck wit' whatever y'all on," G-Boy stated firmly.

Then, almost as if on que, someone's pager started beeping. Everyone except for G-Boy instinctively reached for their hip. But only one of them had been summoned.

Suge didn't recognize the number. It didn't even come with a code. If it weren't for the fact that he was waiting for an important message, he would've ignored it. At least for the time being. It was G-Boy's first night out, which constituted a night off from work.

"Hold up, blood," Suge said. He went to the table, picked up the phone and called the number back.

Buntry and China kept emptying the bags onto the table. They were taking out large amounts of coke, crack and weed for G-Boy. The guns would be his to keep. Although, any one of them could go to him for them if they needed one. The drugs would be for free as well. It was a gangland blessing. One they all knew would be appreciated as well as capitalized on.

Meanwhile, Suge's energy exploded on the phone. "Onda Mob?!? Okay! Okay! Right! On Piru, don't let that bitch leave, blood! I'll be right there!" He slammed the receiver back into its cradle and said, "Buntry, make sure G-Boy gets his issue –"

"Gotchu."

"Where you going?" G-Boy asked.

"I gotta handle some business. I'm 'bout to run up on a mothafucka who been dodging me for a minute –"

"On Lueders, I'm wit' whatever, blood!" G-Boy growled.

"Naw, blood. Don't you see all this work you're getting? Take the snow and fireworks where it needs to be. Don't let no one know where ya' stash spot is. It's good on my end. I got all this other shit handled. You got your own chess board to set up. Let me move some pieces on mine." Suge gave him a look of assurance.

After giving him a thug's embrace, Suge and China Dogg left.

Shortly after they left, G-Boy asked Buntry, "What was all'at about?"

"I can't say for sure. But the homey is chasing a mill ticket. Whatever it is, it ain't no bullshit...

CHAPTER TWENTY

Vanilla Ice loved the strip club scene more than any other aspect of the fast life. In a strip club, specifically a Black one that played hip-hop and R&B, he was able to live his best life. The dancers treated him like a god while his music was played as his money was spent.

There was one "gentleman's club" in particular he loved going to the most. Whenever he was out on the town, he always made an appearance at Barber Coast. Barber Coast had bad bitches, yet it wasn't watered down with the whole high-priced call-girl vibe.

Barber Coast was a top-of-the-line hood spot where Ice could find the type of females that made him feel like a star.

Black girls on Black girls everywhere. Thick bitches with hips, tits and ass. Ice went there often enough to be recognized, yet not enough to be considered a regular by the staff. The loud and smokey joint turned up whenever a star came through. The management was sharp too. They knew who Ice was and what he liked. So anytime he pulled up with his entourage, they would whisk him away to the VIP section where he would be catered to by the darkest dancers in the building.

That night was no different. The DJ started playing "Ice Ice Baby" the second Vanilla Ice and his boys stepped in the building.

He didn't come with a big group this time. He showed up with his manager and childhood friend, Rick. They had showed up intoxicated, runny noses an all. It didn't stop them from buying up the bar, though. They came to get fucked up with some fly Black bitches.

A regular night out...

Ice's friend, Rick, wasn't from Los Angeles. He had just flown in from Texas to visit. So far, he was enjoying himself beyond comprehension.

"Man, you're living it up, bro!" Rick said after guzzling from the champagne bottle.

"This is regular, bro!" Tommy boasted.

Ice laughed, "Yeah, man! I don't know why you don't just move out here. I do this type of shit every other day! L.A. is heaven on earth, bro! Real superstar shit!"

"As a matter of fact," Ice's manager slurred. "Here comes one of his perks right now!"

A slim, dark-skinned sistah locked eyes with Ice as she made a seductive beeline towards their table. Ice saw her coming and naturally assumed he was about to be wooed by a starstruck stripper. A beautiful Black woman with a pen and paper in her hand, asking for an autograph.

He stuck his chest out while tilting his chin up a little. It was his arrogant, player pose. He'd done it a thousand times and it always ended with him getting whatever he wanted.

When the beautiful sistah got to their table she hit them all with a smile. She didn't have a pen or paper in her hands, either.

When she finally locked in on Vanilla Ice she had a look of recognition in her eyes. "Hey, clumsy! You remember me?"

"Oh shit!" he exclaimed. "You're the girl from the airport!"

"Yeah, that's me. My name is Shay," she replied coyly. "How you been?"

"I'm good. Busy, but good. You wanna sit down wit' us?" Ice scooted over, signaling for her to take a seat next to him. To his manager and his friend he said, "I know this girl. I met her –"

"If damn near running me over is meeting me, then we're real good friends," she teased.

The men laughed. She took a seat, then stuck her hand out to each one of them. "I'm Shay."

"Nice to meet you, Beautiful Shay," Tommy said.

She giggled, "Thanks." Then she turned towards Ice and asked, "Busy wit' what? You gotta take a break sometime. If you don't, you'll get burnt out."

"I know," Ice replied. *Damn*, he thought to himself. *She's talking to me like a regular person.* "Hey, you wanna get a private room?"

"Damn!" she said teasingly. "You move fast, don't you!"

"Ice don't play," Tommy joked.

"Naw," Robert defended himself. "It ain't like that. I'm not even on that tip right now. I'm just trying to kick it wit' you. Just talk."

"That's what you call it in California, huh?" his friend teased.

"Yeah. Huh?" Shay agreed.

"Y'all play too much," Robert said with a smile. Then to Shay he said, "I'm not trippin' like that. I really just wanna talk."

Shay stared into his eyes. Bouncing from right to left, searching for his intentions. In her line of work, she had to be on point when it came to reading people. Her intuition had to be spot on because it could be the difference between getting raped or cashing in on a payday. "You're serious, huh?" she asked. "All you wanna do is hang out?"

"Yeah," he smiled. This girl intrigued him. It wasn't everyday he met a beautiful woman who didn't treat him like a star. It was refreshing.

"C'mon," she told him as she took his hand and led him away.

"Hey! Hey! Where you taking our guy?!?" his friend joked. In all honesty, he didn't want Ice to leave the table. He really didn't like his manager much.

"I'll be back, Rick. It won't be long at all. As a matter of fact, get at some of the ladies and get yourselves some private rooms, on me." To his manager, Ice said, "Make sure he has the freakiest night of his life!"

"Gotchu!"

Shay led her date to the back of the club where there was a hallway guarded by two bouncers. The buff security guards both looked like body builders. A white guy and a Black guy with stone faces made sure no one's privacy was violated once they entered the sex dens.

Ice got ready to toss his star-studded weight around when he saw them, but he didn't get a chance to. Shay ended up doing all the heavy lifting herself. She whispered something in the white bouncer's ear that prompted him to look Ice up and down when they reached the men.

After her private exchange with security, Shay took Ice's hand and led him past the burly bouncers. "You don't gotta pay for the room, Ice. It's on me tonight..."

CHAPTER TWENTY-ONE

Suge felt the set's energy as soon as he stepped out the apartment.

By the time he got to the parking lot with China Dogg, the party had lifted a few more notches than where it was when he left a little while earlier.

A non-affiliate would've had a problem breathing in the sea of burgundy that stood shoulder to shoulder in that parking lot. To the active Lueders Park Bompton Pirus, it was all love. A ghetto celebration.

Suge wasted no time. He stepped straight into a crowd with a money-making scheme in mind. "Say, Mob! Say, Mob!" he announced loudly. Still, it was hard to penetrate the loud festivities.

"Hey!" China Dogg yelled. Suddenly, the crowd quieted down. "Check 'dis out! The homey tryna holla at y'all!"

That seemed to catch their attention for the time being. Other than the bass coming from several parked cars, the stage was cleared for Suge to call some shots.

"Y'all wanna go clubbin'?" he hollar'd out over the crowd.

"On Ru's!" several individuals yelled out.

"There's a party at Barber Coast! Everybody gets in free! We movin' the function right now!"

"Onda set!"

"On P's!"

"Let's ride!"

That turnt the crowd all the way up! They started moving, hopping in the nearest car, four and five deep. Suge and China climbed into Suge's K5 along with two other homies and they took off.

Their caravan was deep! By the time the last whip slid into traffic the trail was twelve cars long. Close to sixty Lueders Park Bompton Pirus with an overwhelming number of intoxicants in their systems hit the road ready to paint the town red.

Suge knew the owner, all the bouncers and the DJ at Barber Coast. It wasn't even a flex for him to get his squad inside for free. When they got there, they were met with no resistance. The party was immediately in motion.

The change in their locations worked wonders for the vibe. The club atmosphere turned their gangsta party into a once-a-year type of turn-up. They completely took over the strip club. The booty-butt-naked strippers weren't even the establishment's main attraction once the mob usurped the floor.

The Bompton Pirus knew how to fuck it up. Drinks started flowing. Thick weed smoke floated and hovered over the partygoers dressed in red and black. Suge's people were shoulder-to-shoulder, having the time of their lives. Although the guest of honor wasn't in attendance, G-boy's welcome home party was quickly becoming the function of the year.

The DJ was in heaven. Like any other Disk Jockey, controlling the energy of the masses was his rush. He read the crowd and gave 'em what they wanted.

"Straight Outta Compton" by NWA blasted through the sound system, hyping the club up. Booty shaking and Blood Walking was all you saw! They went wild. Everyone was rapping along to the music. They knew every line to the song, word for word. Except, every time the word Compton came up, the whole club would yell out BOMPTON!

"STRAIGHT OUTTA BOMPTON!" they yelled over and over again. "STRAIGHT OUTTA BOMPTON! STRAIGHT OUTTA BOMPTON!"

The DJ knew what he was doing. He woke up an animal that couldn't be tamed. After witnessing the dopamine-filled wave overtake the floor like a tsunami, he did exactly what he was supposed to do.

He put "Straight Outta Compton" on repeat...

Suge was on his shit. He manifested a scene he had played out in his mind several hundred times over the previous weeks. He was a chess player, a Grand Master when it came to psychological warfare. Every move he made served its individual purpose.

After scanning the club, he chose a specific table and commandeered it. A table that served an extremely specific purpose.

CHAPTER TWENTY-TWO

She's beautiful, he thought to himself as the ambience of the black light danced across her ebony skin.

"You really like mint flavored ice cream?" Ice asked her.

She giggled before replying, "What? I know you didn't think my favorite flavor was vanilla!"

Ice let out a hearty laugh. Then he looked away before looking back onto her big brown eyes. "Well... Yeah. Actually, some vanilla with chocolate syrup on top is always good."

"You got me messed up!" she teased. Then as an after-thought she added, "Shiiit... ain't nothing wrong with ice cream with chocolate on top."

Shay slid over closer to him and rested her arm on his shoulder. *Damn,* she thought while quickly glancing at his crotch. *I wonder if this White boy got a big dick.*

"How Deep Is Your Love," by Kieth Sweat came on over the VIP room's speaker system. It was just the right time, too. Rob was a player at times. When it came to seducing women, he knew how to read the room. He gave the song a smooth thirty seconds before leaning in for a soft kiss on her neck. After lingering for a moment, he pulled back far enough to look into her eyes and then he asked, "Man, what's up wit'chu?"

"Huh? Whatchu mean?" she asked, surprised by his question.

"Why're you working in a spot like this? And don't give me the cliche answer like you're working your way through college. I've heard that one a thousand times."

She looked into his eyes, searching for authenticity. Just like he heard the "working my way through school" statement before, she had fielded the same question he asked before. It was a stereotypical question for tricks who didn't have anything else to talk about.

Shay had a question of her own. She wanted to know if he was real. Her sense of intuition was both active and accurate. But after really studying what was in front of her, she sensed something different. Something unique about him. It was deeper than what she was usually pitted against. *This white boy really likes me*, she thought. *He really does...*

"Okay," she said, ready to keep it real. "I'ma keep it all the way straight with you. I do it 'cause it's easy."

He gave her an inquisitive look.

She met it with a smile. "I'm serious. All I do is dance. Then, after my set I go around to see who wants a private dance. It's easy. I don't sell my ass. I don't do private parties. I don't use drugs. I drink a little, though." She gave him a quick shrug then said, "Easy money."

"So you like it here."

"I didn't say that. It's not like I plan on doing it forever. That's not the program I wanna run my whole

144

life. I can't sit here and tell you I know what I wanna do ten years from now. I can't even tell you what I'll be doing next week. All I do know is I'm living in the moment. I'm moving along with the vibes."

He stared at her soft lips. She could've said she wanted to suck feces out of homeless people's asses and it wouldn't have bothered him. He was on the verge of classifying their exchange as one of love at first sight.

"I get it. Seriously. That's kinda what I do... Just going through the motions. Sometimes it gets kinda heavy. Stressful, even. At times, I feel like I don't even know myself. I never truly get time to unwind."

"What do you mean?" she asked, truly wanting to hear him out. "You're chilling with me right now."

"Yeah. You're right. What I'm doing right now with you is probably the realest moment I've had in months. Everything else has been fake. Fake as fuck! Eighty-five percent of the people I meet are on my jock 'cause I'm famous. Ten percent of the people I come in contact with are only there 'cause they got their claws in my bank roll. But, then there's times like right now. Times when I meet someone from that last five percent of the people who actually keep it real."

A Tina Marie song came on just as he finished talking. Shay didn't rush to say anything. She let the moment linger. The man in front of her was starving for intimacy. On the surface it appeared as if he had everything the world had to offer. But then, after peeling away a few layers, she saw his vulnerable side. A lonely side. A person who actually felt alone in a crowded room.

She was only twenty years old. Most people would've taken her for naive or maybe even uncultured upon first glance. The truth was, neither one of those assumptions were correct.

She was from Bompton! In her two decades on this earth she had seen, heard and learned more than some individuals twice her age. Still, she wasn't a know-it-all. Shay had the wisdom to understand she really didn't know anything at all.

After a moment of contemplation, she took his hands in hers and said, "Other than the fame and fortune, everything you just said describes real life. Look around. It's not just your experience. The world is full of leaches. Everyone is out for self. That's why you gotta do your own thang, Ice. Do what you wanna do! Fuck what the next person's talkin' 'bout! Control your destiny! Pick and choose the players around you!"

He was officially awed. The woman in front of him was a fully-polished gem. After admiring her beauty he smiled and said, "I gotta say this."

"What?"

"I want you to come to my house. It's all the way in Malibu –"

"I'm not a ho."

"I promise it ain't like that."

"Yeah, right!" she said, suddenly crossing her arms across her chest.

"I'm serious. Look. What about you take your own car? I got a limo outside. I'll tell my friends to take that, and I'll ride in your car with you. This way, you can leave anytime you want."

146

Is he for real? she asked herself. *Ride in my car*? Everything about him told her he was being honest. Of course he wanted some pussy. But it didn't seem like he expected it. He actually seemed as if he truly enjoyed her company. For that, she made up her mind. Shay lowered her voice as she looked into his eyes and asked, "What if I get there and I decide to stay?"

"Then I'll wake you up with breakfast in bed. Afterward, we'll take a swim in the ocean..."

CHAPTER TWENTY-THREE

"Boyz n the hood" was blasting out the club's speakers. The strobe light made the sea of flamed-up thugs look like a gangland video shoot.

"Yeah, man, Jennifer put too much on it. I've been trying to talk to you and Ice 'bout all this music I got. My writers are the same exact guys who're writing for NWA," Suge assured Vanilla Ice's manager.

Suge had made his way to their table as soon as he entered the club. Just as they were getting antsy, looking like they wanted to leave. It was one thing to represent a white rapper. Showing up in controlled environments made a lot of the industry leaches feel safe.

That was definitely not the case at Barber Coast that night.

The setting Suge created was spicy to say the least. Anyone in their right mind could look into the eyes of the men and women around them and know without a doubt they were in a pool of piranhas.

"You really know the guys in NWA?" Vanilla Ice's friend asked Suge.

"Yeah! Of course he does," Tommy said. "This is Los Angeles. If someone says they know so-and-so, best believe 'im. This is how true networking happens. Ain't that right, Mr. Knight?"

"You're right, Suge said. "It's really not that big of a town. Especially when you're in the same game." Suge tapped the arm of his nearest homeboy and said, "Blood, find a waitress and order us a round. Make sure all the homies is good, too. Drinks on me tonight."

"Bet, Suge. I gottchu," replied the gangster in a red Dickie shirt.

Suge turned back to the men at the table and flashed an unalarming smile before looking around and finding China. When he found him he gave him a silent gesture conveying one question and one question only: Where's the white boy?

Before he knew it, he got his answer. There was a scuffle towards the back of the club. The energy in the crowd seemed to get rowdy. There was some shoving going on; not like a fight or melee, but it was enough to catch the attention of Vanilla's entourage.

Suge caught their concern in mid drift and said, "Don't worry 'bout that. You know how these youngsters get when they see some ass shaking."

"Ain't that right," Tommy agreed. "That might be Ice coming out right now."

"I hope so," Suge smiled. "Can't wait to see him again."

$$$$$

When Ice and Shay stepped out the VIP room the club's vibe was unrecognizable. It was nothing like how they left it before stepping into their private sanctuary.

The crowd was beyond thick. People were shoulder to shoulder. It looked like a party, yet no one was smiling. Usually, when Ice entered a crowd, he was recognized and met with stargazed stares. But that was far from the case at hand.

It was as if he had entered some sort of Matrix. The gentleman's club he had left a little while earlier was long gone. Ice felt as if he was the new white kid at an all-Black school.

The shoving started as soon as he stepped into the crowd. It was like the partygoers were purposely bumping into him. Looks of disgust mixed with contempt oozed from their eyes. The bouncers didn't even try to offer him assistance. He couldn't even see his friends through the crowd. His only comfort came halfway to his table when he felt Shay's soft hands take his in hers.

When he looked at her, she didn't seem bothered. It was obvious he was, though.

Then, all of sudden, the sea parted! And what he saw at the end of if blew his mothafucking mind. The guy from the Palms was waiting for him next to his manager and friend.

Suge saw the white boy before he saw him. He smiled wide, letting the others see his artificial happiness. But what really got him right was when Robert Van Winkle's eyes shot open like high beams. The cracker was terrified! Exactly how Suge wanted him to be.

"Hey, Rob!" Tommy called out when he saw Ice. "Look who we got here!"

What the fuck! thought Ice. *How is this happening? Why is Tommy acting like this fucking sasquatch is our friend!?!*

"Hey, Ice!" Suge bellowed a little louder than necessary. He reached his hand out and squeezed the hell out of Ice's hand. Although his smile was welcoming, Suge's grip yelled, *WE ARE NOT BOOL!* "How you doin', superstar?"

Ice heard a thick, raspy shot of venom coming from the big man's voice. He snatched his wounded hand from Suge's grasp as soon as he could. Trying not to sound flustered, he replied, "I've been good. Busy as hell –"

"Yeah. Your people told me you've been globe-trotting from the East Coast to the South and back, huh?"

"Super busy. Nonstop flights. As a matter of fact, I'm ready to call it a night."

A buff kid in a red and black t-shirt bumped into Ice. When he looked at him, the guy met him with a hostile glare. Ice was obviously not welcomed at the club anymore.

"You do gotta get some rest," Tommy added. "We got a long day ahead of us tomorrow."

"Is that right," Suge commented sarcastically. "Well, before you leave I wanna remind you about Chocolate's song."

"Oh yeah. Yeah. I haven't forgotten about him."

Suge took his hand again, "I won't let you forget. Feel me?"

"Uh-oh-uh – yeah, bro. I feel you, man," Vanilla Ice stuttered.

That was the moment when Ice's manager finally realized what was going on. Suddenly, the aggressive crowd seemed even more hostile than they had been. Not just hostile, but now they seemed dangerous. He looked at Ice and saw fear and apprehension.

The DJ didn't let up either. He put "Straight Outta Compton" back on rotation and the crowd immediately went wild. "STRAIGHT OUTTA BOMPTON! STRAIGHT OUTTA BOMPTON!"

The whole club sang the words to the hook like it was their theme song. Ice wanted to take off running. The last thing he wanted was to spend another moment in the dragon's nest. But he couldn't just leave. Not without the precious gem he found earlier.

Shay hadn't left his side. She must've felt his vibe because she took his hand in hers. That's all Ice needed. With Shay in tow, he headed for the door.

The dancers weren't allowed to leave the club with patrons. Under normal circumstances, she would've lost her job. But Shay couldn't be fired because she didn't work there.

Suge didn't even try to stop them from racing out of there. He calmly lit his cigar as he watched Ice and his entourage scurry away. His plan had went exactly how he wanted it to. Both Vanilla and his manager had seen his army. The threat of force would always be there. And that alone would eventually pave the way for diplomatic solutions...

CHAPTER TWENTY-FOUR

Shay had been ushered into the back of Ice's limo without a thought. Even though the vibe felt hostile, the move seemed natural.

The ride to Malibu was stuffy. The silence didn't help the aura either. It almost seemed to match.

After pressing the button that lowered one of the windows, the cabin's fear-filled aroma cleared up. Shay was able to sit back and study her surroundings. The inside of the limo was luxurious. A small television was mounted on top of a fully-stocked bar. They were separated from the driver by a tinted glass partition giving them a sense of privacy that could make a person forget they were in a moving vehicle.

As she studied the grim faces of Rob's group, it became obvious they were shook. To her, it was a regular function. She recognized damn near every person that came with Suge. She understood Ice's energy, though. She wasn't blind to the fact that she came from the trenches. In her world, gangs, drugs, sex and violence was normal. In Ice's world it didn't exist at all.

If Shay and her girls would've went somewhere and got dissed, they would've been upset too. But the difference would've been their bounce-back time.

Eventually, one of them would've made a joke and the rest of them would've snapped out of their gloomy mood. She didn't know those men though. She barely knew Ice. Even though she liked and felt comfortable with him she decided to stay quiet and let things play out.

When they pulled up to Ice's house, Shay wasn't immediately impressed.

The neighborhood was in the hills. The houses were new. Even though it was late, the streets were well lit, showcasing the nice homes. Still, she wasn't impressed after her and the white boy were dropped off.

But her whole perception of where she was at changed the moment she stepped inside the home. As she followed Ice through the front door, down a hallway into an extra-large room with the most beautiful view on earth, she couldn't shake the feeling from the opulence she was surrounded with.

The floors were marble. The walls had art decor all over. She could only imagine how much all the crazy looking Picaso-type-of-paintings were worth. The floor-model television stood taller than her. The wrap-around couch was probably the biggest sofa she had ever seen.

Robert went into the kitchen to pour them some drinks while Shay admired the home. The whole back wall was a window overlooking the ocean. His house was perched on the edge of a cliff, hundreds of feet from the private beach.

She couldn't believe the expanse of the ocean before her. The stars lit the Pacific Ocean like a movie scene! It was beautiful.

After a few minutes, Ice came up behind Shay. When she turned towards him she saw the glasses of liquor in his hand.

"Sorry 'bout that drama at the club —"

Shay put her fingers to Ice's lips shushing him. "Don't think about it. Let it go. You're home now, baby. As a matter of fact, I know how to ease your mind."

Ice smiled. Sixty-nine different things that could set him at ease immediately came to mind. His slick smirk betrayed his thoughts.

"Uh-uh... You crazy! Get that smile off your face, Icy-Boy!" she teased. "Where's your bathroom? Your Master bathroom?"

"It's in the bedroom."

Shay leaned her head back, downing her drink before saying, "Show me!"

That's all he needed. Leading Shay to his bedroom made him forget the fear he felt earlier. In Ice's mind, he understood Black women. Their hard demeanors kept soft men off their square. It didn't bother Vanilla Ice. He was aroused by the strong ebony-skinned women.

When they got to the bathroom, Shay's jaw dropped. His bathroom was as big as her living room. There were his and hers sinks and showers. A walk-in closet. A private toilet and door that led to a patio where a jacuzzi sat underneath the stars. It was exquisite.

What caught her attention was the bathtub. It was larger than a normal tub. Shaped in dark marble. She couldn't believe her eyes. It was perfect.

"Oh my god!" she exclaimed when she saw the candles strategically placed all around the tub. *Scented candles! Hell yeah!* she thought excitedly. "Ice, you got a light?"

He smiled at her like one would when seeing a small child opening Christmas gifts. "Yeah, right here." He went to the counter and took a candle lighter out of one of the drawers.

She was already turning on the water by the time he handed her the light. "Take off them clothes."

"Huh?" Ice asked. He wasn't a prude. But the tone of her voice was demanding.

"Boy, take them clothes off. We finna bathe."

"Okay," he replied with a little more surety than he felt seconds earlier.

He started undressing, taking his shirt off first. Shay was not shy. She watched him as he peeled off the layers one piece at a time. She was planning on taking off what little she had on too. But first, she watched him. His chiseled chest and six-pack actually surprised her. The white boy was cut.

Shay stared intently as he kicked off his shoes and pulled off his jeans. He wasn't wearing any underwear. And his dick was hard, bouncy-hard.

Impressive.

"Damn, Icy-Boy! What's that? Eight, nine inches?"

He chuckled proudly. His elongated eight-and-a-half-inch swipe had always been something he was eager to show off.

"Something like that," he replied humbly.

Ice was loving every moment of it. When he got into the water, Shay softly scrubbed every inch of his

156

body. It was something about dark-skinned women that drove him crazy. The way the pink of their insides clashed with the black of their outside pussy lips triggered a lust in him that white women never could. Shay was his type. He could barely control himself once they got naked.

When it was over, he softly dried her off. Then he took her to the bedroom and laid her down on his California King-sized bed. By then, they were intimate enough for love making. He lifted her legs up and took two handfuls of her round ass cheeks. After spreading them wide open he pressed his face between them and stuck his tongue out. He then ran it up and down her crack before kissing her puckering opening.

Shay tried hold in a giggle, but it was hard. He was tickling the hell out of her asshole. His finger started stroking her clit while he licked.

For five good minutes he prodded her asshole with his tongue. His fingers on one hand played with her clit while the other fondled her petite tits. The whole time, his dick started hopping around with anticipation.

Shay wasn't into anal like that. She had never been with anyone who showed as much passion for the job as he had.

"Do it, Rob," she whispered. "Put that pink mothafucka in my booty."

He heard her loud and clear. She was begging for his dick and he planned on giving it to her. He stood up and went to the edge of the bed. First he slid his member into her wet pussy. He wanted to lube his wood for the main event, so he started pounding her love tunnel with no abandon.

"Stop playin' wit' me, Rob! Put it in my ass, white boy! Please!" she moaned. Shay couldn't remember the last time she begged a man for some dick. She didn't mind it though. Not one bit. It was turning out to be one helluva ride!"

Ice pulled his piece out with an audible plop! He grabbed his shaft then ran the tip up and-down her ass crack before slipping the head into her brown eye. He nudged a little bit at a time to get it passed the little ring.

"Dayumm, it feels good," she purred. "Go slow, tho'."

He slowed down even more. He could tell she wasn't used to that type of sex. He even had to stop pushing it in for a moment so she could rest before he pressed play again.

She was experiencing one of the most wonderful sensations she had felt in her entire life. She couldn't describe the ecstasy she experienced when the head of his shaft first penetrated her ring of lust. After that, there were moments she felt as if she were being ripped apart, but she-welcomed the pain as if it were pleasure. One wouldn't have been right without the other.

He waited a few seconds before pushing in deeper. Then he pulled the head out, timing his thrust forward to match her sensual vibe. He was slowly starting to fuck her little asshole. With every thrust he went in deeper and deeper. It was a slow process, but fifteen minutes later, his nuts were banging against her cheeks as he pounded that booty!

Shay felt every inch of his long, pink schlong. She was busting nuts back-to-back. She had gotten so comfortable she was now pushing back, tempting him to hit her deepest realms.

His fingers never stopped working. They tickled her clit through it all.

"Yes!" she screamed. "Fuck this booty, white boy! Fuck this ass, honky!"

Ice felt her rectum squeeze his dick. There was no way he was gonna be able to control himself. "I'm gonna blow! Shay, I'm 'bout to blow!" he yelled. He stopped rubbing her clit and reached for her ass cheeks. After spreading them even wider, he went berzerk on her!

She was all woman at that point. The pleasurable sensations coming from her anal cavity was unthinkable. She could've never imagined it feeling so good. "Cum, white boy! Fill my as wit' yo' cum!"

Ice let out a loud grunt as he shot load after load of cum inside her tight derriere. He could tell she was cumming too, because not only did her ass start quivering, her pussy suddenly squirted woman jizz onto his thighs.

Shay lost all concept of time when she came. Her nut was so intense it brought her to tears. She felt a sense of euphoria. It took over her whole body. It was so pleasurable she felt an out-of-body experience.

CHAPTER TWENTY-FIVE

When G-Boy and Buntry left the bandy lady's house they both immediately noticed how empty the apartment complex's parking lot was. There were still over thirty partygoers in attendance but the difference was noticeable.

G-Boy didn't mind, though. His thoughts were no longer on celebrating his release. The work and guns he was carrying had rerouted the vibe in which his mind was in.

G-Boy scanned the parking lot looking for the group of homies he had originally showed up with. He didn't have to look for long either. He had a whole clique of niggaz waiting for him to come back out. When he saw them, a smirk snuck across his face and he started nodding to himself. His young niggaz were already on point.

Buntry peeped the whole scene and was confident he could leave G-Boy with his team and he'd be straight. Nevertheless, he turned to him and asked, "Blood, you need a ride to ya mamma house?"

"Naw," G-Boy replied. "I'ma ride out with the homies. I gotta holla at them niggaz anyway."

"A'ight, blood. You got my number and you know where I'm at. Get at me tomorrow."

"Bet."

G-Boy was met with five of his dogs. All of them were from Lueders. They had been waiting for him to come home for just as long as Suge and his clique had been waiting.

Baby G-Boy, Bear, P-Dog, CK Brazy and L.B. were all young hitters from Lueders Park Bompton Piru. They had all been running with each other for as long as any of them could remember. G-Boy couldn't have been in better company.

"S'up, blood!" G-Boy greeted each one of them when they met up in the shadows of the lot.

"Where-da-fuck you go?" CK Brazy asked G-Boy.

"I had to touch base with Suge and them."

Bear, a dark skinned, heavyset Y.G. smiled and teased, "So, you already on yo' Mob tip, huh?"

"Nigga... This Lueders!" he replied firmly. "But they the homies. They just put me on."

"What'chu mean?" P-Dog, the pretty boy out the crew asked.

G-Boy held up the duffle bag and said, "Them niggaz just gave me some heaters and thangs. As a matter of fact, I need to go stash this shit. We gotta get up outta here before the rollers pop up on some bullshit."

G-Boy and his niggaz had pulled up to the party in two cars. P-Dog's '72 Cutlass and L.B.'s El Camino.

"I'ma ride with you an Baby G," G-Boy told P-Dog. Then to the others he said, "Y'all follow us. If five-O pull up, make sure they don't get behind us."

"On Piiiru that ain't 'bout to happen!" L.B. announced. "I got you."

"Let's go then," G-Boy told them and they all got in their designated rides.

P-Dog's '72 green and white Cutlass had a 350 Rocket in it. He had been bragging about it's power every time G-Boy called home from Y.A. So G-Boy knew it was the fastest car between the two options they had. He needed that extra assurance just in case the night ended in a high-speed chase.

"So where we heading?" P-Dog asked as soon as they pulled out the of the apartment complex.

"My auntie house"

"Which auntie?" Baby G-Boy asked from the back seat.

"Renee," G-Boy replied.

P-Dog and Baby G looked at one another. Then both turned back to G-Boy.

"Didn't she move to the Kelly's?" P-Dog asked.

"Yeah. She fucks with one of they G's. T-Loc."

"What-da-fuck we going there for?" Baby G asked.

"I already told y'all! Why you askin' me a dumb-ass question, blood?" G-Boy snapped.

"You didn't tell us we was going to the Kelly's."

G-Boy started shaking his head. He looked at P-Dog and said, "Head to Kelly Park, blood." Then he looked at his little homey through the rearview mirror and said, "T-Loc bool as fuck, homey. We been talkin' on the phone for some years. Whenever I called my auntie house and she wasn't there he would accept my collect calls and chop game with me. He's like my uncle, blood. He gets money and he's respected by his set. We'll be good every time we go out there as long as we don't pull up disrespecting and shit."

P-Dog knew exactly how to get to Kelly Park. It was one of the most notorious Crip sets in the city of Compton. He kept driving but still asked, "What I don't understand is why we going there when we 'posed to be stashing all this shit."

"First off, T-Loc got some more work for me. Second, I'm gonna stash some of these straps over there. I'm on parole so they can hit my house anytime they want. This is killing two birds with one bullet. Plus, I wanna see my auntie. Y'all got a problem wit' that?"

P-Dog shook his head, "Naw. As long as we don't run into any of them niggaz, I'm good."

"If we do, y'all stand down. That's they set. We the one's trespassing so we gonna show 'em some respect. As long as we go straight to my auntie's spot it's all good. He's waiting on me right now, anyway..."

With that said the subject was dropped for more pressing matters like which one of the homegirls was going to give G-Boy his first dose of vagina in five years.

That wasn't the first time the red and blue lines of Bompton were crossed on friendly terms. And it wouldn't be the last either.

G-Boy was a Grand Master chess player. He was just as smart as he was dangerous. The majority of his time incarcerated had been spent plotting on his come-up once freed. And he knew the best way to accomplish the moves he was intent on making was by networking with reputables from other sets. The fact that he had cultivated a relationship with such a factor from Kelly Park was a major plus in his eyes. A skillful chess move. One that he was confident would pay off in the long run...

CHAPTER TWENTY-SIX

Robert's bedroom window faced the Pacific Ocean. In the morning, the light that came in was bright enough to appreciate, yet not so much that it made the room hot. The rays weren't disrespectful. They were just enough to slowly wake a person who and fallen asleep to the exhaustion of sex.

Shay couldn't have told anyone what woke her that morning. The scent of the sea, or the aroma of fried eggs and bacon. The two hit her senses at once when he woke her up with breakfast in bed.

"Good morning, beautiful," he told her as she began to stir. *Damn, she's fine,* he thought to himself as he sat the tray on the nightstand next to Shay's side of the bed.

She greeted him with a smile as she stretched out the kinks of the night before. *God, this man is too nice,* she thought when she realized what was happening.

"Not sure if you're a morning person so I let you rest a little longer than I wanted too."

"Wanted to?" she said as she slid a slice of bacon into her mouth. "Shiiit, if you wanted some pussy –"

"Naw," he smiled. He climbed back into bed and leisurely crossed his hands behind his head against a stack of pillows. "It wasn't 'bout sex. I just couldn't wait to hang out with you. Not that watching you sleep wasn't a treat."

Shay cut her eyes at the man next to her. "Uh-huh," she playfully commented while rolling her eyes at him.

He chuckled, "Corny, huh?"

She took a drink from her glass of freshly-squeezed orange juice then smiled at him. "It's cool. I like it. I'm just teasing your cute-ass."

"I know, I'm trippin'. I just got a lot on my mind these days."

She cut her eyes at him again. She could sense his stress. The memory of the previous evening suddenly flooding back into her mental. "You wanna talk about something?"

"It's nothing, really," he said while staring at the ceiling. "Does it got something to do with what happened last night?"

"Yeah. Sort of," he replied, suddenly opening up. "Did you see the big guy who was sitting with Tommy and Rick when we came out the VIP room?"

"Yeah," she mumbled with a mouthful of eggs.

"Well, he's managing a guy I used to hang with back in Texas. He's been coming at me 'bout some money –"

With a wrinkled brow she snapped, "He try'na extort you or something? Is that what all that was about?"

"Naw... Naw, it ain't like he's trying to get over. In a way, I do owe the guy I'm talking about. I just haven't got around to making things right."

Shay sat her plate back on the nightstand and got up. "I gotta pee. But keep talking. I'm listening."

Rob watched her get out of bed and walk across the bedroom to the adjourning bathroom. He couldn't take his eyes off her. She was completely naked. If he wasn't so stressed off the Chocolate situation, he would've prepped himself for another round of love making. But, instead, he just kept talking.

"I did some music with the guy back in Texas. Then we all ended up losing contact. It wasn't really a big deal. Not at the time. But when shit started blowing up everything started moving kinda quick. All kinds of people started coming out the woodworks asking for money and shit. What's so funny is everyone told me it would happen like that and it did."

The toilet flushed and a few moments later Shay came back and climbed back into bed with him. She could tell he was holding back some details. Not that it mattered. She didn't need all the details. He was obviously bothered and needed someone to talk to about it all.

She rested her head on his chest and draped her thigh over his. "Go ahead, baby. I'm listening."

The move seemed so natural that he just kept venting as if there wasn't a beautiful woman laying on him completely naked. "I get it, tho'. Before I got famous, I was just like everyone else grasping for straws. Trying to get a connection from anybody and everybody."

"That doesn't give anyone the right to try and get over."

"You're right. But, Mario did help me out with a few things. He was my partner at one point. He's actually a good guy."

"Hmmm," she thought out loud. "It sounds like your conscious is telling you to give him something. Somewhere in your heart you feel like he deserves something. Is that what I'm hearing?"

Rob didn't say anything. He knew Mario deserved every penny he was asking for. He didn't just write the music he actually helped him perfect his delivery. He was there when Ice was performing at empty hole-in-wall clubs in Houston. In a small dark corner located in the back of Rob's mind, he sometimes felt it should've been Mario rocking those stages with his name in lights.

"... Another way to look at it," Shay continued, "is he seems to have some friends who got his back in a real way. Those guys at the club last night didn't look like they were playing games. I don't think you want that kind of drama in your life. They don't seem to have much to lose. But you do. You're on a whole different level."

"I am."

"Sure, you are. So why not take care of it? Get him out the way and move on with your life."

Again, he remained stitch lipped. He stared at the ceiling for a while then suddenly pulled Shay on top of him. He barely knew her but somehow had a strong affection towards her. If it were up to him in that very moment, he would spend the rest of his life with her. Lost in her eyes. Basking in the vibe of young love...

CHAPTER TWENTY-SEVEN

Close to three weeks had passed since the incident at Barber Coast. Suge was at the Beehive on Bullis tending to his business – it was a full house. A lot of his homies were there to watch the dog fight they had all been looking forward to seeing for some time.

"Ssskkk! Ssskkk! Ssskkk! Time to feed! Feed, Damu! Feed!" Suge's younger homie Silk whispered into his Red Nose Pitbull's ear.

Damu growled menacingly.

The Beehive's backyard was crowded. A barbeque pit was lit. Forties were the drink of the afternoon. The gang stood in a circle, placing bets on the dog fights they were staging.

"I got fifty on CK! Fifty on CK!" another Piru yelled over the crowd.

CK was a Brindle with a track record of tearing his opponents throats out. Damu was a beautiful white pit with blue eyes. Other than the scars on her face, she could've been a show dog. CK on the other hand was hard on the eyes. She was missing an ear and had patches of fur gone, giving her a mangy appearance.

Heron was the ringmaster. In his trademark, deep voice he announced, "Bring yo' bitches to middle of the circle! Let's get this mothafucka started!"

Both dogs were brought into the center of the man-made circle. They were growling low murderistic growls.

"Ssskkk! Feed, Damu! Feed, girl!" Silk whispered in her ear.

CK's owner, Boss Hawg, wasn't as vocal with his animal. But that didn't mean the duo weren't on the same hype. When Heron started counting down, he gave her a simple order, "Get 'im, girl! Get 'im!"

"Three... Two... One!" yelled Heron.

The killers were released! Bam! They hit like linebackers! Snarling! Biting! Scratching!

"Get 'im, Damu!" "Feed, CK!" the onlookers yelled as the bloody fight took place.

Suge was standing on the top step of the porch, right outside the trap's back door. It gave him a view of the whole scene. A picture that promised to end gruesomely.

The screeching sounds that came from the dangerous animals were ear piercing. In a different part of town, the horrific sounds would've prompted several calls to the nearest animal control office. But not in their hood. If anything, it gave their neighbor's a heads up. All they had to do was look over their backyard's fence and they'd get a direct view of the felonious festivities.

"Beep! Beep! Beep!" Suge's pager sounded.

"On Piru, your beeper stays going off!" Buntry commented.

Suge nodded in silent agreement while looking at the number. "Hold on, blood. I gotta call this number back."

"You're 'bout to miss the rest of the fight," Buntry replied.

Suge went inside, not really caring about the outcome. He had millions of dollars on his mind. The dog fight was nonconsequential.

He went straight to the kitchen where the phone was located.

G-Boy was at the table busting down a few ounces of crack. Weighing out and bagging up half-ounce cookies. "What's brackin', Ru?"

"Checkin' on some shit," replied Suge. "Let me see the phone real quick."

G-Boy tossed him the cordless phone before asking, "When you gonna get more work?"

Suge either didn't hear him, or was preoccupied with his own thoughts. Either way, he didn't answer him. Instead, he dialed the number on his pager and stepped into the front room. Everyone was outside, which meant it was quiet enough for him to talk business.

Chocolate picked up the other line on the first ring. "Marion! Marion! He just called!"

Suge didn't need clarification on who "He" was. He knew exactly who Mario was talking about. "I told you he would. What he say?"

"That he's been tryna get ahold of me for over a year!"

"Man, that's bullshit! He's really on some bullshit, ain't he?"

"I already know. But, yeah. He said he wanted to talk. That he's been tryna catch up with me so he can give me the royalties he owes me."

"Is that right... Did he say how much?"

That's when G-Boy stepped in the hallway from the kitchen, "Suge, I gotta get atchu, blood."

"Give me a minute, bro. Let me finish this call," he replied sounding irritated.

G-Boy stared at him for a moment before going back into the kitchen. Suge was his homey, but his tone wasn't warranted. Still, he discarded his own irritation and went back to his triple beam activities.

Suge continued, "What you doin' right now?"

"I really ain't doin' shit. Just sittin' here wit' my girl."

"Don't go nowhere. I'll be there in five minutes." Suge ended the call then walked back through the house towards the backyard.

He needed to have a serious talk with Chocolate. Vanilla Ice calling him was a major breakthrough.

When he reached the back door, he got there just in time to see Silk pull the trigger on the shot that ended his dog's life. It was customary to put a dog out of his misery when it was obvious there was no bringing it back.

G-Boy hopped up and followed Suge when he saw him pass the kitchen *Finally*, he thought to himself. *We can talk business now.*

He'd been hustling nonstop since he got out and managed to get his chips up to a level where Suge told him he would broker a deal with his connect for him.

"Buntry!" Suge called out. "C'mon, blood. Ride wit' me."

"Hey, Suge," G-Boy said when he stepped out the backdoor.

The crowd was still bustling from the fight. The yard was loud enough for Suge not to hear him. Instead of replying, Suge stepped around the side of the house on his way to his truck.

G-Boy felt slighted. It was obvious in his demeanor by the way he stood there staring at Suge walk away. He was stuck, not able to register the disrespect he felt until he was called back to the moment by one of his partnas.

"Damn, blood. What was that all about?" L.B. asked him.

L.B. wasn't from The Mob. He was a hundred percent Lueders Park Bompton Piru. He was more loyal to G-boy than anyone else there that day.

"Fuck dat shit," G-Boy replied. "Blood's just in a rush."

L.B. shrugged it off then said, "Fuck it, then. So, what's up, Ru? You ready to bounce?"

"Yeah. Let's go," he replied. On the surface he let it go without a thought. But, on the inside he felt slighted. It almost seemed as if Suge was acting like he was better than the rest of them. G-Boy jettisoned the negative thoughts just as quick as they came. He had business to handle so he got back to it...

CHAPTER TWENTY-EIGHT

When Suge and Buntry pulled up at Mario's house they found him standing outside. He was leaning against a rusty bucket on crates.

His girl was on the porch on a lawn chair. Suge couldn't help but think of the differences between hood business and cooperate affairs. Here he was, hopping out of his K5 with a convicted felon to talk to Mario about a million-dollar business deal.

At some point he knew he'd have an extension of the same conversation he was about to have in a high-rise office with someone else.

The irony of it all didn't miss its mark.

Suge wasted no time. As soon as they met with Chocolate in the driveway he said, "What's brackin'? What the white boy say?"

"A'ight. So he called and started out with all the bullshit. Talkin' 'bout how he tried reaching out to me, but couldn't find me after I left Texas."

"Bullshit!" Buntry scoffed, along with Suge.

"Exactly. Then he got to talkin' about a bag of money he had for me –"

"What?" Suge asked, looking disgusted. "Bag? Like as in cash?"

"Yeah!"

"Dat's a no-go!" Suge snapped. "Did he mention points off the earnings? Royalties off future sales?"

"Not at all! All he kept saying was he's been holding onto my money. That he had a bag of bread waiting for me to grab."

Suge looked at Buntry, "You hear this shit?"

"Angles! That's what it sounds like to me. The white boy got angles," Buntry shot back.

"Onda Mob!" Suge replied before turning back to Mario. "Did he say anything about how –"

"He told me he was only in town for a few days. That he's staying in a room at the Bel Age Hotel right now!"

"Blood!" Buntry cut in. "Let's run up on 'im! You say he's there right now? Let's go!"

Suge looked at Buntry then back at Mario. He was silently asking them, *Should we?*

"I told him I needed to talk to you first. And that's when he started talkin' 'bout me coming alone. He kept saying there was no need to add other people into our business. That he knew he owed me, and was ready to pay up."

"For real?!" Suge said. "That mothafucka got nerve! Chocolate, on Ru's, don't you find it funny he wants to holla at you alone? If his business is on the up an' up –"

"There would be no need for secrecy," Mario said. "I already know. I told 'im all'at. But he was still adamant 'bout me coming alone. And that's exactly why I called you!"

Suge happened to glance at the porch at Mario's girl while he was talking. She wasn't trying to hide the fact that she was paying close attention to everything

175

they were doing. She was just sitting there staring at them while sipping on her Snapple, peeping the whole scene. When she saw Suge look in her direction, she took it as an invitation to join them.

To Chocolate, Suge replied, "That's right, homey. And you did the right thing by gettin' at me. He knows exactly who I am. He knows I'm your manager. I don't give a fuck how long he's known you, he should've came directly to me with this alleged 'bag of money' he's got for you. Especially since I've been on his helmet for a minute now."

"He's right," Margy told him when she reached the group. "I told you there was something shady 'bout that white boy. He didn't reach out to you till Sugar Bear started pressing him."

"Onda set!" Buntry agreed.

Suge continued, "He wants you alone for a reason. I already know his type. He's gonna lure you into his world. Probably have some bad bitches and drank there. He'll show you a bag of money to make you think there's a lot more coming. Then, when he gets you fucked up enough to blind you with the smoke and mirrors. He'll get you to sign your life away!"

"He's right," Margy said. "He's been around these types of people long enough to know their games."

"I know," he replied. "Shiiit. I know. My question is, what's next?"

"It sounds like he's tryna pull you into a controlled setting," Suge explained. "In his mind, he's got the whole evening planned out. I say we change all'at! The first thing that'll fuck 'im up is when I show up witchu.'"

"Blood! On Ru's, I'm coming too!" Buntry stated.

Suge nodded before asking Mario what time Vanilla Ice asked him to show up at the Bel Age.

"Tonight. At ten," Chocolate told him.

"Bet! I'll be here to pick you up at nine." To Buntry Suge said, "C'mon, dog. I got another spot I need to stop by."

"Let's ride!"

"Be ready at nine, Mario. I'ma pull up, be ready to go."

"I'll be here," he replied.

"Thanks, Sugar Bear!" Margy said before stealing a hug from the thug.

Once they were back in the truck, Buntry asked Suge where they were heading. Suge told him he had to holla at Griffey and Virgil. He was already redesigning his chess board.

Robert Van Winkle didn't know it yet. But, he was about to get pressed in a real gangland fashion. At the same time, Suge had to stay focused. There was an end game that operated within certain perimeters. And that's what Griffey and Virgil were there for...

CHAPTER TWENTY-NINE

G-Boy had business to handle. After bagging up and weighing his work his main objective was hitting the block and getting rid of it. He wasn't happy about the way Suge had ignored him when he tried to talk to him but he pushed the incident out of his mind. He had thick skin and no time for emotions.

Baby G-Boy and CK Brazy were posted up next to L.B.'s all-black El Camino when they walked around the side of the Beehive to the front of the house. The day was still sunny and bright. Perfect for getting money.

When they reached the El-Co, Baby G-Boy was the first to inquire about their next move. The red and white beads on the ends of his cornrows bounced around as he spoke because the Y.G. was hyper in his animated movements. "What's brackin', blood? We fuckin' wit' Tamika an' them? They posted up at the park right now."

Everyone looked at G-Boy. Ultimately, the call would be on him. And he wasn't known for socializing when there was business to be handled. But since the day was so nice, hanging out with some homegirls wouldn't have been a bad idea.

"We can fuck wit' 'em. Shiiit, we can swoop 'em up and set up shop at Tamika's house."

"Bet," L.B. said. "Get in the back, y'all. Let's ride out," he told Brazy and Baby G.

"Hold up, tho'," G-Boy said. "Let's stop by my mamma house real quick. I gotta give her some rent money an all'at. It's almost the first of the month and I wanna look out for her."

"Onda set!" L.B. replied. "Let's go."

They all got in the El Camino. Brazy and Baby G got in the back. G-Boy ended up in the passenger seat next to L.B. The El-Co was fast. Its well-tuned engine was just as clean as its all-leather interior.

When they pulled off, L.B. put a Ghetto Boys tape in the tape deck and they rode to the lyrics of Scarface, Willie D and Bushwick Bill. It was one of those days in the hood when everyone seemed to be out and about.

"That's bool as fuck how you be helping ya mamma out, blood." L.B. told G-Boy. "Most of these niggaz just worried 'bout flippin' low-lows and lookin' good for bitches."

"That's not gonna help them niggaz when they catch a case and end up doing time," G-Boy replied. "That's why niggaz end up doing they bid with no friends or family supporting them. When they out they spend they pennies on bitches that ain't gonna do shit for 'em when they down. I'll be damned if I move like that. I'm not gonna forget who was there for me when I was locked up. My mamma kept me with soups and chips in my locker. So did y'all. So that's where my loyalty lies."

"On Piru," L.B. said.

They passed a boarded-up house with a man on the porch and L.B. shook his head and scoffed. G-Boy hadn't been looking on that side of the street but he noticed his friend's sudden disdain for whoever was on the porch.

"Who was that?" he asked.

"Nobody, blood. A real nobody. This nigga did some fuck-shit a while back that got the set feuding with Park Village. The homies feel salty 'bout the fuck-nigga 'cause he be back here with the rest of the Mob niggaz. Since we be posted up in the front of the set we the ones who end up dealing wit' them crabs when they ride thru shootin' shit up. All while that fuck-nigga stays high all day."

G-Boy had heard about the incident that ended in a high-speed chase and crash in front of the Mob's mad pad. It had stuck out in his mind because of who was in the car.

G-Boy had did time with Bolo a few years earlier. When Bolo pulled up in his building at the Paso Robles youth prison G-Boy embraced him eagerly because they were from the same set. They immediately linked and became inseparable. They ate together, worked out together, even lined it up with their opps together.

Everything was good with them until it wasn't. One day, a riot had popped off between the whites and Sureños against the Bloods and Pirus. The damus were outnumbered three to one so every man counted. In the midst of the melee G-Boy's ace had left him for dead. He ran as soon as the yard got spicy. Afterwards, everyone involved ended up going to the hole and Bolo wasn't one of them. By the time G-Boy and the others had gotten out of segregation Bolo was gone. He had transferred to another youth prison up North.

Not only had Bolo left G-Boy for dead, he had made him look bad. He made the whole Bompton Piru car look weak. So G-Boy had vowed to D.P. the coward the first time he ran into him.

"Blood, turn around!" G-Boy demanded when he realized who L.B. had scoffed at.

"What?"

"Turn the mothafuckin' car around! I'm finna get on dat nigga!"

L.B. didn't have to be told twice. He slammed his foot on the break. He immediately turned into the nearest driveway then backed out and headed back in the direction they came from. While he was turning the car around, CK Brazy and Baby G-Boy knocked on the rear window. They both wanted to know what was going on.

G-Boy slid the window open and said, "I'm 'bout to get on this nigga!"

"Who?" Baby G asked. "You mean, WE finna –"

"Naw! It's just what I said! I'm getting' on that bitch-ass nigga Bolo! Y'all niggaz stay out my business or I'ma need that from y'all too!"

The El-Co pulled up to the curb in front of the house where Bolo was posted up at. When L.B. stopped his whip he didn't break abruptly. He was in war mode and didn't want to give their opp any sort of sign that a squabble was about to happen.

G-Boy hopped out the passenger seat with his 9-millimeter tucked in his waistband. "Bolo!"

When Bolo saw G-Boy get out the El Camino he instinctively smiled.

He hadn't seen his homey since Y.A. and had forgotten the circumstances in which he left him. Bolo stepped off the porch of the boarded-up house and approached his old friend with full intentions of giving and receiving a gangsta's embrace.

G-Boy had different plans for his old comrade. The moment Bolo got within swinging distance he cocked back and hit the nigga with a haymaker to the jaw!

Baaam!

Bolo stumbled but quickly caught his footing. Still, he didn't have enough time to gain his senses before G-Boy took his soul-snatching apparatus from his waistband and started beating him over the head with it.

Baaam! Baam! Bam!

"Bitch-ass nigga!" G-Boy snarled. "Leave a nigga on the battle field and think you can come back to the set! Run now, bitch-ass nigga!"

Bolo's eyesight was clouded by his own blood. The blows he was receiving was making him dizzy and he would soon lose consciousness. Before he knew it, he was knocked out on the pavement. Laying in a pool of his own blood...

CHAPTER THIRTY

Shay was in her robe when she stepped out the bathroom of the room she shared with Vanilla Ice at the Bel Age Hotel. From the time they got there a day earlier, groupies and business associates had been in attendance coming and going. Shay didn't mind, though. She understood what came with the rich and famous lifestyle she had stepped into.

The room was plush. There was a couch with a glass table and top-of-the-line model television in the living area of it. When she stepped out the bathroom, she found three coke-snorting groupies that weren't there when she went in at the table giggling at what she could only assume was a dumb-ass joke one of them had made.

The shades were open so the Hollywood skyline was visible from the fifteenth-floor balcony. A Vanilla Ice song was playing in the background. Which gave the setting a familiar soundtrack.

As soon as she looked at Rob, he stepped to her with a bag and a kiss. Shay took it all with a smile. "What you get me this time, babe?"

"Take a look," he replied. "It's an all-white dress. Beauty for my beauty."

Shay sat the bag on the bed and took out the form-fitting summer dress. The all-white Fendi dress came out looking silky. "Oh my God! It's beautiful! How much?"

"Don't worry 'bout it, baby! Money ain't an issue 'round here."

"Yeah, Shay," Tommy, Ice's manager interjected. "It's all gettin' written off as a business expense."

Ice snapped his head in Tommy's direction, "Nothing I buy her is getting written off as nothing!"

"Whoah!" Tommy replied. "Didn't mean nothing by it, big guy."

In all actuality, Tommy did feel some type of way about all the money Ice had been spending on the stripper. His artist had been spending tons of cash on expensive gifts for Shay from the beginning of their courtship. He had paid for her hair and nails along with a number of other things including clothes and jewelry on a daily basis.

The couple had been attached at the hip from the moment they linked at the strip club. Shay hadn't been home once. Other than a phone call here and there to let her granny know she was alive, she hadn't left the Hollywood fast life since Ice lured her into it.

She held the dress against her frame. The fit would hug her thin frame seductively. That was a given. She was so happy she jumped into Robert's arms and gave him a kiss as intimately as their love affair had molded for them. "I love it! I'm gonna put it on right now!"

"Go ahead! But don't rush," Ice told her. "We're gonna hangout in here tonight."

"No clubbing, huh?" she asked on her way back to the bathroom.

184

He followed her to the doorway. "It's always a club vibe everywhere I go, baby. But tonight, we're chilling here 'cause I got an old friend coming over."

"Rob," Tommy called out from the dining table. "Check this out."

Ice smiled at Shay. His eyes displayed nothing but affection. "Let me take care of this business real quick."

She left the door to the bathroom open as she slipped out of her robe. She was completely nude and in the line of sight of the groupies snorting powder across the room. Nudity meant nothing in Hollywood. Which worked in her favor since she was trying to listen in on Ice and his manager's conversation despite the music in the background.

"... All you gotta do is make sure he signs the papers," Tommy told him. "There's no way he's gonna turn down this kind of money."

"A hundred grand ain't shit, Tommy."

"Who said I'm giving him 100k? He's getting fifty. Not a penny more. Don't forget he's a nigger from the ghetto. He's never seen this type of money before. Fifty thousand to a guy like that is like winning the lottery."

Ice had sat down at the table and was overlooking the contract he was supposed to give Mario. "Fifty G's is a nice chunk of change."

"Exactly! Mothafuckers from where he's from kill each other for fifteen-hundred dollars! This is like a million dollars to him. Just make sure he signs so we can move on with our fucking lives. I'm tired of dealing with that gorilla he's been sending at us.

Shay heard the whole exchange. She couldn't help but think of how fifty thousand would be a lot for a nigga like Mario.

The part that got her was the fact that she had watched Robert spend twice that amount on miscellaneous things over the time she had spent with him. He had spent close to thirty thousand dollars on her alone in their short time together.

Still, none of that was her business. She was there on business of her own. Nothing else pertained to her. She finished getting dressed, then went out and modelled the dress for her benefactor. "You like how it fits?"

"Hell yeah!" Ice replied. "Come here and give me a kiss, baby."

Shay sat on his lap and planted a wet kiss on his lips. She didn't mind making out with her white boy. Feeling his cock harden beneath her was a perk as well. The thought of guiding his soft hand between her panty-less thighs was on her mind until a loud knock on the door caught all of their attention.

"That must be our guest of honor right there," Tommy said. To the red-nosed groupies he said, "You all know what to do, right?"

"We sure do," they giggled.

Shay hopped up off Ice's lap to go answer the door, "I got it..."

CHAPTER THIRTY-ONE

Suge and his hounds hopped out their ride on a mission when they got to the Hotel Bel Age. Buntry, Heron and Chocolate were dead set on forcing the play at hand. The vibe was do or die at that point. Their patience was as low as their fuses by then.

As they stepped towards the entrance of the luxury hotel, Suge looked up the side of the building. He wondered which one of the balconies overlooking the city belonged to the room he was heading into.

Three out of four of them were strapped with dirty weaponry. Although they pushed through the lobby as nonchalantly as they possibly could, the civilians they passed on their way to elevators sensed danger in their midst. No one stared, yet they all moved out the way while Suge and his men made their way through the lobby.

As soon as their elevator started moving upward, Heron turned to Suge and asked, "You sure we ain't gonna have'ta kick the door in? I mean... shiiit... It won't –"

"Shay got us, blood. It's good," Suge replied.

Suge hoped Shay was on point. He'd been around the block too many times to bank on any situation turning out exactly as planned. But he wasn't about to let his doubts seep out in front of his dogs. "Even if she ain't there, or whatever. That door cracks an inch, and we're in there! Point blank!"

"Onda Mob," said Buntry. Then he looked at Chocolate, "So this is it, huh? Blood told you he had bread?"

Chocolate stopped staring at the numbers indicating what floor whey were passing and said, "Yeah. He didn't say how much. But he said he's got cash fo' sho'!"

"None of dat matters," Suge said. "Onda set, it don't! We're talkin' about a platinum selling album that Chocolate basically wrote. There's not enough money in that room to get me to walk outta there without getting' what we got coming. I got somethin' planned that's gonna makes us all rich!"

"And if he don't get wit' the program?" Buntry asked.

The elevator stopped and its door opened just as Suge turned to Buntry and said, "He's gonna dance to this beat. If he don't, I'll sleep 'im myself."

It didn't take them long to find the room. As he approached the door, Suge told himself, *No need to knock too hard*. His knuckles hit the wood and they waited. The sound of music and laughter mixed with weed and liquor seeping through the door's cracks let them know they were at the right location.

When the door opened, Suge saw Shay. He looked into her eyes and was greeted with a head nod. Her job was done. In that brief moment, he promised himself he'd bless her with a lowrider. She earned her spot at the table.

They stepped in like they owned the place. What Suge found when he went in was typical. A star and some groupies. If he would've shown up two hours later, he would've surely found them all red nosed and nude.

Ice did a double take when he saw who came stomping into his room. His eyes damn near popped out of his head. His mouth went dry. He even had to reach for the table to steady himself since his knees were about to give out.

Tommy, Ice's manager had a similar feeling of immediate discomfort.

But his fight-or-flight instinct chose the former prompting him to say, "What da hell! What're you doin' here!?"

"Watch yo' mothafuckin' mouth, chink!" Heron snapped ferociously.

"What did you say?!" Tommy yelled. "How're you gonna come in –"

Vanilla tried to reach for his manager to calm him, but he was way too late. Buntry cut across the room before Heron could and snatched the Asian man up by the nape of his neck.

Buntry picked Tommy up with one hand as if he were as light as a bag of rice. With the force of a three-time felon, he choke-slammed him into the nearest wall, making the whole room shake like a Bay Area earthquake.

The red-nosed groupies screamed. Although the music was loud enough to drown out most of the shenanigans, screaming bitches was an alarm they really didn't need.

Shay looked at Suge and mouthed the words: *I got this*. Then she walked up to the blonde girl with extremely large, silicone breast and "Smack!" She slapped the coke drip out of her mouth.

"Shay!" Ice yelled. He couldn't believe what he was seeing. *Was Shay really with the giant and his goons?*

She ignored him. Instead, she addressed the loose-lipped bitches.

"Y'all hoes betta shut da fuck up before I drag both of you into that bathroom and beat the life outta you!"

Meanwhile, Buntry was on the other side of the room growling into Tommy's ear. "Stay down, chink! My next move is puttin' a hot one in ya' belly!"

Ice had to do something. He was terrified. The whole world was crashing around him. "Hey! Hey! Everybody calm down! I got the money right here!" He looked towards Chocolate, believing he was the only level-headed person in the room. "If you guys came to rob us –"

"Rob you?!" Suge said, calling all the attention onto himself. "This ain't no mothafuckin' robbery! I been told you what this was about! Now, you ready to talk business, or what?"

CHAPTER THIRTY-TWO

All the blood in Ice's body dropped. In that moment he knew he'd been put in a situation he couldn't run from. Tommy was cowering in the corner of the room like a real bitch. Shay had turned into a stranger. And Mario... Mario offered him no reprieve whatsoever.

The ball was in Suge's court. It was now on him to decide how to proceed with his full court press.

It really didn't take much thought on his part. Each move was already calculated days before he ever got the call for this meeting.

With his best set-'em-at-ease grin, Suge told everyone to calm down. "Check this out, folks. This is supposed to be a simple business meeting. There's no reason for anyone to get hurt." To the women of the night he said, "As a matter of fact, let me clarify this: No one is getting hurt." Suge addressed Buntry next, "Let lil man up."

Buntry backed up off Ice's manager, giving him enough space to stand up. He was shaky on his feet so he grabbed the nearest chair and took a seat.

"Chocolate," Suge said. "Pour some drinks, homey. Let's keep the party goin' while me and Mr. Van Winkle talk business."

Tommy looked at his artist. They both exchange panicked looks of fear. Neither one of them knew what to do. They were cornered.

Suge signaled for Ice to follow him as he stepped towards the sliding doors that led to the balcony. "Let's go out here, man. It'll give us some privacy."

Heron saw the hesitation in Vanilla Ice's eyes and wasn't having any of it. "Get out there, blood! Da homey gonna holla at'chu!"

Ice walked the proverbial plank leading out onto the 15th floor balcony. Both Heron and Buntry followed him to the door and took a post on the inside of the room after shutting it behind him.

Outside, overlooking the Los Angeles skyline, the evening was warm. The breeze was strong, yet super refreshing. Any other time, the vibe would've brought peace to anyone stepping out there to enjoy the view.

Suge, being the master manipulator that he was, knew enough to let the awkward silence work its magic. The average man's worst enemy was his own mind. The thoughts that plagued people in fucked-up situations had a way of painting the worst-case scenarios. Suge banked on that phenomenon, knowing he'd be able to capitalize off of it in one way or another.

After the silence finally established itself, Suge looked at him and smiled. "A'ight, man. So, I finally got yo' slippery-ass alone, huh? Since it's so hard to get a one-on-one wit' you, I'ma go ahead and get to the point. You called Mario over here to meet with you because you've obviously come to realization that it's time to pay what you owe him. Am I right about that, or what?"

"Ma-Ma-Mario's a friend of mine. I called 'im when I realized he wasn't getting paid –"

"You're lying," Suge snapped. "The homey been tryna contact you for months! Look, Rob. Let's not start this convo' off on a bad note. It already got ugly for yo' manager. And I can make it a lot worse for everyone else here."

Vanilla nodded, understanding he was standing on thin ice. "This is the god-honest truth: Ever since the album blew up, everything started moving so fast. I tried to get at him, but he moved back out here and we lost contact."

"What dat mean? I know all this. He reached out to you, your manager, your studio, and your lawyer. He basically wrote half your album and you and your team froze him out. Let's keep it real."

"See, that's the thing," Ice replied. "All he wrote was a few songs. I had to deliver it and my team's networking –"

"Dismiss me with the bullshit, homey! You and I both know writers are the heart of the industry. Plus, networking isn't his job. But writing music is. Stop playing me like I'm stupid, bitch-ass cracka!"

Suge had raised his voice enough for Heron and Buntry to hear him from the other side of the sliding glass doors. It got them to both look out onto the balcony. This raised Ice's anxiety level way past bearable levels.

"Alright, man," Ice began. "The truth is, I called Mario over here to give him some money. I got an okay from the label to give him a lump sum for the rights to the music he wrote."

"A lump sum, huh? So, what's the plan? You gonna hit 'im wit' da okey-doke? The 'check is in the mail' routine?"

"Naw, man! I'm not even like dat, homes!"

"Homes!? Boy, don't play wit' me! It's Knight! Suge Knight! I'm not yo' mothatfuckin' Homes!"

•

CHAPTER THIRTY-THREE

"C'mere, white boy!"

"Huh?"

Suge's sudden gruffness made Ice flinch. The last thing in the world he wanted to do was step an inch closer to the ex-NFL player. But what was he to do? It wasn't as if he had much of a choice.

"Take a look at this," Suge told him when he came over. "Look down there, Rob."

Vanilla Ice peeked over the balcony's railing. Fifteen stories up never looked as far from the pavement as it did that night.

"It's a long way down, aint' it?" Suge commented right before setting his heavy arm over Ice's shoulders.

Robert Van Winkle tried not to shake under Suge's embrace. Even though they were both outside overlooking a great expanse, he felt claustrophobic. Suge's weight leaned on him, pushing him a little too far over the railing. Then, just as Ice reached the peak of his discomfort, the gangland landlord whispered in his ear, "It'd be a damn shame if you happened to slip, huh?"

The visual was extra loud and clear. He was about to lose his life over a fucking song. A song he didn't even write. In that moment, Vanilla Ice made the conscious decision to do right by Mario Johnson. Instead of belly flopping from the fifteenth floor of the Bel Age Hotel, he'd give Suge Knight whatever he wanted.

Suge read his mark's pulse. The scent of fear mixed with an uncontrollable tremble told him all he needed to know. He took his arm off his prey, reached into his back pocket and took out an envelope. After handing it to Ice he knocked on the glass door and told Heron to hand him a pen. When the pen materialized, he gave it to Ice.

Suge didn't smile until the contract was handed back to him.

It was done! All he had to do was get it back to his lawyer and the rest would fall into place. "Let's go," he told his team after stepping back into the suite. He made sure Shay had her things and was out the room first. Then, as an afterthought he glanced at Tommy and asked, "Where's Mario's money?"

The bewildered-looking Asian wasn't as confident as he seemed when the evening first started. He looked at Ice for some sort of sign as to what took place outside. Vanilla Ice looked away. The only thing he wanted at that point was for Suge and his goons to leave and never come back.

Tommy got the message. He gave Suge the money and sat his ass back down...

$$$$$

Later on that night, after dropping everyone off, Suge found himself seated at the edge of his bed. He was receiving a shoulder massage from the love of his life.

The ten thousand he got from Mario's fifty was safely tucked away in a shoebox in his closet. The cash had been evenly split between everyone there that night. It was a nice chunk of change. But it wasn't the prize. The pieces of paper in his hands were the real trophies. He couldn't stop staring at them.

"It all worked out, huh?" Sharitha asked softly.

"Yeah, baby," he replied, still staring at the contract. "This move right here is about to change our lives. I own the rights to 'Ice Ice Baby,' plus a few other songs. Vanilla Ice can be who he wanna be. Do the shows in the world. I don't give a fuck 'bout all'at. But one thing I do know is, I'm gonna get paid every time his album sells."

"We gonna get a house now?"

Suge turned around to face his high school sweetheart. He then kissed her, knowing deep in his heart he'd give her anything her heart desired. "Give me a few days. I already talked to Griffey. He's gonna give me and Chocolate an advance. A major lump sum. I was just waiting for this contract to get signed. And here it is...

CHAPTER THIRTY-FOUR

The bedroom in G-Boy's new apartment was warm. He kept the whole apartment at a comfortable 72 degrees at all times. The electricity bill didn't matter to him. All the years he spent living in captivity made him keep a promise to himself that he would never experience another cold night of sleep. Not if it was up to him.

He was currently getting comfortable on his queen-size bed next to a Mexican girl named Jacky. They had been watching porn for close to forty-five minutes and were both extremely hot and bothered enough to start their own 'bout of sweaty sex.

The couple had been slowly taking off their clothes one piece at a time. First, Jacky took off an item then G-Boy reciprocated the action. It was a sexy game of give and take that turned them both on.

In the end it was G-Boy who had the last article of clothing on. He couldn't help but smile when she said, "You're next," while staring down at his red and black striped boxer shorts.

"No problemo," he replied before lifting his hips and sliding them off. As soon as his boxers were discarded Jacky boldly admired the size of his swipe. It didn't take her long at all before she reached out and touched it. She was cheesing as she grasped and squeezed his shaft.

It was obvious she liked what he was packing. With no hesitation she climbed on top of him and slid down onto his member, forcing it to stand straight up between her legs. They then started kissing as she slid his dick up and down against the lips of her pussy.

The sudden heat of her cunt along with her feminine juices made the slide slick and easy.

By the sound of her moans G-Boy could tell she was enjoying herself just as much as he was. It felt so good he wanted it to last as long as possible. But his urge to feel her deeper crevices didn't let him lay there for too long.

G-Boy eventually grabbed her hips and rolled her on her back placing her legs over his shoulders. *This bitch bad!*' he thought to himself while moving her into position. He watched her eyes open and close as he rubbed his mushroom shaped tip against her slit. She was beautiful.

"Fuck me," she softly whispered into his ear then took a deep breath as he gently pushed inward against her entrance.

Her pussy was tight. Her jaw clenched as he entered so he pulled out, spit on his dick then went in a little deeper. It seemed to help so he started doing it every time he pulled out. Soon he was able to dive all the way in her.

Jacky was lustfully rubbing herself as he stayed deep inside her just grinding himself against her. She started holding her breath longer, a sign he interpreted to mean she was close to cumming. So he started pulling out a little, then going back in. Every time he pulled out he could see she was getting wetter so he would pull out further.

He could tell she was having small orgasms because she was getting wetter and wetter. But when she stopped rubbing herself and started pulling him towards her harder he knew she was on the edge. She wrapped her legs around him with her hands. Her eyes shut tight and she let out a loud gasp. That's when he started pounding into her faster and harder until he felt her tighten up. There were sloppy sounds filling his bedroom as he buried his shaft into her warm pussy. In the end, when she relaxed her legs and opened her eyes, he knew he had given her what she came for.

She then laid her legs flat and G-Boy started sliding in and out of her. In the midst of the changing of position she pulled him close and whispered, "Cum inside me," and started pushing her hips up. She was now fucking him as he stood still enjoying the feeling her cunt muscles gripping his member. A few minutes later he started cumming with his jackhammer buried deep inside her.

When G-Boy finally rolled off her she started pulling the cum out of her pussy with her fingers while smiling. "It tastes good," she told him as she licked the remains of it off his dick. The next thing he knew, she was wildly deep-throating his hammer.

He had his hand on her head with his eyes shut tight when the phone on his nightstand started ringing. Part of him wanted to let it ring. He didn't wanna do anything to stop the sloppy head he was getting. But he couldn't let any calls go unanswered. Not in the life he was living.

As he reached for the receiver, he suddenly remembered paging Suge. He had been trying to get ahold of him for some time because heeded to re-up. Assuming it was him he put the receiver to his ear and said, "What's brackin'?"

"G-Boy, this Unc," T-Loc, G-Boy's aunt's boyfriend said.

A smile eclipsed G-boy's face. "Man, what's good? I been meaning to slide out there but –"

"Don't trip, nephew. It ain't shit. I already know you been busy."

"Busy is an understatement," G-Boy replied. He then tapped on Jacky's head singling for her to stop what she was doing. Then he put the receiver against his chest to muffle the sound of his voice and told her, "Let me get a minute alone on the phone. It'll be quick."

She offered no resistance whatsoever. She just nodded then got up and walked out the room completely naked.

G-Boy got back to his call the second the bedroom door shut. "Yeah, Unc. I been having to put niggaz in they place lately."

"Onda set, I already heard. Your name been ringin' all the way out here. Heard y'all been goin' at it with Park Village too."

Suddenly G-Boy saw a vision flash before his eyes. A double homicide he had committed less than a week earlier filled his line of sight. He would never speak of it out loud, but the memories were vivid.

"It's all kinds of shit going on out here, unc. I'm waiting to hear form the homey right now 'cause I ain't got no work. It's all kinds of money in these streets and every day I ain't got no work be killin' me."

"Selling crack ain't the only way of makin' money. You know it's different ways for a real nigga to eat out here, right?"

"Yeah. I feel you."

"As a matter of fact, that's why I'm calling you."

"What's good? I'm all ears."

"There's a chess move some homies from the set tryna put together. It's a backdoor movement on one of the big locs. Shit that gotta be hush-hush since some of the homies won't understand –"

"The politics," G-Boy cut in. "I already know. I ain't new to the game, unc. Homies be killing homies out this way all the time. Niggaz just don't talk about it."

"Onda set. 'Cept this time, in this case a few locs is putting bread together so the job can be outsourced."

T-Loc stopped talking so the proposition would sink in. G-Boy soaked up the silence as if it were being read out loud.

"Things understood need not be said, unc. If the mathematics is right and exact, a clean-up crew will take out the trash for whoever needs it done."

"It's a messy job. Niggaz tryna eliminate a whole bloodline. Ya dig?"

"Onda set."

"A'ight. Stop by the house in morning. Ya auntie finna cook a big breakfast. We'll talk then."

"Can't wait. Oh, shit –"

"What's up?"

"Can I bring a bitch wit' me?"

"Of course, nigga. And, about that problem you been having with finding a plug. Don't trip. I got you on that too."

"That's what I'm talkin' 'bout!" G-Boy replied. "I'll be there..."

After ending the call G-Boy called Jacky back in the room and resumed their late-night shenanigans...

CHAPTER THIRTY-FIVE

Two weeks later...

G-Boy was annoyed with the dog in the backyard behind the yard him and Little G were squatted down in. The mutt kept barking, trying to alert its owner of the two trespassers. In the time he spent watching the house they were currently camped out behind, he managed to count three children, a hood rat and her nigga. G-Boy knew their schedules and sleep patterns. But the one thing he hadn't taken into consideration of was their loud-ass neighbor's dog.

It was too late by then to do anything about the mangy mutts. G-Boy had already created their plan of attack and it was currently in play. It was a cold plan that ended in the deaths of all five of the home's inhabitants.

G-Boy and his lil homey had hopped the fence on the side of the house while CK Brazy and Bear took their spots at the front of the house with their Molotov Cocktail bombs.

G-Boy repositioned himself in the shadows. His leg had gotten stiff from the position he was squatted down in. G-Boy had a lot on his mind. The hood had turned cold after the pistol whooping he gave Bolo.

The Mob felt salty about what he did to their member. And it didn't help that the rest of Lueders had applauded his actions

The consensus on his side of the set was Bolo deserved the D.P. Bolo had started a war with Park Village Compton Crips. Which wouldn't have been a big deal if it weren't for the geographical setup of their sets. His homies weren't feeling the way Suge was moving either. Which didn't make sense on his part since Suge had basically enlisted G-Boy's assistance in keeping the peace between the factions.

The layout of their territories mattered because the Mob's mad pad was all the way in the back of the Lueders Park neighborhood. Which meant whenever their opps slid on them, they would shoot at niggaz at the front of the set. That had the Lueders Park niggaz feeling slighted.

On top of that, Suge's clique seemed to have been eating a lot more than the rest of the neighborhood. Those closest to Suge were shining in new lowriders, brand-new clothes and everything else that came with having an influx of revenue.

G-Boy had only been able to cop from Suge a few times before the faucets went dry. There were rumors circulating that Suge had cut G-Boy off purposely because he had gained too much power since his release. Of course, that wasn't the case, but you couldn't tell that to the streets.

Still, G-Boy did his thug-thizzle. He managed to keep just enough work to feed his homies. And when odd jobs like the one he was currently on came up, he took them.

He was suddenly snapped out of his thoughts when he heard the first 40 bottle shatter the front window of the house they were ambushing.

CRRSSHHH! CRRSSHHH! CRRSSHHH!

Several different bottles were thrown at the front door and surrounding windows. Causing the house to burst into flames.

"Blood! You bee that?" Baby G-Boy observed.

"Yeah! Get ready!"

Baby G stepped out from the shadows followed by G-Boy.

BLOCKA! BLOCKA! BLOCKA! sounded several different guns from the front of the house.

G-Boy took his eyes off the back door long enough to glance at his younger homey. "Get ready, blood! And, remember … No survivors!"

"Onda set!"

Suddenly the whole house went up in flames. The roof was engulfed in fire. Thick black smoke shot out the windows. The inhabitants had nowhere to go. No way to escape the fire except through the sliding glass doors that led into their backyard.

And just as G-Boy had expected, the sliding doors opened and out came the mother of the children with a newborn child in her arms. For some reason G-Boy hesitated for a moment. Instead of pulling the trigger in his hand he looked at Baby G wondering if he would freeze up when it came to killing a woman and child.

BLOCKA! BLOCKA! BLOCKA!

Baby G's Tek 9 sent bone-shattering slugs into the mamma bear and her cub. The look in his eyes openly displayed his blood lust. The only thing lacking was guilt. Baby G-Boy harbored none of that. On the contrary, he savored the moment hoping he could be the one to kill the next human to exit the house.

A few seconds later, another kid, maybe nine years old, froze in the doorway. Shocked to see his fallen mother and sibling. He didn't know what to do. Step over them or run back in out of the line of fire. A decision he didn't get a chance to mull over since G-Boy decided his fate for him.

BLOCKA!

A headshot knocked the Top Ramen out of the boy's head. After that, both G-Boys unloaded several more shots into the shattered glass doorway.

Inside the house, their main target was stuck between deciding which fate would end his and his four-year-old daughter's life. Smoke and flames or hot lead. In desperation and necessity, he pulled a Hail Mary trying to save his child as well as himself.

The G-Boys waited him out knowing their mark would have to come out some time. They both had enough bullets left to finish the job. But no one came out of the house. For several moments, which seemed more like an eternity, everything went silent. The was no longer darkness with their death filled bonfire illuminating the sky. Yet silence dominated their adrenaline flooded senses.

Then, from the flames came a father clutching his child against his smoke-filled chest as if both of their lives depended on his blitz through G-Boy's offensive line.

BLOCKA! BLOCKA! BLOCKA! BLOCKA! BLOCKA-BLOCKA!

CHAPTER THIRTY-SIX

Two months later...

"Fuck all this shit, baby! We don't need none of it! Leave it all! We're coming new-new with everything from our furniture to our shoes!" Chocolate told his woman. "We on now!"

Margy was beaming from ear to ear. She was somewhere in between believing and not believing her fortune. She was in a deep sleep when she heard his deep laughter coming from the other room. He wasn't alone, he had been with Sugar Bear. By the time she got herself together, Suge had left and she had found Mario in the kitchen standing next to a stack of cash on their dining room table.

"Oh my god!" she yelled when she saw it. "How much is it?"

"It's enough to change our lives, baby! Enough for us to move and get a few cars with numbers on the back! That's what I'm thinkin'. Fuck the furniture. Fuck our clothes. Fuck everything in this bitch! We're rich!"

"We're moving? Where?"

"It don't even matter," Chocolate told her, lowering his voice to a more intimate leve. "Suge kept it real, girl. They paid up for my songs. This is enough to change everything! And, it ain't even all of it. The money ain't gonna stop coming!"

She stared into her man's eyes while hers filled with tears. She thought of the nights they went to sleep hungry. Times they had to wash clothes with dish detergent. Their bus ride from Texas was hard, but she didn't care. She was in love with him, so she would've followed him to the end of the earth if that's something he wanted her to do. And, now... Now they were rich!

All because of Sugar Bear...

"C'mon, baby," Chocolate told her as he led her to the stack. "Help me count it –"

Margy cut him off with a loving hug and kiss. When they got to the money, it looked intimidating. Neither one of them had ever seen that much cash in one place at one time. "How much you think it is?"

"He said it was a quarter mill'."

Her neck snapped, "What?!"

"I told you, we're rich," he said while making a money pyramid with the ten-thousand-dollar stacks as bricks. "I'm gonna keep writing more music, too. We're starting our own record company!"

Margy screamed with all her excitement. She grabbed him and started jumping up and down, "You did it! You did it!"

"Yup! But I couldn't have done it without Marion. He kept it real with me, and now we're on!"

Chocolate had all kinds of thoughts shooting through his mind. His body had him counting his piece of the pie. It wasn't just the perks of having money that was changing his life. Mario was wise enough to recognize that. It was way more than that.

It was vindication...

The money was a slap in the face to his doubters. Everyone who called him a liar and laughed in his face whenever he told them he wrote that song had taken a piece of him with them. The embarrassment he felt every time "Ice Ice Baby" came on over the radio when he was flipping burgers had crushed his ego. At one point, the whole debacle had him questioning his own sanity. But that was over now. He won!

He finally won!

$$\$\$\$\$\$$$

Several weeks later...

Sharitha came into the living room with a heavy plate of eggs, hashbrowns and ham and placed it all on the coffee table. "Here you go, babe."

Suge leaned in for a kiss then said, "Mmm-mmm."

"And you betta eat it all, before you even think about hittin' them streets."

"I wouldn't miss a plate of your home cooking for the world."

"Says the man that only sleeps at home three nights a week."

"Stop playing," he replied before pinching his wife's backside.

"Boy!" she hissed. "Don't start nothing you can't finish!"

"Girl, come 'ere!"

Sharitha let him pull her onto his lap. His neck kisses tickled her in ways that made her pussy wet. "Stooop! You gonna spill the food, boy!"

"Spill it? I'm thinking 'bout pouring it on yo' titties and eating it off them melons!"

"You betta not, nigga!" she hurried up and scooted into a seated position on the couch, next to him. She cuddled up against his large frame and whispered, "I love yo' crazy-ass so much."

"I love you, too, baby."

Two and a half months had passed since Vanilla Ice signed over the rights to Mario's music. Dick Griffey had worked out a publishing deal with Sony and got Suge and Mario an advance on the monies Vanilla Ice would have to pay once the court proceedings were finished. That advance was enough to turn a pauper into a king.

Suge was in his twenties and was richer than anyone from his set. In one move, he surpassed several tax brackets. Still, he remained the same person. Other than his new house in the suburbs and the Corvette he bought for Sharitha, no one would've known he had hit for so much money. He still remained the same person who bent corners through Lueders Park in his K5.

Sharitha was spoon-feeding her man when the house phone rang. After picking it up from the coffee table she handed it to Suge.

"Who dis?" Suge said into the receiver.

"What's brackin', P-Funk?"

Suge immediately recognized DJ Quik's voice on the other end of the line. "On Piru, I've been waiting to hear from you, blood!"

"My bad, homey. I been busy as fuck. On top of that, the homies been hunting for some off-brand niggaz. The streets is lookin' like Vietnam!"

"Onda set?"

"On Tree Top!"

"I got some shit still in the crate. Some military grade heavy metal. Send somebody to the set and I got'chu."

"Nuff said. Now, on another note, is it true you got the white boy to pay up?"

"I own all that shit now. The white boy can't take a shit without payin' me and Mario. Why? What's up?"

"For real?"

"Yup. It was the goal the whole time. I already know how the industry works. It's all about who owns the publishing rights on everything from beats to lyrics. I rather have the publishing rights to a song than the rights to perform it. It's true equity."

"Onda set!"

"It wasn't easy, though. The game is full of sharks. But I'm a B-Dog, feel me? They can't fuck wit' my push. Now it's time to start on the next phase of the plan. I'm tryna put a team together so we can take over the music industry on a national scale."

"I'm listening."

"This last deal just put me in a position to play in the big leagues. I hooked up wit' Dick Griffey –"

"Solar Griffey?"

"Yeah. I'm in there with real movers and shakers. They gonna help me start my own label. That's what I'm on right now. So, I'm coming at you 'cause I wanna bring you wit' me. I need a bomb producer who can come hard on every track."

"Is that right?"

"On Piru."

"Both Suge and Quik were bosses in their own right. When they spoke, men moved. Neither one of them got their ranks without seeing how ugly the streets really were. They knew the seriousness of creating alliances with other wolves. Creeping into the shadows without thinking things through properly could get a person smacked.

Thus came the quiet...

Then, after a few moments of contemplative silence, Quik said, "I'm wit' it."

CHAPTER THIRTY-SEVEN

The sexy waitress set two bottles of champagne on the table where Suge and D.O.C. were seated. Giving both men a full view of her Double-D cleavage. Suge gave her a full body glance, boldly letting her know he was interested in more than liquor.

"Bitch bad, ain't she?" D.O.C. commented as she sashayed away.

"She keep eyeballing a nigga, I'ma end up taking her outside real quick. See if she can swallow some kids without choking."

D.O.C. started laughing at his friend's antics. "I'm on that one right there," he said, motioning towards the stage.

When Suge looked up, he saw a thick redbone bent over displaying all her private parts. He lit his cigar while admiring the girl's sexy slit. "My lawyer's drawing up some papers for the record company. Gotta make sure all the paperwork is right, from the gate. This shit gotta be proper in every aspect."

"Everything on the up-n-up. I feel you. We're gonna take over the game. I can feel it. All the pieces of the puzzle are there. Shiiit, I bet you Mario's on one, huh?"

"Hell yeah. He went brazy! The nigga bought two Porsches and an all-white Beemer the same day I gave him his advance."

D.O.C. chuckled. "I did the same thing with my first check. I copped my first Benz immediately!"

"Quik went out and got 'im a load, too. He bought a 'Maro with the signing bonus I gave him."

D.O.C. nodded. Suge was showing signs of a true businessman. One who knew how to split the spoils of war evenly. They were able to hang out a lot more since Suge had gotten his money. But, other than that, D.O.C. couldn't see a major difference in the man. Marion seemed to move a certain way with or without money.

After taking a swig straight from the champagne bottle, D.O.C. got a light from Suge for his own cigar. Then he shared his thoughts.

"Quik is straight. He's a good ear and he knows what the streets want."

"His production skills are top shelf. And that's without the unlimited studio time of a high-end studio."

"I already know. He seems like the type that can make a whole album with some turn tables and a tape deck. The thing is... he's not Dre. We need Dre."

"That's on you, Tracy. It's all a progression. We really need him, and it'd be nice to get his bitch, too. That's step one."

"Step two is to get Heller and Eazy to release us from our contracts," said D.O.C.

"Step three will be to start our own label. Just get me and Dre in the same room. He's gotta realize he's getting robbed. Maybe he's already seeing it but doesn't got an outlet. Make it happen, man. Put me in the same room wit' 'im and I'll lay it all out for 'im."

"I've been in his ear. I really don't know what he thinks. On some real shit, he's sketchy 'cause he still trusts Eazy's bitch-ass."

Suge let out a large plume of purple smoke to that last statement. He took his time, choosing the right words to say. Then he said, "Consistency. Consistency and persuasion is the key. A blind man can see y'all not getting a king's share of the cut."

"We not even gettin' a knight's cut!"

"Onda set! He's gotta see it. So we just gotta let blood know we got a plan. We got an end-game. We not operating blindly. We gonna win like Cube's winning."

"I get it –"

"Excuse me," cut in a stripper. She surprised both of them when she pushed up to their table unannounced. "Are you D.O.C. from NWA?"

Tracy looked at Suge, who met him with a smirk. Suge had seen that scene play out too many times to count.

"Yeah, I'm D.O.C.," Tracy replied. "Why? What's up?"

The starstruck stripper didn't believe the girls who pointed him out in the crowd. And, now that it was confirmed that he was indeed a world-famous rapper, her eyes saw nothing but dollar signs.

D.O.C. thought it was funny. He didn't let her see his amusement, though. He was about to say something, but Suge beat him to the punch.

"Why don't you take my nigga into one of them private rooms and show 'im what you can do. Maybe afterwards y'all might end up in one of his mansions in the hills."

She didn't need any more coaxing at all. Without even asking D.O.C., she took his hand and said, "Come on, D. I'll show you a good –"

SPLASH! KRSHHH!

The sexy stripper was stopped in her tracks when the bottle girl bumped into her with a tray full of drinks. Alcoholic beverages splashed everywhere, drenching the dancer.

The sexy stripper took a millisecond to go off. She reached back and slapped this shit out of the clumsy waitress. If they hadn't had a history of haterism between them, she probably wouldn't have reacted so quickly. But there was a history. So, in her mind, the mistake was done on purpose. It was a strategic move to dislodge her from the bag she would've gotten if she did spend the evening with D.O.C.

And just like that, a cat fight started. Except these bitches weren't scratching and pulling hair. They locked like pits. Throwing blows like seasoned street fighters.

Suge and Tracy didn't move. They sat back and enjoyed the show. They weren't there for long, though. Before they knew it, two more dancers slid into their presence. In the midst of the chaos, they were led into private rooms in a much more secure part of the club.

Once they took refuge in their sex dens, clothes were adjusted so orifices could be jackhammered. It was a regular night. Late night shenanigans were always expected, never neglected. It was the life of thugs...

CHAPTER THIRTY-EIGHT

G-Boy's one bedroom bachelor pad was decked out in all-black leather couches and glass end tables. All of it accentuated the black and white framed posters of Tony Montana and Malcom X. He had made sure to make his apartment look exactly how he had visualized it to look while he was locked up.

The complex he stayed in was in the heart of his set's territory. Which meant his homies were always around. He had just finished losing eight hundred dollars to CK Brazy and Baby G when his homegirl RiRi walked up with two of her relatives. G-Boy didn't care about the money he lost because he was making triple that on a good a night. Plus, he liked seeing his homeboys eating.

If anyone else would've taken his money G-Boy would've been ready to fight. But Baby G and CK Brazy were his niggaz. If anything, he was happy for them. That's part of the reason he had been smiling when the females walked up.

G-Boy liked RiRi. He had been watching her from a distance ever since he came home from doing his bid. He never seemed to have the time to really pursue her though. On that particular evening, the timing was perfect. She was obviously in a flirtatious mood by the way she was eyeing him. And the set was crowded that night so no one was really paying him or her too much attention. So G-Boy decided to make his move by inviting her into his apartment.

He had slipped out of his black tank top, tossing it on the couch as soon as they stepped inside. After hitting the light switch and locking the door he stepped towards RiRi invading her personal space.

There was an intensity in the way he stared into her eyes. He didn't reach out to touch her or anything, yet she didn't have anywhere to go even if she wanted to move. It kinda frightened her, but then again she really didn't want to move away from him.

"Wha-what're you doin', G-Boy? Let me go!"

G-Boy held his ground, not moving an inch. "Let you go? I'm not doin' shit, RiRi. You can leave anytime you want."

"That's-that's not what I mean," she shuddered, knowing she had exposed her secret turmoil.

G-Boy lifted her chin, forcing her to look into his eyes. His lust filled eyes...

"What?" she asked with a whisper.

"Your homegirls were giggling when y'all walked up to the dice game. I saw you look at me then look away hella fast. What was so funny?"

"Tanisha said you had a BBC," RiRi whispered then looked away embarrassed.

"Onda set?" G-Boy chuckled. "You think she was lyin'?"

"Naw. She be sayin' it every time we see you." That time, RiRi's smile betrayed her lust.

G-Boy straightened his posture and his hands went down his body until he was fingering the zipper on his

Dickies. "You wanna see it, don't you? You wanna see a nigga swipe one time, huh?"

RiRi wasn't a ho. As a matter of fact she was the last one out of all her friends who had held onto her virginity. She was actually terrified, but underneath it all her pussy went from moist to wet-wet.

"We shouldn't –"

"Shouldn't what?" he asked innocently.

RiRi let her gaze drop down to G-Boy's and suddenly they widened in surprise. "You're so hard," she whispered, barely controlling her urge to reach out and grab the bulge.

"I'm a man," G-Boy smiled. "It happens when I'm wit' a bad bitch."

The warmth of her pussy was rising with every second. It was pulsing and a tremble passed through her whole body. "I'm not a bitch," she responded with more confidence than she felt. "I'm a woman."

G-Boy lifted her chin again and said, "You are. You're a beautiful woman, RiRi."

Her heart fluttered like a tweeter on the dashboard of a Chevy. G-Boy moved his hand to her cheek and her will to resist crumbled like some cocaine under the pressure of a snorter's ID. She nuzzled his slight embrace; surrendering to whatever he wanted of her.

"What if someone sees us?" she asked.

"This my shit, baby. The door locked. Ain't nobody gonna see shit and you know it."

G-Boy leaned in for a kiss. His tongue glossed her lips, urging them apart. She accepted his tongue intimately into her mouth. His kiss was hot and demanding. She felt as if she would melt.

"What're you doin', G-Boy?"

"Givin' you what you want."

"I never said I wanted this."

"Then tell me to stop."

Her mind screamed the words but they refused to form on her lips. Then the moment passed and her mouth was smothered by his kiss. They went from slow and sensual to hot and insistent. "Oh, God, G-Boy, please be gentle with me."

"I will." His soft whisper hypnotized her and calmed her fear as she gave herself to him.

He slowly undressed her. When she was fully nude she cupped her exposed breasts in her palms. Her cheeks burned as G- Boy's gaze fell on her caramel-colored skin.

"Damn, RiRi. I didn't realize you had a body like this." G-Boy pulled her hands away from her titties.

"Hold on! Stop! I can't do this. I can't believe you're doin' this to me!"

"I'm not doin' nothin' you don't want done. I know how much this turnin' you on. I know you want this."

G-Boy started kissing her passionately. He kissed her throat and sucked on her lips all while rubbing his shirtless chest against hers.

She felt him reach between them and seconds later she felt his pants drop. "Oh my god," she said as she felt the length of his member pressing against her stomach. It felt hard and heavy on her skin.

"You feel that, RiRi? I'm so mothafuckin' hard right now! I can't wait to slide inside you! G-Boy started sawing his swipe between her pussy lips. "I've been wanting to fuck you for a minute."

He was grinding his dick on her clit. Sawing it back and forth. The friction radiated through her body and soon her hips were meeting his thrusts. The tension was driving her crazy. Her pussy was getting wetter and wetter by the moment. Suddenly she couldn't take it anymore.

"Stop teasing me! If you're gonna fuck me then do it, G-Boy!"

He reached behind her and grabbed both of her ass cheeks. He was about to lift her up when he heard a sudden commotion outside his apartment.

Several voices sounded like there was an argument starting and then he heard shots!

BLOCKA! BLOCKA! BLOCKA-BLOCKA! BLOCKA-BLOCKA!

G-Boy immediately went into murder mode. He ran to his couch and snatched a Mac 11 from underneath one of its cushions before running outside.

He made it outside just in time to see several of his homeboys shooting at a fleeing vehicle. Somebody yelled, "Is Baby G alright?"

Then the ghetto cries began...

"Someone call an ambulance!"

"Baby G got shot!"

"They got Baby G-Boy!"

G-Boy saw the crowd surrounding a body on the sidewalk. He didn't want to see who they were crowding around. His heart dropped. He didn't want to face the cruel truth of what he knew was strewn across the pavement...

CHAPTER THIRTY-NINE

The Foxhill Mall was packed. Dre was lucky to have found a secluded parking space under a shade tree. Even though the sun was bright it didn't take from the Southern California breeze. The birds were chirping and the natural mood was smooth.

Dre was seated behind the wheel, tweaking on the knobs of his equalizer. His Cadillac had a top-of-the-line stereo system.

The sound quality was good, so he used it as a listening booth every time he put a new track together. The highs, mids and lows gave the music he made a studio quality sound that allowed him to hear what he needed to tweek before mixing and mastering a track.

He looked up through the passenger side window when a 4x4 with loud music pulled into the space next to his. He already knew who it was. So when Suge hopped out, he motioned for him to get in.

Dre turned the music down when Suge slid into his passenger seat. But he kept the track playing.

After giving him dap, Suge heard the music playing and quickly put two and two together. His instincts told him to slow down and listen. Instead of jumping straight into business he took in the music.

After a few moments he looked at Dre and asked, "This some new shit?"

"Yeah. I'm still working on it."

"Sounds dope!"

"It's missing something. I don't know what. But, it needs something added or taken out. I can't figure it out yet. But I will."

Suge smiled. "I'm trippin' right now, Dre. You're one of the hottest producers in country and I'm sittin' here watchin' you work. We ain't even in the studio –"

"The 'Lac got studio sound. It also gives me a feel of what the streets really hear."

Suge studied Dre for a few seconds. He was a regular nigga. From the hood. That part didn't bother Suge, though. He welcomed that type nigga around him. It meant he could talk to him in a language they could both understand.

Dre was the one to bring the meeting to the open. After a minute or two, he stopped the music and addressed Suge. "I told Tracy I'd hear you out. He told me you're talkin' about startin' a label and all'at."

Dre wasn't easily influenced. The comment made about him being the best in the country went in one ear and out the other. He came to see if Suge was a real nigga. If he detected any fakeness, he'd cut the meeting short. *Chances are*, he thought on his way meet Suge, *It's a waste of time.*

Suge nodded. "I feel you. I fucks wit' D.O.C. I've been following y'all progress since the beginning of this of shit. Been watching from the sidelines. As artists, the line-up is epic. Once in a red moon type shit. After talking to people, I'm hearing shit ain't right with y'all numbers, though. None of it sounds kosure. I haven't seen any contracts with my own eyes. But shit don't seem right."

"How can you assume shit ain't on the up and up from the bleachers. We've all been eating on levels never seen before."

"A hundred K a year? Is that what you get paid? I don't care how far I'm up in the nose-bleeds, a hundred G's ain't shit compared to what NWA is really making. All your records go platinum. Eazy is living like a millionaire. Doesn't seem like you or Tracy is. Cube surely wasn't. And you do the beats. You produce the actual music. D.O.C. writes it, but you produce it. If anything, you should get more than all of 'em."

"It ain't about more. This was supposed to me and Eazy's company –"

"*Was*? What'chu mean? If you started one way, what happened? Where is the 'was' coming from?"

Dre didn't say anything. His mind was suddenly flooded with thoughts of NWA's manager, Jerry Heller. He felt angry. But he managed to push the thoughts out of his head.

"Check it out; Cube is smart. I met him before. He's young as fuck, but the nigga ain't the type to let himself get played. I don't think he's crazy, Dre. If he left the hottest rap group in the country – no, let me fix that: the *world*! If he left the hottest rap group in the *world*, he left for a reason."

"He blamed Heller an' Eazy. Said he wasn't gettin' his proper cut. That none of us are."

"I can see where he's comin' from. But I can do better than just talk. I got my nigga Mario paid for one song and he bought a house, two Porsches and a BMW.

One mothafuckin' song! With all the work you puttin' in, you should be a millionaire. Not ten years from now. I'm talkin' 'bout now!"

"It ain't like –"

"Like what? Y'all got the hottest group in the world. You're killing the game. Man..." Suge paused. Giving himself time to get his words together. Knowing he had just one shot at this, he didn't wanna fumble. He had to be precise. "This what I can tell you. We all know the industry is full of sharks. These white folks got us working for them like slaves. They get all the real money and give us the crumbs. That's just how it is. But it doesn't gotta be like that. You see how you said you and E started this? Well, I bet it was all good till Heller got involved. I bet if I got ahold of your contract and let my lawyer look at it, he'd find some bullshit! The way I see it is, if you guys would've stuck to the script and shit got split evenly, every single one of y'all would be rich right now."

Suge was in his element. At that point, there was no stopping him. "That's why we're starting our own label. Dre, I'm not only tryna become your manager. If you let me represent you, I know I'll get you all the green you deserve! But, I'm also starting a record label so the team can get every penny they got coming. It beats givin' most of it to a honky."

Dre's mind never stopped moving. He heard everything Suge was telling him. He even understood what he wasn't telling him. "I really sat down with Tracy and he told me you was on your shit."

"I'm makin' moves. Moves that includes everyone involved. It's gonna be ran like a family. If you sign wit' me, I'll push for you like you're one of my real niggaz. And, for the record, I meant what I said about you being the best producer in the game. D.O.C. is the best writer. Chocolate already wrote a platinum-selling song, so he's on the squad fo' sho'. I got my nigga from Tree Top, Quik. He's a good beat man. But he's not you. With you, we become a force. A problem. An issue that can't be ignored."

"So, what you talkin' 'bout? What's the first move?"

"Just to show you I'm on some real shit, do this: Get me a copy of your contract with Eazy and Heller. I'll have my people look at it. If it's good, it's good. We can act like I never stepped to you. If it's bad, then at least you know the truth and can move accordingly. Either way, you need to think about coming over with us. Fuck Ruthless, homey. You need to get on the team. With us, you won't have to worry 'bout shit like this. There's enough money to go around."

Dre nodded. He had a lot to think about. It was a serious decision. Something that needed honest contemplation since there was no turning back when it was all said and done.

"Alright," Dre said. "I'ma holla at Heller about the contracts. Let me think about everything else for a few days and I'll get at you."

"Bet! Do what you gotta do. I'll be setting up a few things so when you do come over, everything will be ready."

That concluded their meeting and Suge left. Dre didn't move just yet, though. He sat there thinking about the conversation he had just had. He believed Suge could make things happen. His track record spoke for itself. And, the idea of being part owner of a start-up record label was appealing too. Being an artist was one thing, but a record label owner was something totally different. It was a major step in the direction of real wealth.

Dre made up his mind as he pulled into traffic. Yes, he'd talk to Eazy and Heller. But, his mind was already made up. Even if they offered him a bigger bag, he was seriously leaning towards fucking with Suge and D.O.C.

CHAPTER FORTY

Dre couldn't ignore the thoughts spinning through his head. The truth of it all was that he did feel like Eazy was robbing him. He couldn't get away from it. Yeah, he had a house now. He had some cars, too. He was famous for doing something he loved. That counted for something. His life had changed since he hooked up with Eazy. Yet, the facts also included other things. Heller and Eazy were eating on a whole different level. They were most definitely working from a different tax bracket than the rest of them. Something wasn't right, and they couldn't deny it.

Before he knew it, Dre was at Eazy's house. He pulled up just as Ren and Eazy were stepping out the front door of the mini mansion Eric lived in. From afar, the two thugged-out Crips didn't match the high-class neighborhood they were in.

"What's up, Dre," Eazy said when he met Dre in the driveway. "I didn't know you was coming over, cuz. We 'bout to go to a party in the Hills."

"That's coo," he told Eazy. Then, to Ren he said, "What's crackin', loc?"

Eazy asked, "What's up, Dre? Holla. You rocking wit' us? We finna –"

"I wanna talk about the contracts."

Eazy smiled; "You startin, to sound like Oshay, cuz."

"Naw," replied Dre. "It ain't 'bout Cube. Niggaz getting cheddar off this shit."

"Yeah, we getting' millions," Eazy said. "You're eatin'. You got a big-ass house. Ya baby mamma's ain't been trippin'. And, how many low-lows you got, cuz?"

Suddenly a vehicle coming up the block thumping a stupendous amount of bass distracted them for a moment.

"There go cuz right there," Ren announced. "Damn, he already got some bitches wit' 'im!"

"On Crip," Eazy stated. To Dre he continued, "We all getting' paid. You're a millionaire compared to how you were living when I bailed you outta jail."

"Shit don't matter," replied Dre. "Ever since Heller got involved –"

"Our lives changed!" Eazy snapped. "Everybody wanna talk about Heller this, Heller that! Cuz took us to a whole 'nother level. We wasn't takin' trips across the country before I met him. We was takin' trips to the Swap Meet to sell tapes out the trunk of my Impala! The best money I ever spent was the seven-fifty I paid to meet up with cuz! On Crip!"

DJ Yella hopped out the Astro van he had pulled up in and approached the fellaz. With a smile on his face and a forty ounce in his hand he greeted them, "What's crackin', cuz! He gave everyone dap! This is what I'm talkin' 'bout! We all fuckin' wit' it tonight!"

"Hold up!" Eazy barked. "Dre, who's been in ya ear? Where's all this coming from?"

"Ain't nobody been in my ear. But –"

"But, what?" Ren cut in harshly.

Dre sensed the hostility, and immediately met it with aggression. "Ain't nobody talkin' to you! You need to check yo' tone –"

"I ain't checkin' shit, cuz!"

Both of them stepped towards one another with fists clenched. But Eazy got in between them. "Ren, stall that shit out, cuz. Yella, get this nigga!" He turned to face Dre and added, "You trippin', man!"

"Naw, E! You niggaz is the one on some other shit."

"Look, cuz. We finna ride out. We on some other shit. You wanna talk business, come through tomorrow," Eric told Dre.

He was hot. Watching them get into the van and leave was annoying as fuck! He was dismissed like he was one of the groupies who are always coming around looking for a signature. He stood there shaking his head, not believing his eyes.

Dre then got into his Cadillac and drove to the nearest gas station. He got out and called Heller's office from the payphone. When the receptionist answered he said, "Molly, this is Dre. Can you put Heller on the phone?" He sat there for almost five minutes before his manager got on the phone.

"Andre, hows it going on, my friend?"

"How you doin', man. Hey, I was wondering if I could stop by and talk to you about somethin'."

"That doesn't sound like a problem. But, what do you wanna talk about? Maybe I can help you right now."

"I'd rather talk about this in person."

"Okay, but I'm going on a business trip soon. I'm not sure if I'l be around. But if it's not an emergency then I'm sure it can wait."

Damn! Dre sighed. *This can't wait!* Outloud he said, "Can I come in right now?"

"Well, yeah, sure. I don't see why not. But, what's it all about Andre? Maybe I can get things moving along if you can tell me what it is we're supposed to be talking about."

"It's about my contract," Dre said, knowing he shouldn't have as soon as he did.

"What about your contract? You know, Eric's who deals with the contracts. That's not really my department. Why are you asking about them?"

"Well, you know this is a business. So, I'm thinking about having someone overlook mine."

"Oh... I see. Well, it's like I said. That's Eric's department. I'll get ahold of him for you."

"Yeah, but –"

"I have to leave the office, Dre."

Before Dre could get another word in, he was met with the sound of a dial tone. Heller had hung up on him. He stood there with traffic passing by oblivious to the anger fuming from the man in the phone booth.

These mothafuckaz is really playin' wit' me! Dre yelled in his head as he slammed the receiver in its cradle. *Bitch-ass niggaz!*

Dre got into his car, slammed the door, and turned the music all the way up. He headed home with a freshly-lit flame burning.

To say he was angry would've been an understatement...

232

CHAPTER FORTY-ONE

Suge was on the tenth floor of the Marriott, overlooking the Los Angeles skyline. He loved scenic views. It reminded him of his childhood, when the only times he would see a view like that one was on the television.

On this particular evening, instead of enjoying the bird's-eye view of the city, he was admiring the roundness of a fat ass.

He was in the room with a brown-skinned honey from Watts. He'd been eyeing Tamika for a while. Every time he went to the Nickersons, she'd happen to show her face. She lived in one of the units on the way to Dave's spot.

He had seen her other places too. They exchanged numbers weeks earlier. But he never had the chance to catch up with her until that very evening. When he called her, she was game to meet up, so he swooped her up on his way out of the projects.

Suge had Tamika bent over in the shower while the warm water beat down on his back. Her round booty alone made him want to cum. Her silky crevices were another temptation holding him in a position where he could barely contain himself.

Soft moans filled the room with sounds of lust. "Damn, that dick feels good, Suga! That's it, Big Daddy. Fuck this pussy!"

Suge held himself in check. He wanted to call out her mothafucking name, but he kept his composure. The blood was rushing into his pipe, swelling it past recognition. On top of that, her pussy was squeezing his dick like a cock ring. *Damn, this bitch tight! I can't believe this shit* he thought while slowly sliding his swipe in and out of her silky slit.

Tamika turned it up a notch. "Suga Bear, you feel so good!"

She held onto the wall, using it for leverage as she started pushing her hips back at him to the rhythm of his sex. The sound of his stomach slapping against her ass cheeks got louder and louder with every plunge.

"You like this dick, huh?! Feel it in ya stomach, huh, girl?!" he told her as he pounded his member into her love tunnel. Harder and harder with every pound. Faster and faster with every plunge! All while he rubbed her cunt ferociously!

Feeling a man's rough hand on her pussy was a luxury Tamika appreciated. It got her to her precipice a lot sooner than if she were using her own fingers. Her arms buckled and she fell against the wall.

But Suge caught her before she could hurt herself.

He knew what he was doing. Sex was a game he practiced for years. Suge spun around, ready to dive into her from the front, but Tamika had other plans. She squatted down, putting her face at dick level. Without a word, she took Suge's hips in her hands, quickly lining his pipe up with her face. Then she started deep throating his massive member.

"Dayumm! Goddamn!" Suge mumbled. This time it was him who fell back against the wall. Tamika slurped harder, pressing her warm tongue against his head, trying to squeeze the cum from it!

She took her mouth off him for a moment, then looked up at him while stroking his meat muscle. "You like that, Daddy? I can't wait for you to cum in my mothafuckin' mouth!"

"Naw... Naw, Baby... I don't wanna nut like that!" Suge fought the urge to cum. He felt the feeling swelling in his stomach. He knew he was seconds from splashing all over her face, so he pulled her back up into standing position.

Tamika bit her bottom lip with anticipation. Watching his dick bounce around uncontrollably was turning her on-on! Suge leaned in and mumbled something she couldn't understand.

"Give me dat dick, Suga Bear! Stop playing wit' me!"

Hearing her sexy voice begging for his man meat gave Suge a purpose. He reached behind her, pulling her by the ass cheeks towards him. She wrapped her arms around his neck while pressing her back into the shower wall for leverage. At that angle he could do all the damage he wanted. His dick had stretched out as far as possible, giving him a full jackhammer to pound in her guts!

"Damn! Damn! Damn!" Tamika cried out after each pound. She reached down with her left hand started rubbing her clit in mid-air.

"Don't stop, Daddy!"

Suge could feel her pulsating pussy puckering along the length of his penis. "Cum, bitch! Cum on this dick, Tamika!"

All that talking was driving her crazy! She started rubbing her clit frantically. "Dig me out, Daddy! Dig me out! I'm gonna cum!"

She went into convulsions when her climax exploded between her legs. She immediately felt her fluids gushing out her snatch, onto and all over Suge's dick while he continuously slammed it inside of her.

She was moments away from passing out. Suge saw it and became even more aroused. He sped up, thrusting himself into her with more force on every pound. Suge was going berzerk in the pussy! He was pulling himself all the way out before diving all the way back into her velvet rose.

"I'm there, bitch! Oh shit, I'm there! Damn... I'm cumming –"

"Cum in me, Daddy!"

"Oh shit! Oh shit!" and with that, Suge gave one final thrust, stuffing ten-and-a-half inches of veny muscle deep into her silk folds. The explosion sucked the life from him. He just stood there leaning all of his weight onto her.

A few moments passed before they both stepped out the shower and started drying off. Suge was still dripping when his pager went off and he saw a number he never called before. For some reason, the number invited him to call it. So he went straight to the phone by the bed.

The call was answered on the first ring, "Suge..."

"Yeah."

"You know who this is?"

"Yup. What's brackin', Dre? You a'ight?"

"Hell naw! I was thinkin' 'bout what we was talkin' 'bout earlier. It keeps replayin' over and over again in my head. You really think they looking at me like a slave?"

CHAPTER FORTY-TWO

Dre was at home, in his studio babysitting a glass of Cognac. Every few minutes was marked by a sip from his cup. He was trying to figure out what his next move would be.

He'd been in the music industry for a few years by then. From DJing at different clubs, to being part of an R&B group called the World Class Wrecking Crew. Although it gave him experience, none of it had blown up like NWA had. Fucking with Eazy ended up making all of his dreams come true.

That part was real. All of them had more than they had ever dreamed of. The problem was something wasn't right. Cube saw it. D.O.C. saw it. Michel'le and a few others saw it too. Now that Dre was beginning to wake up, he needed to ask himself if he would stay, or would he go. And, if he chose the latter, which route he would take.

As he sat there drinking, all kinds of thoughts started shooting through his head. All the times Eazy and Heller walked away from the group to have their private conversations came into perspective.

He did the math on all the times Eazy walked away with better deals than the rest of them, whether it was a bigger room on their tour buses, to certain meetings with powerful individuals in the industry. It all started becoming a lot more clear.

Dre had never been a hater. He loved the fact they all had their specific shine. The issue was simple: It was obvious the money wasn't getting split properly. If Suge hit for several hundred thousand dollars off one song that a nigga wrote, then every single NWA member should've already been millionaires several times over.

So, why weren't they? Where was all the money going?

Dre drank to his thoughts in the dark. At some point he started staring at the phone next to the sound board. Then he took Suge's pager number out and stared at it for a while. It took him a minute, but eventually he called it and left his number. He still hadn't figured out what he was gonna do, but he was sure Suge would help him in whatever direction he chose.

It didn't take long for his phone to ring. When it did, he answered it; "Suge..."

"Yeah."

A slight pause took place. Dre sat up from his slouched position and asked, "You know who this is?"

"Yup! What's brackin', Dre? You a'ight?"

"Hell naw! I was thinkin' 'bout what you was sayin' earlier. It keeps replayin' over and over again in my head. You really think they looking at me like a slave?"

Suge took a moment to think of his reply. The phone went silent for a few seconds before he started. "I know the industry, Dre. I'm not takin' from what you've seen and experienced. Actually, I'm bankin' on utilizing your knowledge and expertise. So, before I answer that I'm gonna ask you this: Do you think the mothafuckaz behind them desks give a fuck about anyone other than themselves? For real, Dre. When's the last time you seen some honkies really give a fuck about any nigga?"

Dre just shook his head. He didn't have to give an answer because they both knew and understood what was being said.

"White people can't help it. They're born with a sense of entitlement They're bred to believe Blacks are inferior. They come at this music industry just like the slave trade. Heller is a plantation owner. Eazy is his House Nigga. You, Tracy, Michel'le and them are their field hands. It's the same concept. On Piru, I believe they treating you like a slave! They're making millions off you! Without you, they wouldn't have the product they got. All you gotta do is say the word and I'll change everything. We'll get you out from under their grasps and set you up in your own studio. We'll cultivate some artist and create a gangsta Motown! A ghetto Def Jam!"

"I'm thinkin' 'bout it. I know I need to fuck wit' you. So, yeah, I'll do it. Let's do this, Suge!"

"Bet! That's all I needed to hear! First step is to get you up from outta Heller an Eazy's thumb. But, before we can do that, there's a payday we gonna have to cash in on. We gonna get you the money you deserve, 'cause I feel like they been playin' you even worse than they been doin' everyone else."

"I'm wit' it!"

"A'ight. Let me make some calls. I'll get back at you in a couple days..."

Dre was now filled with an energy that matched his feelings. He felt like a man with a mission! He no longer felt defeated. The energy triggered his creative side, and he got up and turned the lights on. A few minutes later, he was at the sound board with his headphones on mixing and mastering the beat he had been listening to all day...

CHAPTER FORTY-THREE

Suge was standing on the porch at the Beehive when two cars pulled up to the curb. It was a sunny day. The set was filled with movement; felonious activities. Close to a dozen other Pirus were spread out from the porch to the sidewalk, just hanging out.

One of the cars that parked on the curb was an SS Monte Carlo that belonged to China Dogg. The other was a BMW ridden by D.O.C. He had been waiting on them to show up. And now that they arrived, he was ready to have a meeting of the minds.

China Dogg made sure he acknowledged the soldiers posted up in the yard on his way to the porch. D.O.C. gave a few head nods himself. Neither one of them knew what Suge had on his mind. Whatever it was it couldn't have been too bad; he was definitely on a winning streak.

"S'up, relly," Suge greeted Tracy. "Step inside. Buntry and Heron already in there."

"Bet," D.O.C. replied.

"P-Funk!" China Dogg gave Suge a hug when he reached the porch.

"What's good, blood! The SS looking clean, nigga!"

"I just had that bitch waxed. It's the perfect day to ride with the T-tops tucked."

"Onda set," Suge remarked. He opened the door and they both went inside.

They went into the kitchen where Heron and Buntry were waiting for them. They all greeted each other then found a spot to settle in at. D.O.C. took a seat at the table with Buntry and Heron. Suge and China stood with their backs against the counter.

Buntry hadn't seen China in a couple of weeks. Things were moving so fast that sometimes traffic kept soldiers on the move instead of in the trenches. Before Suge could inform them of what the meeting was about, Buntry asked China, "Where you been, dog? I heard you went and copped you something hot."

"Onda set," China replied. "Just snatched up a SS. It's outside right now. Ready to race for pink slips when ya nuts drop, nigga."

"What?! Blood, you ain't said shit! We can run it right now!"

"Both of y'all full of shit," Heron teased. "Neither one of y'all finna give up your babies! Let that shit go, blood."

"Shiiit, my engine hot!" China continued.

"I bet," agreed Suge. "But right now we need to chop game. Anybody know where G-Boy at?" Everyone looked around, but no one replied. Neither one of them had seen him in weeks.

"I heard you talked to Dre," D.O.C. said. "He said Michel'le is on the same accord. We all ready to do this."

They all looked at Suge. The meeting officially in motion. "Yeah. Blood finally realized what's going on. Eazy and Heller on some bullshit. Dick Griffey is all in with us, too."

"So, what's the hold-up?" Buntry asked. "What's the next move?"

"We start a label. Record some albums and take over the game. But I can't do shit until we get these niggaz out they contract with Ruthless."

China looked at D.O.C. and said, "You still under contract?"

"Yeah," Tracy sighed. "I been knowing they was on some bullshit. But every time I step to 'em, they give me the runaround."

"That's what I wanted to talk to y'all about," Suge said. On Piru, I been callin' Ruthless tryna set up a meeting with Heller, but he's ignoring me. They stonewalling me."

"So," Buntry began. "What exactly do you need? What's the process?"

Suge glanced at D.O.C. before addressing Buntry's question. "The deal is, half of their label is ready to jump ship. Niggaz heard I'm hooked up with Griffey, and how I hit for Chocolate. So, they ready to ride with us. But all this shit tied up in contractual technicalities."

"That shit brazy," Heron commented.

Suge continued. "I wanna roll up on them fools. I've been tryna holla at them diplomatically. But that shit ain't workin'. I'm really ready to turn up the heat on 'em."

"Whatchu mean?" China and Buntry both asked at the same time.

Suge circled the room with his eyes. Making contact with each one of his men was important to him.

244

What he was about to say was serious. It would include the set, so they would all have to be on the same page.

"Eazy-E got his whole hood behind him. I'm talkin' about snatchin' up half his label. The way I'm 'bout to press is gonna escalate shit. Which means we're probably gonna go to war with Kelly Park."

"They crabs," Heron stated. "The homies is itching for a squirmish. Niggaz ain't got a problem with deep-sea fishing."

"But this ain't set business," China commented. He understood Suge's concern. He was asking to involve their whole gang in a situation that was quasi-personal. "If an all-out war kicks off, niggaz on both sides gonna die. In order to sanction something like that, we gonna need to make sure it's worth it. If not, the homies is gonna politic on us."

"Exactly," Suge said matter of factly. "Onda set, if I can make this happen, we all gonna hit a whole different level. This shit is bigger than any other move I ever made. We're talkin' millions on millions. Takin' over the whole music industry. In my eyes, it's worth it. That's why we needed G-Man in on this!'"

"On Ru's," Heron agreed.

China and Buntry both nodded. They believed in Suge. But they also realized that neither one of them were bigger than the set. Everyone would have to benefit from their move. Especially since all of them would lose in one way or another. If a war with Kelly Park Compton Crips was activated, the body count would be high on both sides.

"Right now," Suge continued, "I'm tryna pull up at the studio. Not by myself either. It's past the point of friendly conversations. It's time to flex."

"You're right," D.O.C. agreed. "Eazy ain't tryna hear nothin' I gotta say. I'm ready to get this shit over with. I'm ready to start getting real money."

"What we waitin' fo'?" Heron asked. "Let's go! Let's roll up there right now. We got enough homies outside right now!"

Suge looked at his men. They all had that familiar look in their eyes. Loyalty was the vibe of the moment. They trusted his judgement. And were all willing to put it all on the line for him.

After a moment, he nodded. A smile crept across his face and he said, "Let's mob!"

That was all they needed to hear. The meeting was adjourned and they headed outside. They had a clear mission ahead of them, but Suge had something on his mind in addition to everything else that was going on.

Away from everyone else, he pulled Heron to the side and asked, "What happened to G-Boy? I wanted him to hear all this."

"I told 'im we was having a meeting, but he was acting funny."

"What? What you mean?"

"I don't know. Blood could've been in a hurry. You know he's running it up out here. But, then again, he said some off-the-wall type shit. Talkin' 'bout every time you got an issue, you want everyone there. But, when niggaz come to you with shit, you don't got no time."

Suge looked at Heron for a moment without saying anything. He was trying to process what he had just heard. "Damn. Blood trippin'. I'ma holla at 'im tho'. I've been so caught up with this shit, I haven't really had a chance to make my usual rounds lately."

After that, Suge followed the others outside, where a cadre of Pirus were waiting for him. From the porch, he addressed them.

"We finna handle some business right now! There's four cars out here, but we're only takin' niggaz with straps. If you not packin', don't get in, 'cause we 'bout to set-trip on some niggaz."

This wasn't the first time the Mob had been called to arms. They were all seasoned war veterans. None of them asked for an explanation as to where they were headed, or who they were expected to press.

Set trippin' was what they lived for.

When the caravan headed out, they had eleven blood-thirsty Mob Pirus with them. Each one of them were clutching their blowers. One after another, the cars followed one another on their way to Ruthless Records recording studio.

Suge was focused. He had one mission in mind: To obtain his artist's contracts from Heller or Eazy. He didn't give a fuck if he had to bust some heads to get them, either. Diplomacy had ran its course.

It was time to show force!

CHAPTER FORTY-FOUR

Eazy was posted up outside of his recording studio with a group of his locs. The parking lot was looking like a sideshow with Low-Lows parked next to one another with their doors and trunks open. Music was blasting from their speakers providing a soundtrack to their Crippin'.

He was enjoying his time at home. Being on tour with NWA kept Eazy on the road for months at a time. So, whenever he got the chance, he made sure he did regular hood shit with his day-ones.

"Ain't that T-Loc right there?" Eazy's homegirl pointed when a dark-green Corvette rolled into the parking lot with its trunk pounding.

Eazy, clad in his trademark white T and blue 501's smiled behind his Locs. "Yeah. That's cuz. He ridin' clean, ain't he?"

"On Crip," she remarked.

T-Loc double parked behind Eazy's '64 Impala. When he stepped out of his ride, he was shaking a pair a dice in his hand. "Which one of y'all niggaz ready to lose ya bank, cuz?"

A dice game was all they needed to accentuate their afternoon shenanigans. Regular hood shit.

Eazy loved Craps. He was a hustler who saw a dice game as an opportunity to get paid. "On Crip, I got first fade! Hand me them dice, cuz! I'm callin' all bets!"

A circle was created between the back of Eazy's Impala and his homeboy's Vette. The Loc'd-out rapper was feeling himself that afternoon.

Roll after roll, he hit his numbers. This was his world. He felt comfortable in the midst of his heathens. Squatting down in a circle of gamblers was something he'd been doing since the first game he played when he was nine years old.

Although he could've easily bet five hundred per roll, he didn't high side on his homies. They shot five dollars a bet unless it was raised. This way, they all had a chance at the money.

The Game Gods favored Eazy that afternoon. Before he knew it, he was three hundred dollars richer. A small amount when considering what his net worth was. But that wasn't what had 'im smiling.

It wasn't about the money. His enjoyment came from the energy he felt from being in the middle of all his homies. He was surrounded by Crips who had been through hell and back for one another.

That's what it was really all about for him.

The dice game was in full affect when the rumble of an approaching caravan of cars with their own booming systems suddenly pulled into the parking lot.

Someone on the outskirts of the dice game said, "What da fuck is dat, cuz?!"

"Ain't that Buntry and Heron from Lueders?" someone else asked.

Those two names alone was enough to call the attention of all who heard it. Every set in Compton had its reputable gang bangers. Some had got their names from fighting, robbing, selling drugs, or putting in work. Most of the people in Suge's immediate circle were known factors. Reputables known for spitting fire from their flame throwers. Buntry and Heron just happened to be two of the most known steppas from Da Mob.

Eazy left the dice on the asphalt when he heard the commotion.

The smile that was on his face moments earlier was suddenly forgotten and replaced with a scowl.

"Nigga, that's D.O.C. wit' dem niggaz!" someone from Eazy's camp observed.

Eazy's disdain was apparent when he saw the Judas approaching his crew. "What da fuck is dis'?" he said out loud, while thinking, *These niggaz gotta be crazy!* The demeanor of the crowd had changed instantly. Eazy took the lead, stepping to Suge and D.O.C. After scanning the opposition, he addressed D.O.C. directly. "S'up wit' dis, cuz?"

"The homey Suge wants to holla atchu," D.O.C. replied coldly. "He's my manager now."

"Is that right?" Eazy scoffed disrespectfully. Then, to Suge he said, "You need this many niggaz wit' you to have a conversation?"

"On Kelly Park Compton Crip, we ain't worried 'bout none of these niggaz, E!" T-Loc announced as he took his place next to his loc.

Eazy glanced at his homey before turning back to Suge. His shades covered his eyes. Not that he needed the tint. Fear was null and void. Everyone in attendance was just as hard as the next man. It didn't matter if it was bullets flying or fist being thrown, each one of them was ready for whatever, including Eazy.

Towering over the shorter man, Suge said, "I stopped by in person 'cause you obviously ain't taking my calls. I'm reppin' several of your label-mates now –"

Eazy looked at D.O.C. and said, "You a bitch, cuz?"

"Nigga–"

Suge stopped D.O.C. before he ran up on Eazy. "Hold-up, blood. Let me handle this," he told D.O.C. before addressing Eazy again. "See, that's your problem. No respect. That's why D.O.C., Dre and Michel'le are my artists now. So we need to reach an understanding no matter how you feel about it. I need copies of their contracts."

Eazy's anger was apparent by the way his jaw muscles clenched. Still, even though he was burning up inside, he kept his composure. "If Dre or Tracy wanna see they contracts, they can holla at me themselves."

"Naw," Suge stated while shaking his head. "You not hearin' me. I'm their manager now. All their business goes through me now."

Eazy scoffed before cutting his eyes at the Judas standing next to his opp. He couldn't believe what he was seeing. *This nigga Suge has gotta have a death wish fucking wit' me like this*, Eazy thought to himself. *I'ma kill this nigga!* Outloud he said, "I'm not gonna repeat myself too many more times, cuz!"

That's when China Dogg stepped towards Eazy with full-on aggression.

"What's up wit' dat tone of yours, blood!? The homey already told you what it is!"

Eazy knew exactly who he was talking to. China Dogg was a hunter ten-times over. It didn't matter, though. He wasn't backing down. Not then. Not ever!

"On Kelly, y'all got me fucked up!" Eazy snapped. "How da fuck you gonna show up here like you runnin' shit! This my record label! Ain't nobody runnin' shit over here but me!"

Suge anticipated China Dogg's next move. He already knew if he didn't do something quick, Eazy was gonna find himself knocked out.

He extended his arm across China's chest, stopping his homey from demonstrating his knockout skills. Everyone saw it, and it triggered the already simmering tension into a full on boil.

"I'm tryna handle this professionally. But, if you feel some type of way about this push, we can take it behind the building," Suge said. "We can line it up wit' all yo' homies if that's what you lookin' for. But that's not what I came for. I want copies of D.O.C.'s, Dre's, and Michelle's contracts. You and me can step inside and get them thangs printed out real quick. Then, I'm gone. No harm, no foul."

"I already told you it ain't happening, cuz!" Eazy barked.

Suddenly, the scene got even more tense when someone from Suge's camp yelled, "On Piru, they got us fucked up!"

"Line it up then, slob-ass nigga!" the opposition called out.

"Hold-up!" Suge bellowed over the crowd. It was important he kept control of the situation. His immediate goal wasn't violence. He wanted the contracts. To Eazy, he calmly stated, "I'ma let yo' attitude slide, homey. This ain't what I came for. The fact is, whether you like it or not, you have several of my artists under contract. On some professional shit, it's my job to make sure their affairs are in order. If you ain't on no shady shit, it shouldn't be a problem for you to cough up them contracts."

Eazy balled up his fists. It took all his energy not to sock the giant in the mouth. He was standing face to face with a wolf who was coming after everything he had. He couldn't remember the last time he wanted to kill someone as bad as he wanted to murder Suge in that very moment.

"You need to get the fuck outta here, cuz!" Eazy hissed coldly. "On Kelly, I'm done wit' this conversation."

"On Kelly, huh?" Suge said. "You know what you're sayin', lil man?"

T-Loc had had enough. He took a step forward growling, "On Crip, fuck what you talkin' 'bout, cuz! Y'all heard the homey! Get the fuck on!"

The line had been drawn. Neither crew was gonna back down. Both sides drew their weapons, filling the parking lot with sounds of pistols getting cocked. They were way to close to one another for a shootout to take place without casualties. The first shot was about to be fired when a police cruiser chirped its siren.

They all looked towards the street where the cop car with two officers were passing by at a snail's pace. It was one of those situations where Los Angeles sheriff deputies would not step out of their cruiser. The tension was visibly obvious. The looks on the gang member's faces told them this wasn't the time for their usual harassment tactics. The most they could do was show their presence in hopes of bluffing the crowd into dispersing.

That's when Suge motioned for his men to stand down. He couldn't risk having so many soldiers arrested for the dirty weapons concealed in their waistbands.

Guns quietly disappeared. Both groups retreated. But not before someone from Eazy's gang called out, "D.O.C., you rockin' wit' dem, cuz?"

Even though the question came from someone else, Tracy addressed Eazy. "It is what it is, E."

"C'mon, blood," Suge told D.O.C. as he put his arm around his shoulder. "Let's go." Then to Eazy, he said, "I need them contracts."

Eazy was beyond livid! If it weren't for the Sherriff deputies pulling up when they did, things would've turned out extremely different. After Suge's group headed back to their cars, a few of Eazy's niggaz approached him with questions and statements about what had just taken place. But, he wasn't listening. His world was on fire. He couldn't think straight.

He was so angry his hands were shaking. Still, he reached through the window of his lowrider and grabbed his brick-sized cell phone. He had one person he needed to talk to. And, the outcome of that conversation would dictate his next move.

CHAPTER FORTY-FIVE

It was actually a good day for a funeral. The skies were clear. The weather was nice. Not too hot, not too cold. Still, it didn't mean the vibe of the day matched Mother Nature's blessing.

As G-Boy stood by in his black and red suit, Baby G-Boy's mother cried uncontrollably. Her wails were loud and piercing. Meanwhile, their church's pastor spoke of blessings carried by angels. Pearly white gates and eternal forgiveness. All language that G-Boy had heard before yet never listened to.

Their gang was in full attendance. Over fifty active Lueders Park Bompton Pirus were dressed in matching suits for the occasion. Some wore t-shirts with Old English lettering that read: P.I.P. Baby G-Boy... Lueders Park Bompton Piru!

Since Baby G's family was heavy in the church the gangland presence was overshadowed by law abiding, church going mourners. To a civilian not privy to the Bompton politics nothing would have seemed out of place. But that couldn't have been further from the truth.

After laying Baby G to rest G-Boy got into the limo he had ridden in along with Bear, P-Dog, CK Brazy and L.B.. At first, the trek back through the set was silent. The crew as a whole were in pain. One of their main niggaz had been taken from them so it was under-standable. The unified loss they felt was excruciating.

Bear along with everyone else had taken their recent loss hard. He had tears in his eyes when he announced, "I'm shooting up Park Village every time blood's mamma cries."

"On Piru!" L.B. agreed.

"Man, fuck all'at!" P-Dog growled. "Where were the Mob niggaz today? That bitch-ass nigga Bolo started all this shit wit' dem crabs and they homies didn't even have the respect to show up to blood's funeral."

"And they was nowhere near us when them niggaz hopped out on us!" CK Brazy spat. "They been startin' shit with other sets, but when it's time to ride they nowhere in sight."

"On Piru!" L.B. agreed. "Sugar Bear got them niggaz smoking good; riding clean; looking like a million bucks–"

"Wit' big guns too!" P-Dog interjected.

"Them niggaz all getting' fat!" L.B. continued. "But when it's time to ride they not wit' the movement!"

G-Boy hadn't said a word the whole time his day-ones were venting. He just stared out the window looking at nothing. He had went through all the emotions one experiences when losing a loved one. He heard his homies gripes. He too saw the lack of attendance from Mob members. At that point Mob Piru and Lueders Park were still technically one entity.

Their groups were barely indistinguishable from one another. So they usually functioned together.

Things were changing though. It all started when Suge started flooding his circle within a circle with money, guns and drugs. G-Boy pistol whooping Bolo didn't help their internal feud either. Still, G-Boy had never actually spoken ill of the man who had put him on when he first came home. Nevertheless, things were changing.

"None of them niggaz were there, huh?" G-Boy asked no one in particular. "I could've sworn Buntry was somewhere in the back. But it seems like the Mob ain't pushing with us no more."

"They not!" CK Brazy spat. "The homey got killed and they whole clique is M.I.A."

L.B. looked at G-Boy and asked, "You talk to Sugar Bear lately?"

He shook his head silently before saying, "Fuck 'dem niggaz, blood! None of them niggaz my homie!"

As fast as the words left his mouth was as fast as the message was sent and understood. Things like that weren't taken lightly when they came from the mouth of a reputable like G-Boy. His words were interpreted and taken as a gangland decree.

"We need to worry 'bout ridin' on them Mark Village niggaz," G-Boy continued. "I'ma kill at least one of them fools every night until Baby G's mamma stops crying!"

"Onda set!"

"On Piiiru!"

"On Lueders Park Bompton Piru!"

"Onda dead homey Baby G!"

CHAPTER FORTY-SIX

Michel'le watched Dre as he took in the sound of her last take of a song they'd been working on. It always amazed her to watch him work because she appreciated his genius. She knew what the world hadn't figured out yet: That Dre was one of the greats.

"What is it, Andre? You don't like it?"

Dre leaned back in his seat. She was so cute. He loved her smile. But he wasn't gonna let her off that easy. "It's the way you deliver that high note at the end of the second verse. You gotta push up a little."

"Uh-huh, Dre! We been workin' all morning! It's been three hours on this same track!"

"I hear ya, but –"

"No! You don't hear me, baby. My throat is getting sore." She was used to her man's grueling work schedule. He was a perfectionist in every way. It was good at times. But she had to put her foot down every once in a while.

Michelle went to Dre and took his headphones off his head. Then she sat on his lap. Their work day was over if she had anything to do with it. Their bedroom was just down the hallway and the music they made in there was just as good as what they made in the studio.

"What you doing, Michelle? We ain't done –"

"Yes, we are. At least, for a little while. You need some food in your stomach. And so do I.

She leaned in to kiss him on the lips. Work always came first.

Dre was addicted to making music. But he was also a Pussy Hound, too. Feeling her soft booty squirm around on his lap was beginning to wake up his beast.

"Okay, ma. We can rest a little bit. But we ain't done with this track. This mothafucka gonna go platinum by the time I'm done with it."

She leaned in for another kiss. "I know it will." Michel'le turned her whole body around as she straddled his lap. Her pussy was moistening. She was ready to continue their recording session on a whole different level.

Dre stared deeply into her eyes. She was everything he wanted in a woman. Beautiful, sexy, loyal and she loved music. They matched perfectly. Then, just as he thought of how well they meshed with one another, something else crossed his mind.

"You know, that nigga Suge supposed to be gettin' at Heller 'bout our contracts. I been

Thinkin' –"

"About my album? The release date, huh?"

"Yeah. You might not wanna hear this, but it might be best if we wait. I know we been putting it off for a while –"

"It's almost finished."

"I know. I've been thinkin' 'bout that. I just don't wanna submit it to Eazy until we figure out where we stand with our contracts. If we wait, there's a chance Suge can make it a bigger payday."

"How much bigger?"

"I can't be sure. I'm thinkin' from hundreds of thousands to a couple million if it goes platinum. I'm thinkin' this because there'll be a lot less hands dippin' into the pot."

"Ring-Ring-Ring-Ring," sounded the cordless house phone.

Michel'le looked at it then back at Dre. She had no problem ignoring it. She wanted to spend some quality time with him… time with no clothes on. It was really on him. Yet, after staring into his eyes for a moment, she knew he wasn't gonna let the call go unanswered. Which was okay with her. She'd take her time setting the mood while he took care of whatever was on the other end of that line.

"Let me get that, baby. It might be Suge with an update."

"Alright, honey," she replied as she climbed off him. "I'll get us some lunch ready. I'll be back."

Dre answered the call while watching Michelle's plum-shaped booty shashay away. "What's happenin'? Who dis?"

"What's this bullshit I'm hearin' about that slob-ass Lueder's Park nigga being yo' manager?"

Dre was surprised by the call. Eazy was clearly pissed off. It's not like he didn't think that specific call would eventually come. He just wasn't expecting it right then and there. Nevertheless he put his game-face on and dove straight into it.

"Yeah, I'm fuckin' wit' 'im. What's the problem?"

Eazy scoffed, "On Crip, you trippin'! You been talkin' 'bout how you feel yo' money ain't right. Then you go and invite that leach into our business! That nigga really 'bout to rape your pockets!"

260

"Like you and Heller been doin'?"

"You been on some bullshit! You soundin' just like the rest of these niggaz! I never thought you'd let some outsiders in your head. Especially after everything I did for you!"

"What?! Everything you did for me?! We came into this shit together! Or, did you forget that? I've been tellin' you for months that somethin' ain't right! The numbers ain't been kosher since the honky came in the picture. And you know it. But you ain't trippin' 'cause you eatin' more than the rest of us!"

"We're all eating, Dre! We all getting' rich!"

"Naw," Dre said, shaking his head. "We ain't all getting rich! You and Heller getting rich! On some real shit, if you ain't in on it with 'im, he's probably robbing you too! You just cool wit' it 'cause you're getting more than the rest of us!"

The line went silent.

Eazy didn't reply. It was as if he was mulling over the statement. Then, after a few moments he came back in a much lower, more calculated tone. "You're makin' a mistake, Dre. You bringin' outsiders into our business. We could've handled all this in-house."

"I've been tellin' you that this whole time! You're the one who ain't been listenin'. It's too late for all that now. I'm lettin' Suge take care of it. We need them contracts, E. That's the program I'm runnin' wit'. Point blank!"

"Point blank, huh?"

"Damn right!"

Michelle came back with two glasses of wine in her hands. She found Dre in a totally different mood than how she had left him. "You alright? Was that Suge?"

"Naw!" Dre snarled. He was fuming over the call he had just had. "It was Eric. He must've just talked to Suge, or somethin'. He was trippin'. Bitch-ass, nigga."

"We knew that was gonna happen."

Dre was staring at the soundboard, shaking his head. "Fuck 'im! I'ma let Suge do what he do. We're gonna get from under them mothafuckaz and do our own thing!"

"What did he say?" she asked as she took a seat on the couch.

"He was on some stupid shit. Talkin' 'bout we could've handled everything in-house. That I shouldn't have involved Suge. This ain't nobody's fault, but Eazy's! If he didn't have his head so far up Heller's ass he'd see what's going on!"

"Dre, he probably does know what's goin' on. Everybody knows he's getting' more money than everybody else..."

$$$$$

"Bitch-ass nigga!" Eazy said after hanging up on Dre. Most of his boys had gotten in their cars and left after the police had shown up. But the ones who lingered had heard the whole conversation.

He really didn't give a fuck at that point. He was hot! The realization of everything that was happening was starting to sink in. Dre was really on board with Suge. Suge was tryna take all his artists.

"Damn!" he yelled as he pounded on the roof of his Impala.

"Fuck dem niggaz, cuz!" someone said.

He wasn't listening to anyone. His mind was swirling. His whole crew was irritated with what had just taken place. The hostility was thick. He got into his car without saying anything to anyone and was followed by three other locs. No one had to voice what was to come next. Da Mob had crossed a line they shouldn't have. There was only one course of action after that.

"On Kelly Park Compton Crip, them niggaz finna get served! Comin' to my studio with all that ra-ra just signed they death certificates!" Eazy announced more to himself than to anyone else. Seconds later, he was in traffic with several other vehicles following close behind.

"Who da fuck he think he is?" Blue Rag, Eazy's homey said from the backseat. "And ya boy D.O.C. was wit' 'em, cuz! Lookin' like a mothafuckin' hood-hoppa!"

"On Crip, that nigga deserves a hot one to the chest!" interjected the loc in the passenger seat.

Eazy couldn't think straight. He almost ran a red light until he remembered all the guns they had on them. When he stopped at the light he grabbed his brick phone and called Ren.

"Yo, Ren!" he said as soon as the call was answered.

"What's crackin', cuz?"

"You'll never believe what just went down. The nigga Tracy just pushed up on me at the studio with some Lueders Park niggaz!"

"What?! What you sayin', cuz?"

"D.O.C. showed up at the studio with Suge and three carloads of slobs! They was talkin' 'bout Suge is his manager. And, get this, cuz! The bitch-ass nigga Dre is on board wit' them too!"

"Dre was wit' em too?"

"Naw. I just got off the phone wit' him, tho'. He talkin' 'bout Suge is his manager too!" The light turned green, Eazy took off a little too fast. "I can't believe these niggaz, cuz!"

"Onda set."

"I'm hot, cuz!"

"Where you headed now?"

"I'm 'bout to hit the hood up. On Kelly, I'm not lettin' any of this shit slide! The first person on my list is that nigga D.O.C. cuz was outta line for bringin' them niggaz to the studio."

"Fo' sho'!" I'll meet you in the set."

Eazy dropped the phone on the seat next to him. He already knew exactly what to do. Growing up in the trenches taught him to recognize and eliminate all threats...

CHAPTER FORTY-SEVEN

Three days later...

D.O.C. was in his Benz, in a dark spot towards the back of Eve After Dark's parking lot. He'd been smoking and drinking all night, and had decided to get a night cap before heading home.

His seat was leaned all the way back, giving the skinny white girl currently bobbing her head in his lap just enough room for her not to bump her head on the steering wheel.

The liquids mixed with the smoke he ingested throughout the night had him right. But the head he was receiving sent him over the edge. He didn't even have to put his hand on the top of her head. She was a pro who left no room for question.

Baby was deep throating the thug fast and hard. When his balls finally overheated, he couldn't hold the tsunami back. Tracy busted in her warm, wet mouth. And she swallowed every drop! Afterwards, she didn't act clingy. Nor did she hint that he owed her some sort of fake affection. The nameless groupie wiped her lips with the back of her hand and got out of the car on her own accord.

I love this life, he thought to himself as he pulled into traffic. Stardom gave him a fast life incomparable to any other. The perks that came with fame was worth millions by itself. Add real money to that and you had a dream come true.

D.O.C. had sense enough to drive extremely slow. He was shitfaced. So intoxicated, at times he felt out of his body. The last thing he needed was to get pulled over by L.A.P.D.

Tracy was used to driving under the influence. He actually had a tactic he used on nights like that. Driving on main roads was out. He did everything in his power to stay on the side streets. Preferably, residential ones.

On that night, he made sure he headed home under the shade of backstreets. Less traffic also made things better. After about ten minutes into his trip, he got the feeling he was being followed. At first, he wasn't sure if the black Trans Am with three heads inside was really trailing him. But after hitting a few unnecessary corners, it became overwhelmingly obvious.

Suddenly sober, he reached under his seat for his .357. There was no telling who was in the load behind him. But there was no way they were friends. If they were, they were in store for a rude awakening. D.O.C. had full intentions of shooting first and asking questions never.

In a last-ditch effort to get away from who he assumed were would-be robbers, he decided to hop on the freeway. It didn't work out how he hoped, though. Initially, he though his Benz would outrun the cheaper sports car. But the Trans Am was just as quick on the gas as his foreign ride.

The highway was void of traffic. This gave them a wide-open throughway which played straight into

Tracy's pursuer's hands. With no witnesses in sight, they saw the perfect opportunity to press play on the mission they were on.

The muscle car's engine came to life in a real way when it's driver slammed his foot on gas. It not only caught up with the Benz, it pulled up next to it, giving the men inside a clear shot at their man.

BLOCKA! BLOCKA! BLOCKA!!

KRSHHH! KRSHHH!

D.O.C.'s passenger side window exploded, sending shards everywhere including his face and neck, cutting him open in the process.

Still, he managed to let off a few rounds in defense.

He fought to keep his eyes on the road. The glass had cut his face so bad, that blood was in his eyes, affecting his sight. High speeding down the highway didn't help, either.

The Trans Am stayed on his tail. Realizing he was running from an engine just as powerful as his own, he decided to take the next exit back into the city. His only hope was losing them in traffic.

The chase was tight. One of the shooters was hanging out the side of the passenger window, shooting at his Benz. He could hear the bullets puncturing his ride.

KRSHHH!

The back window shattered.

The explosion of glass made him swerve. He fishtailed, but managed to maintain control of the steering wheel. He hit a corner sideways.

A few seconds later, he slid into another. For a moment, as he approached an intersection, he thought he had lost his pursuers.

Then he saw them again! "What da fuck!" he yelled when they popped back up in his rearview. The intersection was coming up quick. He slammed his foot on the gas preparing to hit the corner sideways.

BLOCKA! BLOCKA! BLOCKA! sounded the bullets as they riddled his ride. D.O.C. hit a hard left. The car behind him never slowed down. As he slid into his turn, they kept their forward momentum, ramming into the back of his Benz!

D.O.C. lost his handle. His car spun out of control. Suddenly he was heading straight into the headlights of an incoming Burrito Truck!

CHAPTER FORTY-EIGHT

Suge had just lit his cigar and blew out a thick cloud of smoke when Mario's girl came in the room tripping. "Watch where you ash that, Sugar Bear!"

He was startled for a moment by the way she ran towards him with the ashtray in her hand. You would've thought he was burning the house down by the way she was acting. Amazed, he chuckled and said, "All of a sudden... You wasn't trippin' off ashes when you stayed in the set."

Margy gave Suge a smirk, knowing he was right. "You right, but I always kept a clean house. It's just now we got things worth looking after. Like the eight-hundred dollar couch you sittin' on. I rather stick this ashtray in ya face before I let you burn a hole in that leather.

"Can't argue with that. You right."

"She been on me too," Chocolate commented as he entered the living room with several glasses of Hennessy in his hands. He gave one to Heron, China, Silk and Suge before taking a seat on his La-Z-Boy.

"Your girl trippin'," Heron teased.

"Yeah," China chimed in. "She told me my Dickies were too dirty to step inside with —"

"No, I didn't!" Margy argued. "Y'all better leave me alone. It's hard keepin' four bedrooms, a den, and a clean backyard. It's a twenty-four hour a day job."

"You dead right, baby," Chocolate told her as he grabbed her by the waist and pulled onto his lap. Then to his company, Mario said, "Ever since we moved out the hood she been acting like my mamma. I barely got her to take the plastic off the couches!"

"Boy, you betta stop!" she exclaimed. She playfully punched her man on the chest before getting up and leaving the room.

Suge took his pager off his hip for the fourth time in thirty minutes. No messages. He was getting antsy and it was beginning to show all over his face.

"What's up, Suge?" Mario asked. "What's on the agenda for today?"

Suge looked up and shook his head, clearly annoyed. "Waiting to hear from them mothafuckaz at Ruthless. I got everything lined up. D.O.C., Dre, Michel'le... they all ready to come home. But we can't do shit without their contracts."

Heron took a drink from his glass then commented, "You know blood ain't gonna call, right? Eazy thinks he can't be touched."

"On Ru's," China agreed.

"You're right," Suge said.

"Then what's the holdup?" China asked. "Why you treating this with kid gloves?"

"What you mean? I just pushed up on blood at his own studio! In front of his so-called riders!"

"He ain't sayin' you didn't press blood," Heron interjected.

After looking at Heron, Suge addressed China. "Then what're you saying, P-Funk?"

China Dogg sat his glass down on the coffee table then leaned in and said, "Remember when B-Rock stole your pit bull in eighth grade? How we handle that?"

Heron answered for Suge. "We went to his house, hopped the fence and stole it back."

"Okay," Suge replied, not sure where they were going with the conversation.

China then continued, "What did we do when your sister's boyfriend stole Heron's watch?"

"Me, you and Pineapple went to that bitch-ass nigga's house and took it back!" Suge said.

"We went to his house, jumped him and took the homey's shit back! So if we ran up on niggaz over a fake watch and a mutt —"

"Sheba wasn't a mutt," Suge said.

Heron cut his eyes at Suge. "Sheba wasn't full-blooded."

Everyone started laughing except for Suge. He loved that dog. But her pedigree had always been disputed by his friends.

"Onda set Sheba was a pit. But, fuck all'at! I see where you going wit this."

"Do you?" China asked.

"Yeah," Suge replied. He understood their language. How couldn't he? They were his day ones. They shared experiences that pre-dated puberty. They were basically asking him why he wasn't treating his current situation like any other situation where someone had taken something that was theirs. Why were they sitting in Chocolate's brand-new house in the suburbs when they should've been in the trenches aggressively attacking the obstacle at hand?

Suge nodded his head more to himself than to his friends. A light switch had been turned on in his head. He looked at his dogs and said, "Y'all ready to mob?"

"On Ru's! Let's go!" they replied.

"Let's go!"

$$$$$

Jerry Heller loved the ocean. Something about the steady flow of its waves always seemed to calm his senses. An ocean backdrop cleared his mind, especially when he was in a jam.

From the deck on his thirty-foot yacht, he stared off into the expanse of the Pacific Ocean. He was on top of the world. Below deck there was a cabin filled with several duffle bags full of cash. Tons of it!

He wasn't alone on this journey. The boat was carrying a group of naked groupies, all starstruck by Eazy-E's presence. Eric saw Heller looking up at him and called out from his seat in the yacht's jacuzzi, "Jerry! C'mon, man! Come up here and get in! The water's warm and full of bitches!"

Jerry grinned. Eazy's crassness would always amazed him. Besides, Eric knew he didn't like girls. "I'm okay, Eric. Just enjoying the breeze." He then turned around and reached for the deep-sea fishing pole resting next to the railing. "This is the life," he whispered to himself as he casted his line out into the water.

The skies were blue. There wasn't a cloud in sight. His goal was to lure in something big enough to mount on his wall at home.

Then, out of nowhere, just as the hook hit the water, he heard a loud crashing sound behind him. The sound was clear, yet distant.

Assuming it must've been Eric and his groupies, Heller continued watching the waters, waiting for a tug on his line from something extra bulky. Meanwhile, the ruckus behind him got louder. There was an argument somewhere in the background. It sounded serious, so he turned around to see what was going on when suddenly a loud clap of thunder snapped his attention right back to the ocean.

The once clear blue skies had turned dark. Almost ominous. The waves had instantly turned hostile. A storm had came from nowhere.

"Mr. Heller! Mr. Heller!" a woman's voice yelled over the storm. He grabbed a handful of railing in an attempt to steady himself. The woman's voice became more insistent. Then a loud crashing sound brought him to his senses. Jerry woke up from his slumber to find himself in his office. At his desk at Ruthless Records recording studio.

"Mr. Heller!" his receptionist called out. "I told them they couldn't come in!"

"Shut up, bitch!" a tall muscle-bound Black man barked. "Get somewhere before you get yourself knocked out!"

Heller's secretary scurried out the office into the hallway. Leaving Heller alone with Suge and his thugs.

"What do you think you're doing?!" Heller bellowed, still believing he had some sort of authority over what took place in his office.

SMACK!

Heron slapped the taste out of his mouth. Heller was knocked straight back into his seat. "Sit yo' bitch-ass down, honky!"

Suge stepped in between Heller and his homeboy. He then calmly took a .38 revolver from his waistband and placed it on the desk. With a set of Grim Reaper eyes he stared straight into the old man's face and said, "Where you been, Heller? I've been calling the front desk every day for three weeks. I spoke with Eric. Told him I was managing a few artists who are on your label. I've been asking for copies of their contracts, but you guys haven't been replying to my messages. I've been trying to handle this business diplomatically. As civilized as possible. It doesn't seem to be getting through to you, though. So, now I've taken it upon myself to come down here to handle this once and for all."

I g-got your messages," Heller stuttered. "There's a problem —"

"Don't tell me there's a problem, Heller!" Suge said. Then he turned to China who was standing next to Heron. "You hear this mothafucka? He remind you of someone?"

"Yeah. He sounds just like Vanilla Ice."

Suge was well aware of the rumors floating around the industry about how the agreement with Vanilla Ice came about. It was as good a time as ever to cash in on that notoriety. Then, just as he was about to re-address Heller, Silk called him from across the room.

"Suge!" Silk said, while holding several folders in his hands.

"What's up?"

"I got 'em."

"The contracts?"

"All of 'em!"

Suge looked at Heller and scoffed with disdain. "I ain't even mad at you for lyin'. That's what you do for a livin'." He then picked up his gun and told the others, "Let's go. We got what we came for."

Heller watched them leave without saying a word. He was speechless.

He was used to dealing with thugs from his days dealing with the Jewish Mafia on the East Coast. Yet, in all that time he had never had a firearm pulled out on him.

His receptionist came running back into his office soon after Suge and company left. "Are you okay? Did they hurt you? The police are on their way."

At first he didn't say anything. The cops weren't gonna be able to do anything about what had just happened. He was in Los Angeles. It was gangland. There was no doubt in his mind what would happen if he involved the law.

"Call them back. Tell them it was a mistake."

"But, Mr. –"

"Call them back and tell them not to come! Nothing happened! Do what I'm telling you to do. Then get me Eric on the line! Tell him to meet me at my fucking house!"

CHAPTER FORTY-NINE

Heron kept glancing to his right, watching Suge leaf through the folders they took from Heller's office. China and Silk were in the back seat of his Cadillac doing the same thing. It was an easy lick. Almost too easy.

Then, just as they stopped at a light ten minutes away from their previous location, Suge announced, "This is it! On Piiiru! This is it! I gotta get this to Virgil ASAP! We got 'em!"

That lightened the mood in the 'Lac tenfold.

"So, what exactly are you looking for in 'em?" Heron asked as the light turned green.

Suge didn't look up from his reading. "First, I'm tryna figure out what kinda deal my artists made with Eazy and Heller. There's too much money involved for Tracy and Dre and them to be getting their full share. I'm looking for that. Just to prove to them they've been getting fucked. This way, no one has second thoughts 'bout jumpin' ship."

"He's also looking for who owns the publishing rights to the music they made," Mario added.

"Exactly," Suge agreed. "It'll help if Dre owns the songs he produced. If so, I might be able to cash in on some of the music NWA put out."

"Just like you did with 'Ice Ice Baby,'" China said.

"Onda set," Suge continued. "And, most important of all, I need to know if any of them signed anything that says they can't do music. Some deals include shit like the artist has to drop a certain amount of albums with their Iabel before they can do music on their own, or with someone else."

"Damn!" Heron said. "What if they signed some shit like that?"

"If they did, I got Virgil for all'at. As far as this music industry shit goes, they're the top of the food chain. Virgil's the type of lawyer that's seen it all. He'll find a loophole. I'll bang dat, too!"

Hearing that got the crew even more excited. Even China Dogg, who was the most reserved out the bunch leaned forward and said, "So, you tellin' us what you got in your hands right now can possibly be worth a mill-ticket?"

Suge stopped reading. He looked at his partna with a straight face and said, "Onda Mob."

Suddenly, the sound of someone's pager caught all of their attention.

They all checked theirs, but it ended up being Suge's. There was a 911 behind the number.

"Pull over at that gas station up there," Suge said. "I gotta see who this is."

Heron pulled into the Chevron station and parked in front of the pay phone. Suge immediately hoped out to make the call then realized he didn't have any change on him. Silk had been watching his every move. As soon as Suge turned around to ask one of them for a quarter, he was already reaching his hand out the window with some change.

Suge didn't recognize the number. But it didn't take him long to realize where he called once the person on the other end answered.

The news he received was crushing.

"Damn! Damn!" Suge yelled as he slammed the receiver in its cradle. "Fuck!" He got back in the 'Lac and told Heron, "Take us to the fuckin' hospital..."

CHAPTER FIFTY

The smoke from T-Loc's barbeque pit was floating into the cloudless sky filling the air with a soulful aroma. G-Boy was at the domino table a few yards away watching his nieces and nephews run around. A chess board was set up in front of him with a game already in play.

It had been a minute since G-Boy had made it to his aunt's house in Kelly Park. The streets had been a nonstop tumble of drama so he hadn't had the chance to get away from the set. But when T-Loc called him and told him they needed to talk, G-Boy made his way over there ASAP.

T-Loc came back to the table and sat down across from G-Boy. They were both nursing their own bottles of Corona. A blunt was also seated comfortably in the ashtray on the side of their chess board.

"The ribs smell good, unc'," G-Boy said before taking a drink of his beer.

"It's the sauce. I keep dousing the meat in it every time I flip 'em. But none of it's gonna have anything on ya aunties potato salad."

"I already know."

T-Loc stared at the board. They had been playing for only twenty or thirty minutes but both sides had already pulled out and set up their offensive pieces. T-Loc moved his king's bishop into play. Then he looked at G-Boy and asked, "How you holdin' up?"

"I don't know. I mean, I'm good but this shit hurts, unc. Baby G's death hit me harder than with the other homies I've lost. Shiiit, when I was locked up we lost a few thugs. I shed some tears but this is different. Real different."

"Onda set. I feel you. And, as far as that pain goes, it gets even harder when you lose a family member. I remember I was doin' a bid at Chino when my mamma died. That shit ripped my heart out, cuz. That shit changed me. Onda set. That's why I spend so much time with these kids. You never know when ya time is up, neph'."

G-Boy slid one of his knights in position to cover the pawn T-Loc's recent move had threatened.

T-Loc continued; "It don't help that you dealin' with them Park Village niggaz on top of all the other shit that's going on in your set." T-Loc didn't look up. He spoke as he studied the board. "I always trip off how niggaz in power be hiding behind niggaz with power. How shit gets started and homies are told it's 'cause one reason when it's really a whole nother reason."

G-Boy was staring at T-Loc as he talked. T-Loc always laced him up with real game but his style of teaching was vague at times. One time when G-Boy was still locked up he asked T-Loc why he spoke in riddles and T-Loc chuckled. He went on to tell him that his messages weren't sent in riddle form.

T-Loc went on to explain that he spoke in ways that made the listener listen closely in order for them to come to their own conclusions. As G-Boy sat there playing chess with him he knew it was one of those times when he was expected to listen and decipher."

"Whattchu mean, unc?"

"Well, the way I see it is money is power. But a person with an army of loyal followers is just as powerful as the man with money. Let's say you got the army. But there's someone in your set with more money than you. We both know this lifestyle we live revolves around a constant fight for power." T-Loc pushed a pawn forward. "You catchin' what I'm droppin'?"

"Yeah."

"So let's say you got the army and there's someone with more money than you that wants your power. Especially since you are, or can be a formidable threat. He's gonna have to use his head to knock you out your position. And, it won't be easy if your strength lies in loyal soldiers. He's gonna have to use strategy since brute force won't work. One tactic that could be used to make you weaker would be to misdirect your attention. Keep you at war with an outside entity. Meanwhile, makin' sure you can't get your money up. Everybody knows wars cost money."

G-Boy countered T-Loc's move with a bishop. "Onda set," he commented afterwards.

"The whole time you at war with this other entity, the threat at home becomes bigger. Bigger, 'cause his money getting longer while your soldiers are getting killed or locked up. Niggaz like that are chess players. Most people don't even know moves like that are takin' place until it's too late. But the thinkers, strategic warlords recognize shit like that. So they move accordingly. That's why you hear about so many backdoor moves that take place in strong sets. That's how nigga's big homies get killed and mothafuckaz don't be knowin' who did it."

"There's never a murder where no one knows who did it," G-Boy said. Repeating the bottom line of a previous lesson he received from T-Loc.

"Onda dead homies," T-Loc agreed. Then he positioned his other bishop on the board. "So, anyways, I got a proposition for you."

G-Boy stopped looking at the board and zeroed in on T-Loc. "What's brackin'?"

T-Loc leaned in over the chess board, at the same time lowering his voice. "What I'm 'bout to say is classified. Even if you decide not to fuck wit' it, I need you to keep it under wraps."

"Understood."

"The homey that came to me wit' this has fifty G's and a crate full of AK's for whoever takes the contract. The only catch is this shit has to happen ASAP!"

"Who y'all need downed?"

"Someone you know. Someone who if you take out will make room for you to hit boss level. If you take this contract, your set will never be the same. At the same time, you'll go down in history. And you'll be securing your spot at the top of your set for years to come."

G-Boy didn't say anything. Everything that T-Loc had said that afternoon was now coming into perspective.

"This is how bosses are made. It's a big decision. And it has to be made now because it needs to be executed immediately. So, is you wit' it or not? I gotta get an answer before you get any more details..."

CHAPTER FIFTY-ONE

Crowded hospital rooms weren't new to Suge Knight. He'd been in them many, many times. Not only was the one he found himself in when he went to see D.O.C. packed, but there would be a lot more scenes like that one that would take place throughout his life.

When he first got there, D.O.C.'s female cousin was there with his mother. They had flown in from Texas. He was coherent, but he couldn't speak. His face was mangled. And his neck was bandaged up.

"What happened?" was a question that kept coming up.

Since D.O.C. couldn't speak, Suge ended up getting a pen and some paper from one of the nurses. "Tracy just scribble somethin', nigga! Was you drinking and driving? You get hit by a truck or somethin'? What happened?"

Even though D.O.C.'s hands were bandaged, he was still able to grip a pen. With an unsteady hand he wrote the following note:

I WAS CHASED! EAZY SENT SOME NIGGAZ AT ME! I RECOGNIZED ONE OF THEM. THEY WAS FROM HIS HOOD!

Suge stared at that note for a long time. All the blood in his body seemed to rush to his head all at once.

"What does it say?" someone asked in the background.

Suge didn't reply. Instead, he handed the note to Heron. Then he walked up to D.O.C.'s mother and said, "Tracy's gonna be alright. I'm sorry this happened. I give you my word, the people who did this won't live to do it to anyone else."

Suge's niggaz knew what that speech meant. The note didn't have to circulate for them to know a target was acquired.

"C'mon," Suge told his homies. After everyone gave D.O.C. dap, they all left.

Once they got in the elevator, Heron told Suge, "We got this. It's on you. Tracy ain't from the set, so it's on you."

Then China Dogg added, "Yeah, Ru. We can put a green light on Kelly Park, or –"

Heron cut in, "We can kill Eazy's bitch-ass!"

They all looked at Suge. His mind had never stopped moving. Never stopped calculating moves. He had been through that type of warfare so many times he could actually anticipate the gangland inquiries way before they were presented to him.

"Eazy made this call," Suge started. "He was hot when we went to the studio. He kept looking at Tracy like he had given us some secret information, or something. Crab-ass nigga made the call. But I can't kill 'im yet. We got big moves in the making. We're talkin' 'bout millions. If the nigga disappears, we'll be stuck in the courts for years."

"Just like when we was dealing with Rob," Chocolate cut in.

Suge nodded, "Funkin' with Kelly Park ain't gonna do nothin' but create a bunch of back and forth that'll make the set hot. And it won't affect blood's movements."

The elevator stopped on the ground floor. All four men got in. They didn't say another word until they got back into Heron's whip.

As soon as they were all in the sedan, Silk broke the silence, "So, we going after Eazy's inner circle?"

"Yeah," Suge replied. "I'm in the process of takin' his whole label from him. Other than him and Heller, everyone else can go. We can start knockin' his niggaz down one at a time. Once he starts seeing his closest comrades dying, he'll start fumbling. In the end, he'll wish he never got in the rap game.

"On Ru's!"

"Onda Mob!"

CHAPTER FIFTY-TWO

"I had no choice! The son-of-a-bitch came barging in with his goons. He pulled a gun on me! Look at my face, Eric!" Heller yelled.

Eazy had rushed to his place as soon as he got word Suge had stolen the contracts. Heller didn't want to meet at the studio.

He was spooked.

"I'm not goin' for this shit! If that slob-ass nigga think he's gonna do me like he did Vanilla Ice, he's got the game fucked!"

Heller was frantically going through his Rolodex looking for the number to a security firm he had used years earlier. "We're gonna have armed guards everywhere we go from now on!"

"Armed what?! Look, Jerry. I got somethin' better. I'm gonna have Suge killed. It's as simple as–"

"What?!" Heller exclaimed, hoping he didn't hear him correctly. "Killed? Do you hear yourself? You're a platinum-selling artist! You can't go around killing people!"

Eazy looked at him like he was a crazed lunatic. "Jerry, I've been tellin' you from the beginning that I'm not a studio gangsta. I'm a mothafuckin' Crip! I'm a Kelly Park Mothafuckin' Compton Crip before all this rap shit! I'm gonna be a Compton loc way after all this rap shit! That nigga Suge is in the streets too! He's not playin' by the rules you live by. He's tryna take everything I have and he's gonna use any tactic he knows. The niggaz he runs wit' are killers! Serial killers! The type of killers mainstream society don't even know about. 'Cause if they did, half the country would be up in arms."

"I hear you. But I'm hiring security –"

"You must not hear me if you think security guards are gonna stop these niggaz." Eazy let out a nervous laugh. "You just don't understand, Jerry. In the streets, it's only the strong who survive.

It's the law of the land. We're at war! And the only way to win wars like this is to take the head off the snake."

"You just can't do it, Eric!" Heller stopped fingering his Rolodex. He went to his bar, poured to glasses of liquor and handed one to Eazy.

"I don't want this shit," Eazy snapped angrily.

"Drink! Listen to me! Eric, you are a mega-superstar! You aren't a petty act performing in hole-in-the-wall clubs anymore. You are years ahead of guys like Knight! We're already established. Even if he manages to talk Dre and Tracy into leaving, we'll have them all blackballed! The industry isn't listening for D.O.C.. They don't care about who 'Doctor Dre' is," Heller said while making quotation marks with his fingers. "They want Eazy-E! They want *you*! If you lose your career over this two-bit thug, you'll be the dumbest person in history!"

Eazy leaned against Heller's kitchen counter. He still had his glass in his hand. Heller might as well have been talking to a brick wall. He knew how to handle Suge. He already took care of D.O.C.'s bitch-ass. Next, was Suge's turn.

He watched Heller calm down and go back to his phone to call his private security people. Heller was terrified. Suge had him shaking, which wasn't surprising. The niggaz Suge was pushing with had the ability to spook seasoned gang bangers with decades of prison time under their belts. He could only imagine the fear they actually instilled in Jerry.

"Alright, man," Eazy told Heller. "I hear what you're sayin'. You're right. I'm gonna let you handle this your way. I got way too much to lose. You're dead right!"

Heller knew Eazy well enough to detect a lie when he said one. But, that whole situation had him discombobulated. He was so intent on securing a security detail that he totally missed Eric's deception.

"A'ight, man. I'm gonna head out. Call me if anything comes up, Jerry."

"Okay, Eric."

As soon as Eazy got into his Impala, he sat his .44 Magnum on his lap. Then he took out his brick-sized cell phone and called one of his closest loc's. "Meet me at my house, cuz. We gotta take care of some shit..."

CHAPTER FIFTY-THREE

Virgil Roberts was leaning against the front of his desk talking to Suge and Co-Co when his office phone rang. When he answered it, his receptionist told him it was Dre and he told her to send him up. Then he told Suge, "He's here."

"Good," Suge replied. "You gonna need to explain all this shit –"

The door opened and Dre came in. He looked around the room and saw all smiles. They were real, yet strained. After giving and receiving some daps, he took a seat along with everyone else.

Suge started, "Virgil was explaining some shit he found in your contract. But I told 'im to wait for you." Suge scoffed then continued, "You gotta hear this."

Virgil took his cue and said, "Okay. So, Andre, after reading these contracts I came up with a plan that can be utilized to free you and the others from it. But, man... I can't believe the terms I've been reading. To call them draconian would be a major understatement. I've never seen anything like it."

"You hear 'im?" Suge asked Dre.

Dre didn't reply. After repositioning himself in his seat he nodded towards Virgil to continue.

"According to these contracts," Virgil continued, "Heller's been skimming off the front as well as the back end. I know there's been assumptions about theft. I'd have to see the accounting statements to verify something like that. But I don't think he would steal from you guys. He doesn't have to. He's been raping you legally since the inception of Ruthless Records."

"Whatchu mean?" Dre asked.

"Let me show you," Virgil told him. He then gave him a copy of the contract before handing another one to Suge. "The lines I want you to look at are highlighted. Go to line 4 in paragraph 32. It plainly states Heller gets ten percent of all Ruthless Records gross revenue earnings. That means his ten comes off the top. Before taxes. Even before any of it gets dispersed to the artists. Next, I want you to find the highlighted section in paragraph 54." Virgil gave them a few moments to find the part he sent them to look at. "This section gives him another ten percent off of all the artist's earnings for his managing fees. Keep in mind, ten percent altogether is the going rate. Secondly, he's making a killing off the revenue he's making off the top. And, we're talking about big names. NWA, JJ Fad, D.O.C. and you, Dre."

"That honky's cold, ain't he," Suge commented.

"Onda Mob," Co-Co agreed.

Dre was shaking his head. He couldn't believe Heller and Eazy's audacity. *Yeah*, he thought to himself. *Eazy knew about this shit too! That's crazy.* Out loud he asked, "What we 'posed to do?"

"There's always a loophole," Virgil replied. "I found a way to get you a publishing deal with another label. Dick is already talking to some people at Sony.

See, I don't think Heller realized how gifted you or Tracy were when he had these contracts made.

"These stipulations say you only have one song agreement. It means you didn't agree to a term deal. A term contract would've had you locked in with them for a period of time. Like five to ten years. You're not signed to anything like that. Which is good. The bad news is your contract, Dre, has you locked in for four more albums. Which means –"

"I gotta produce four more albums before I can go," Dre said.

"Yes. But something else I found is what's not in the contract: There's nothing in here that prohibits you from starting another company. This means, legally you can start your own record label if you choose to."

Suge and Dre exchanged a look. It was their greenlight to proceed with what they talked about. The opening they both needed. What Suge was planning on the whole time.

"You talk to everyone else 'bout this?" Dre asked Suge.

"You're the first one to hear this part. No one else knows about the contractual issues. They're all with us without this. Mothafuckas know Heller and Eazy been snakes."

"Suge," Virgil said, "The biggest issue I see is the four-album contract clause. Dre's not the only artist with those stipulations in their paperwork. Dre and D.O.C. can venture off to create a record label. But other acts like Michel'le and J.J. Fad have to finish their agreements. If they don't, they won't be able to put out their own music."

Dre couldn't take it anymore. His anger was boiling over. Suge watched him closely. He saw Dre's jaw muscles clenching. A sign that meant he was getting angrier by the moment. Suge nodded, hoping everything he was hearing was adding fuel to Dre's discontent. Dre stood up and walked to the office's window overlooking the city. He blocked out what the others were saying as he thought about everything he had just heard. Him and Eazy started out with the understanding they would be fifty-fifty on Ruthless. The simple truth of the matter was that he was only an employee.

He was mad. Mad enough to kill.

In the background, Virgil told Suge, "You're gonna have to get the artists out of their contracts. Or, you can start the company with all new acts. The problem with it is the litigation can take years. Everything is under Eric Wright. It's almost as if him and Heller planned it all. Anyways, you'll have to persuade Mr. Wright to let them out of their contracts."

Dre kept staring out at the skyline when he said, "E ain't 'bout to let anyone go. The nigga got a bounty on Cube's head. Look at what just happened to D.O.C. That nigga's a bitch!"

Suge didn't like Dre's tone. The scent of defeat was on his breath, and that was unacceptable. He got up from his seat and went up to Dre. "Leave the technical shit to me, Dre. You wit' me now. All of y'all are –"

"Onda Mob!" Co-Co agreed from her seat across the room.

"On my dead ones, I got this," Suge assured him. "I'ma make that little nigga see things my way.

Watch!" Then he turned towards Virgil, "Draw up the contract he needs to sign to release my niggaz! I got this!"

"I figured you'd say something like that," Virgil smiled. He took some papers from his desk and held them out for Suge to grab. "Here you go. All you need is three signatures. Eric Wright's and two witnesses."

Dre turned away from the window and saw the contracts being handed to Suge. Suge Knight really was who he said he was. He had a team of professionals working every angle. Dre was really starting to see things from a whole different point of view. Suge was dead serious about pushing his line. Even if it included taking things to the streets.

Suge took the contracts then looked at Dre, "Onda set, I gotchu!"

CHAPTER FIFTY-FOUR

There's a common feeling every gang banger experiences when crossing back into their territory after being gone all day. It's calming. It's a feeling one gets when they feel safe. That's exactly how Suge and Co-Co felt when they got back to Lueders Park after leaving the meeting they had with Virgil and Dre.

Co-Co was in the passenger seat of Suge's K5 humming a melody to herself, while Suge, who was lost in his own thoughts, navigated his 4x4 into and through the trenches.

Suge had a million-dollar dream fueling his million-dollar schemes.

Getting the contracts to Virgil was a feat within itself. Which led to the next phase of the plan. Now he had to get Eazy to sign the release forms. He knew it wasn't gonna be easy, though.

Eazy-E wasn't about to give up his acts without a fight. And, who could blame him? Dre was the hottest producer in the game.

D.O.C. was the rawest writer. On top of that, the truth was out. Heller was robbing the whole label. Suge halfway expected the other half of Ruthless Records to come to him too. It wouldn't have surprised him at all if they did.

The sun was bright that afternoon. Their futures shun just as bright, matching its energy. When Suge first entered Lueders Park territory, he was hit with a smooth level of calmness. The set was quiet. No one seemed to be outside which was out of the norm, but it didn't register at the time.

When the K5 turned onto Bullis, the calmness was suddenly shattered.

On the frontside of the apartments where the Mob hung out, the street was crowded with people. None of them civilians.

Co-Co shot up in her seat. Quickly scanning the block, she said, "You see all'at, Suge?"

"Yeah."

"Something went down. I hope none of the homies got shot. I'm not in the mood for this type of shit!"

Co-Co took her .45 out of her waistband and sat it on her lap. As soon as Suge pulled up to the curb where the main crowd was standing, he reached under his seat and brought back a seventeen-shot Berretta.

"Suge! Suge! Co-Co, blood, com'ere!" a chorus of people called out.

The duo hadn't even made it to the sidewalk before they were bombarded by their homies. Everyone started talking all at once. They were all so frantic, neither Suge nor Co-Co could fully decipher what was being said.

Suge bellowed, "Hold up! On Piru, I can't understand all of y'all when you talkin' at the same time!"

That's when Heron came out the crowd and addressed Suge. "What's brackin, blood?"

296

"I just got back from hollerin' at Dre and the lawyer. I gotta talk to you 'bout all'at. But fuck all'at! What's going on?"

"I just got here 'bout twenty minutes ago. The homies said G-Boy came over here with some Y.G.'s from the other side of the set, and them niggaz got to set-trippin'!"

"What!?"

"Yeah! Blood came over here with a couple carloads. Tiny B-Rock and Lil J.R. squabbled up with two of his lil homies."

"G-Boy?! *Our* G-Boy?!" Suge asked. He couldn't believe his ears. It had to be true because the set was up in arms. But it didn't make sense.

That's when Tiny B-Rock, a big light-skinned teen walked up to them. Suge immediately noticed his busted lip and ripped tank top.

"You good?" Suge asked him.

"I'm good, big homey! I squabbled up wit' that bitch-ass nigga Brazy."

"The homey just told me what happened," Suge replied. "But I wanna hear it from you. Where J.R. at?"

"I'm right here, Mob!" a much shorter, stalkier Y.G. replied. "Fuck dem niggaz, blood! On Ru's!"

While that conversation was taking place, a group of homegirls pulled Co-Co to the side and started telling her what happened while she was gone.

As Suge listened to his young niggaz explain how G-Boy came with several carloads of his homies, he began to understand what was happening. A civil war had officially started.

He knew something like that would eventually happen. No matter how much he tried to keep things kosher, the outcome was inevitable. From the outside looking in, it looked like Suge and his inner circle had just hit for millions. With whispers of that type of loot circulating, it was only a matter of time before somebody tripped.

"G-Boy, P-Dog, CK Brazy, L.B. and all they homies pulled up talkin' 'bout Da Mob ain't Lueders no more! On Bompton, they said we been bringing funk to the hood. They said we expect them to fight our battles while we the only ones 'round here eating!" B-Rock explained.

Suge looked at Heron and said, "Ain't no way G-Boy sanctioned this."

"He did, blood," Heron replied. "Don't you hear 'em? G-Boy was wit' dem niggaz who pulled up!"

"Did you call 'im yet?"

"I paged him right before I came out here to holla at you."

"C'mon, blood," Suge said. "Let's go by blood's house."

BLOCKA! BLOCKA! BLOCKA!

Suddenly, an older-model Buick slid onto their block with two shooters hanging out the windows busting!

BLADADAH! BLADADAH! BLADADAH!

Suge instinctively pulled out and started squeezing in the direction of their attackers.

BLOCKA! BLOCKA! BLOCKA!

Suge and his thugs took cover behind several parked cars. At least nine of them were strapped. And every single one of them returned fire. The brazen daylight drill had turned into a full-on shootout!

For a quick moment it seemed as if Da Mob had the upper hand on their attackers. That was until a black Chevy truck slid to a halt behind the Buick with a whole other set of shooters. The second group all had burgundy bandanas wrapped around their faces.

Two of the shooters from the Chevy pick-up hopped out the back and started sprinting towards Suge. The fact that he was bustin' back did nothing to stop them. They obviously had a specific target and were on their way to tag him.

He saw them heading straight towards him. He had a clear shot on the closest man, who was about twenty yards away. Suge knew who it was despite the burgundy bandana on his face. It was a homie he actually went to school with. But none of that mattered. Suge aimed at his chest and pulled the trigger.

Nothing!

He squeezed again, demanding the gun to go off. Bullets whizzed dangerously close to his head as he fought with his jammed Berretta.

His homies were firing at their attackers as well. But Suge knew how chaotic a battlefield could be. There was a chance he was the only one who noticed his two would-be assassins closing in on him. He started backpaddling, looking for more cover when, suddenly, he lost his footing.

"Fuuuck!" Suge yelled when he slipped and fell. The end was coming for sure, he thought to himself. "Fuck!"

BLOCKA! BLOCKA! BLOCKA! BLOCKA!

BLADADAH! BLADADAH! BLADADAH! BLA-DADAH!

The firefight continued. Loud and violent bullets with no names whizzed past people, riddling the cars and walls they landed in. Windows shattered. Flesh ripped open! The air was filled with the scent of gun powder.

Then, all of sudden the shots became even more insistent! *More guns?! More shooters?!* Suge thought in a panic. Everything was getting louder. The scent of gunpowder became thicker.

"Bitch-ass niggaz!" a female Piru yelled. "Dis Da Mob, bitch! Fuck all you niggaz!"

The first of the two gunners heading for Suge fell. The other one stumbled. Co-Co and two other homegirls ran towards them with their guns blazing! They created a protective scrimmage line between Suge and their opps.

The tide was turned. The drill team began to pull back. Within seconds, the sound of tires burning rubber filled the void of gunfire.

"Suge! Suge!" Co-Co yelled. "You good?"

Heron ran up to them, "Blood! You bool?!"

Suge was hot! The adrenaline coursing through his veins made him feel like he was floating. "On Da Mob, all them niggaz is dead!"

Sirens sounded in the distance. Someone yelled out, "Five-O on they way!"

"Co-Co, bring them niggaz!" a homegirl called out.

They were ushered into a nearby apartment where all the curtains were shot. In Compton, it didn't matter who the aggressor was. To the Law, if you had melanin in your skin, you were guilty before proven innocent.

No one wanted to be around when the law dogs showed up with their own guns drawn.

Inside the apartment Suge and Heron were taken into, everyone was still pumped from the overdose of adrenaline they had experienced. Suge was livid! He picked up the house phone and called the first number that came to mind. It was answered on the second ring.

"China!"

"Blood, you a'ight? On Piru, I heard the shots! I'm on my way!"

"Naw!" Suge replied. "Police everywhere, Ru! Just tap in with the fellas. Tell everyone to meet up at the Beehive in the morning.

"Blood —"

"It was G-Boy, blood! He turned against us!"

The line went silent. China Dogg had to process the information he was slapped with. "On Piru, I'ma rally the troops. Damn, blood.

Suge didn't wanna believe it either. "I know, blood. We'll talk about it tomorrow."

"Bet."

CHAPTER FIFTY-FIVE

"Dayummm! Dayummm! Dayummm, Eazy! I feel that mothafucka in my stomach!"

"Stop playin'! Slide all the way down on it!"

Eazy had his hands on the sexy sistah's hips. Pulling her as low as she'd let him, every time she dropped down on his pole. She was taking a lot of it already. More than some. But, still, she wouldn't sit all the way down onto his humungus member.

"Give me dat dick, Eazy!"

"I'm tryin' to!" he said as he squeezed and pulled her hips as far as she let him pull her.

"Ahhh! Dayum! It's so fucking fat! I got it! I got it, tho'!" she exclaimed while dropping and lifting her body faster and faster. She finally caught her rhythm. Up and down she moved. She steadied her hands on Eazy's backboard. It was sturdy so it easily withheld the pressure she was bringing after she opened up enough to use Eazy's dick like a pogo stick.

"Yes! Yeah! Uh-huh!" she yelled.

"Don't stop, bitch! I'm 'bout to cum! I'm 'bout to —"

RING! RING! RING!

Eazy immediately stopped fucking her when he heard the phone ringing. "Holdup!" he told her. "I gotta get that." She couldn't stop. The short haired red-bone was at the precipice of ecstasy. She was at the doorstep of one of the most intense orgasms of her entire life. Then, just as she was about to explode, Eazy pushed her all the way off him, knocking her onto the bed next to where he was just lying.

"What da fuck, nigga! Whatchu do that for?"

Eazy snatched the receiver off its cradle on the nightstand and spoke into it. "What's crackin', cuz?"

"E," a raspy voice on the other end said.

"Is it good?" Eazy asked while focusing his stare on the portrait of Tony Montana that was on his wall across from the bed.

The girl he was just fucking was in her own world. Rigorously rubbing her clit in hopes of catching the tale-end of the orgasm she had missed.

"It went bad."

Eazy was in disbelief. He slowly started shaking his head from side to side. "Them slob-ass niggaz acted like they had it in the bag!"

"Shiiit, two of G-Boy's Y.G.'s got shot. They pulled up and hopped out. But I guess that nigga's homies started bustin' back."

"What did they expect? Suge got hyenas 'round him every fuckin' day. All day!" He was so angry the room started spinning. The venom in his voice was apparent when he finally said, "Fuck, cuz!" before letting the phone drop.

Somehow his gaze ended up landing on the girl lying next to him. The sexual vibe they were riding moments earlier was long gone. His mind was nowhere near the plush bedroom they were both in at that moment. His stare was deep. As if he were looking through her instead of at her. If the situation would have been different, he would've completed the task at hand. But after receiving the worst news he could possibly get he just sat there fuming.

"This is some real bullshit, cuz!" he said to himself.

"E... Eazy," the person on the phone called out.

Instead of putting it to his ear, Eazy snatched the phone up and beamed that bitch against the far wall. "Fuuuck! I should've just downed that bitch-ass nigga my-mothafuckin'-self!"

"What's going on?" the girl asked meekly.

"What?!" Eazy snapped. "Bitch, get out!" Before she had the chance to even download his demand, Eazy literally kicked her off his bed.

"Damn, nigga!" she said as she quickly stood up from the carpeted floor. "What's wrong wit' you!?"

"Shut up, bitch! Get up outta here before I have one of the homegirls whoop yo' soft ass!"

She snatched up her discarded clothing and left the room, slamming the door on her way "...Punk-ass nigga..." was the last thing he heard before she stomped down the staircase.

Eazy sat there steaming. His thoughts were whirling through his head. *This nigga gotta die! Bitch-ass nigga think he can take mines? He got the game fucked up! On Kelly, cuz gotta die!*

He found his boxers on the floor next to his pants. After putting them on, he went downstairs to the kitchen where his other house phone was. The number he dialed was memorized...

Ren answered it on the second ring; "What up, cuz? They put the dog down?"

Eazy didn't reply immediately. He still couldn't get it in his head that Suge wasn't dead. As far as the streets were concerned, the kill squad he activated was seasoned. Young, but experienced, he was told. But that was all bullshit. Finally, after a moment of awkward silence, he said, "Naw, cuz. Onda set, it went bad."

"That's fucked up," Ren stated. His mind was already beginning to come up with their next move. "I'm gonna tap in with Cuzzy Blue and dem. Don't even trip, loc. This ain't nothin' but a minor setback for a major comeback. Cuz got an X on his back. You can bet dat!"

"Nuff said."

"Be safe."

"Always."

Eazy leaned against the counter and crossed his arms. He fought to catch his thoughts as they raced back and forth. Then all of a sudden he thought of Jerry. He grabbed the phone again and qucikly dialed the number to Heller's house. It was answered on the first ring. "Jerry!"

"Yeah. What's wrong? You sound stressed out."

"I'm good. I'm calling to check on you."

"Why? Did something happen? What's going on?"

"Did you ever get to hire the security guards you told me about?"

"Yeah. I hired Mike Klein. And he's more than just a security guard, Eric. He's an ex Mosad operative. All his employees are armed with semi-automatic weapons. They're professionals. Trained to kill."

"Is there a team at the house with you right now?" Eric asked, hopping Heller was protected.

"Of course not, Eric. What's going on? I know you didn't go out and do anything stupid. We talked about this –"

"I ain't got time to explain. Just call the bodyguards, man. I'm not playin'. Get 'round-the-clock security! It's about to get real ugly 'round here."

"Eric –"

"Call your people, Jerry. I'll check in with you in a little while. If they don't show up, I'll send some of my loc's over there."

Eazy hung the phone up. There was no doubt in his mind what would happen next. It wasn't supposed to be this complicated. With a ten-thousand-dollar bounty on his head and a little gangland instigating, the fat mothafucka should've been executed by now. But now, since the hit failed, there was gonna be an all-out war.

He knew the men he was dealing with weren't to be taken lightly. In Compton, bangers with reps like theirs were meant to be taken seriously. Even though they were Bloods, they were still just as dangerous as any of his homies.

Yella and Eazy's couzin Squabbles and a couple homies were in the den playing Nintendo. After telling them to strap up, he went back upstairs and got dressed. The color of the day was black. Black Dickies, black hoody, black Chucks. After tucking his Ruger in his waistband, Eazy put his Locs on and headed out.

It was officially funk season and he vowed to be the aggressor.

CHAPTER FIFTY-SIX

Ren pulled up to a decrepit-looking house in the trenches. His black-on-black BMW didn't match its surroundings. But that didn't bother him one bit. He was home. The ghetto was his true element. The only people out that late were those whose character traits were as dark as Compton's darkest shadows.

It was game time; press play and blitz time. Ren had spent thousands flooding his hood with guns over the last few years. Not because he anticipated friction. That was regular. He didn't even expect anything in return for his donations. He did it because he was gang member. He had homies he came up with who pushed like they were a part of a militia. In a world where candles and memorabilia of fallen soldiers were set out on the sidewalk where they are murdered, guns could mean the difference between life and death.

Needless to say, Ren was a factor in his set. A reputable whose voice held weight. When he handed out death sentences his orders were followed with no inquiry.

After calling a meeting with close to fifteen of his closest locs, the opening line was asked by his homey Blue-Note, "So Lueders is set trippin'?"

"Not Lueders," Ren clarified. "It's dem Mob niggaz. Suge, Buntry, Heron and China's set."

"Cuz," Zay, an OG cut in. "You know we get at any one of them niggaz you just mentioned, and it's goin' down, right? The whole city finna go up in flames over them niggaz."

"So what!" Blue-Note snapped. "They slobs anyway! Fuck dem niggaz! Onda set, fuck 'em!"

"I hear what you're sayin', big homey," Ren told the OG. "But some things can't be overlooked. We talkin' 'bout bread and butter. Them slob-ass niggaz is tryna destroy everything we built. The nigga Suga Bear playin' a dirty game. This ain't about a block. Or some regular set trippin'. Cuz comin' for the crown. If he succeeds, where does that leave us? The whole set eats off NWA money."

"He's robbin' us!" someone in the crowd said.

"Naw," another Crip commented. "He's robbin' *them!*"

Upon hearing that, Ren went from zero to a hundred real quick. "What! Robbin' me? Eazy? Man, who da fuck been puttin' on for the set like us? No one! Name another loc whose been droppin' off crates full of artillery to the homies for nothin'! Me and Eazy been droppin' off AK's in the set since we got on! If you don't see this as a hood situation, you blind as Stevie Wonder! If it ain't for NWA, who gonna put Kelly on?"

"The homey's right!" Blue-Note agreed along with several others.

Ren continued, "I hear what you sayin' about hittin' them specific niggaz, and what's gonna happen after we do. I feel you. In all actuality, all we gotta do is kill that nigga Suge. He's the head of the snake."

"Cuz do got a death wish," someone commented.

"Onda set!" Ren agreed. "He's runnin' 'round here like he can't be touched. Disrespectin' the set like we suckas! I'm just askin' for a green light before this shit gets outta hand."

Ren watched as the others looked around, gauging one another's thoughts. It wasn't as if there was anyone there who was objecting to his proposal for an all-out war. This was Compton. Every Crip set hated all Piru gangs. Nevertheless, a decision of this stature had to be well thought out based on the inevitable outcome of violence it would induce.

"Nuff said!" Blue-Note announced. "On Kelly Park Compton Crip, it's on sight with Da Mob!"

"Fuck 'em! On Crip! Fuck all dem niggaz!" the group chimed in.

That concluded their meeting. The war was on. Someone handed Ren a cigarette, and he asked, "Is this wet?"

"Yeah."

"That's wazzup!" Ren lit it and took a small puff. He knew better than to take a large hit before checking it's potency. He suddenly felt the full body glow hit him. Ren loved Sherm. He'd been smoking it since he was a teen, so he knew how to handle himself when he was on it.

Someone turned the house stereo on, which managed to lighten the mood despite the decree that had just been declared. They were now at war with Da Mob. Every Crip there was officially on active duty. Which didn't seem to bother anyone at all. On the contrary, the vibe became festive. Before they knew it, some homegirls started dancing and the gangland meeting went from handing out death sentences to a full-on house party.

A little while later, a nineteen-year-old rhyme spitter named Crip Crazy pulled Ren to the side and said, "Cuz, I need you to listen to this song I wrote. On Crip, it goes hard in the paint!"

"Go ahead. Spit that shit!" Ren told him.

That's when another one of Ren's homies, Cuzzy Dru, walked up. "What's up, cuz?" Ren replied.

"Let's get some drank," he said while handing Ren a plastic cup with Hennessy in it. "This the last of the Yac."

Ren took a sip then said, "Fuck it. Let's go."

"Uh-uh!" a pretty dark-skinned girl named Laticia said as she walked up to the guys. "You ain't leaving me this time, Ren!"

"What you talkin' 'bout, cuz?" Ren said with a smile.

"You know what the fuck I'm talkin' 'bout! We was 'posed to kick it the last time you came through –"

"And I told you I'd come back."

"And that was three months ago, nigga!"

"You's a lie!" Ren teased, knowing he could fuck if he wanted to.

Then another homegirl who had been watching the exchange play out yelled over the music – "You betta give Laticia some dick, nigaaa!"

Ren chuckled before turning back towards Laticia, "C'mon, baby. You wit' me tonight."

"You ain't gotta tell me! I'm telling you! You ain't leaving me this time, Ren."

The house had been bombarded by people once word circulated that Ren was in the set. They had to push their way through a crowd to get outside. Even the front porch was crowded. Everyone was having a good time smoking and drinking. Ren, Laticia, Crip Crazy and Cuzzy Dru all went to Ren's Beemer.

Just before hopping in, Ren tossed his keys to Laticia, "You know how to drive somethin' foreign, right?"

"Tsst!" she sucked her teeth. "I drive like I ride dick. Hard and fast!"

"Ha!" Cuzzy Dru laughed. "The homegirl finna put dat pussy on you, cuz!"

Ren got into the front passenger seat before replying, "I gotta see it to believe it, cuz. I ain't met a bitch yet who can take this dick without running."

Crip Crazy was behind Ren when he tapped him on the shoulder and handed him a tape he had recorded. "Put this in the deck, cuz! I'm tellin' you, it's raw!"

"A'ight, homey," Ren replied as he took the tape and put it in the deck.

Laticia put the key in the ignition and started the car, but didn't put it in drive. Instead, they stayed there to listen to Crip Crazy's music. Within moments, a deep bassline started thumping from the trunk. Ren liked what he heard. He started bobbing his head.

Then, just as they were about to pull off, the sound of automatic gunfire sounded over the music...

BLOCKA! BLOCKA! BLOCKA! BLOCKA! BLOCKA!

The BMW started rocking back and forth like an earthquake was shaking it. Glass shattered everywhere, stinging everyone inside. Instinct made them reach for their weapons. The Compton-bred gang bangers automatically chose to return fire, but the fireworks couldn't be ignored.

Laticia screamed!

Ren yelled out, "Get down, cuz!"

The screaming ceased.

Ren was slapped in the side of the face with a handful of brain. The slimey substance splattered everywhere. Laticia's head was gone. The gunfire never stopped coming.

BLOCKA! BLOCKA! BLOCKA! BLOCKA!

The Beemer was filled with holes before they all heard the sound of screaching tires signalling the end of the drill.

The world was spinning when someone snatched Ren's door open. "Cuz! You alright?"

He looked up with a blood-stained face and slowly replied, "Yeah. I'm good. But..." He looked at Laticia and got quiet. Her once beautiful face was no longer connected to her head. The only things left were dead tissue and shattered bone.

Crip Crazy and Cuzzy Dru both hopped out with their heaters drawn. But it was too late. The ambush was over.

For a brief moment, the trenches were silent. The evening had gone pitch black.

Then someone screamed, "They killed Laticia! They killed Laticia!"

"Who did it?!" the group inquired.

Ren didn't need a positive ID to know who was behind the massacre. "It was dem Mob niggaz! On Crip – it was China Dogg and them..."

CHAPTER FIFTY-SEVEN

Suge was unfolding one of the blankets Ms. Davis had given him to sleep on. Him and a few others who didn't live in the set had opted to sleep at her house that night. The whole area was saturated with law enforcement. K9's and Ghetto Birds were heard in the background, looking for a scapegoat to roast.

A knock sounded on the bedroom door just as Suge was about to settle in on the air mattress he was given earlier. He glanced at his pistol, it was on the floor next to his things. If he would have been anywhere else he would've grabbed it. He was safe though. A person would have had to get through three other gunners in order to get to him where he was at.

"Marion," Ms. Davis said from the hallway. "Sharitha is here. Boy, you decent?"

"Yes, ma'am," he answered.

Sharitha came in and rushed into his arms. "I was so worried! I thought you got shot! The phone was blowing up with people telling me what happened. I didn't know what went down!"

"It's good, babe. For real, I'm alright."

Ms. Davis backed away, shutting the door behind her. Suge let go of Sharitha so he could get a good look at her. He couldn't help but think about how different it felt being next to her after being within an inch of losing his life. She definitely made things better. Yet, in the back of his mind, it made him angry knowing some niggaz from his own hood had came for his head.

"Did you eat yet? You want me to get you something to drink?" Sharitha asked caringly.

"I'm good, baby. I just wanna lay down. I'm tired as fuck. Is your brother okay?"

"Yeah. He's at my mamma house."

Sharitha's feminine instinct to nurture kicked into second gear. She scanned the room, saw a table with a scale against one wall, and an air mattress on the floor a few feet away.

"Okay. Let's rest, baby," she told him. She put her purse down on the table and stared at the mattress. "Let's get some sleep."

He looked at her, suddenly feeling even more affectionate towards her. Sharitha was amazing. A real woman. His woman.

A short time later, the couple was comfortably laying on the air mattress together. The light was out and they were still both fully dressed. Sharitha's head rested on her man's chest. His heartbeat set her at ease. It was steady and soothing, something she so desperately needed to hold onto.

Several minutes passed before Sharitha whispered, "Marion."

Suge was still awake. He had been laying there staring at the ceiling since the light went out. His mind was crowded, but he liked having her with him. Looking at her made him feel like everything would come out right.

"Yeah, baby. I'm here."

"Are you okay? I mean, for reals. I know you're fine physically. I'm not talking about that. I'm talking about mentally. From what people are saying, it sounds like it was G-Boy who came at you. Baby, I need you to keep it real wit' me. If there's something I need to know –"

"I hear you," Suge said before taking a deep breath. He usually kept street shit away from her. Her world wasn't in the trenches. But, she was his wife. So he trusted her. "Well... the sum of it's rooted in the crab-in-the-bucket metaphor. Niggaz feel the movement is getting too big, so they mad about not getting a bigger piece of the pie."

Suge paused for a moment. For the life of him he couldn't understand how G-Boy could turn on Da Mob like that. The game was shady like that, though. It wasn't as if the scenario was impossible to picture. But G-Boy was one of his guys...

"It was bound to happen," he continued. "Better now than later."

"Why?" she asked with a concerned look in her eyes.

Suge lifted his head from the pillow to look at her, "Oh shit. I didn't tell you, huh?"

"Tell me what?" She repositioned herself so they were face to face.

"Virgil finished going over the contracts. He found some holes. It's all good. Dre and D.O.C. can start another company. Which means we can create a whole different label."

"That's great news!"

"Yeah, but that's only part of it. As far as the music goes, they're stuck with Ruthless till they finish a few more albums. And, that ain't cool. It could take 'em years to drop. Eazy can play games with their release dates if he wants to."

"Oh... okay. I can see where that can be a problem."

"Virgil gave me a contract that can clear them and everyone else that's coming with them. The problem with that is I gotta get Eazy's signature."

"The same guy you're taking these people from. Yeah... I can really see where that'll be a problem."

"True. Very much true. But, I'm gonna make that happen. I don't give a fuck what I gotta do. He's gonna sign them papers. It has to happen, and I'm not 'bout to wait. I'm pressin' play."

Sharitha didn't say anything at first. There were too many thoughts to decipher. When Marion said he was gonna do something, he did it. And if everything he was talking about came to fruition, their lives would change dramatically. House-in-the-Hills kinda change.

They fell asleep in each other's arms. Two lovers resting in the trenches of Bompton...

CHAPTER FIFTY-EIGHT

Eazy woke up in his old bedroom at his mother's house feeling both irritated and paranoid. He hadn't slept well, especially since he got word there was an attempt on Ren's life the evening before.

Not knowing who he could trust, he went straight to the studio.

As soon as he pulled up, he knew something was up. There were two black sedans parked next to one another in front of the studio's entrance. Inside the lobby, there were several armed guards.

"Mr. Wright," one of the guards said as soon as he stepped through the door.

Eazy had never seen him before, but the guard holding an Uzi knew exactly who he was. "What's happening?" he replied as he walked right passed him.

When he got to the end of the hallway, Heller's office had another guard sitting in a chair outside the door. This guard wasn't as friendly as the first one. He was a big musclebound white man who wordlessly studied the young gheri-curled thug. The door was open so he saw Heller and went straight in.

"What's up, Jerry?" Eazy said as he took a seat.

"I'm fine. I called Mike as soon as we finished talking."

"I see that," Eazy said while thinking, *These honkies ain't bulletproof. They strapped, tho'. But, I gotta be more proactive wit' my security.*

"Are you okay?" Heller asked him with genuine concern.

"They tried to kill Ren last night."

"I heard. How's he doing?"

"He's mad. He feels just like me. We can't let this shit ride. We're goin' on the offensive."

"Eric –"

"Look, Jerry!" he snapped. He was tired of all the passive aggressive shit Jerry had been talking about since everything started hitting the fan. "That mothafucka just sent some people to kill Ren. They ended up shootin' one of the homegirls we grew up wit' in the head. Blew her fuckin' brains out! Her mamma ain't stopped cryin' yet! It's already happening, Jerry! They comin' for me, and I'm comin' for them. Point blank!"

"Killing people just isn't an option, Eric. I thought I got through to you."

Eazy stared at him. Jerry just didn't understand. Probably never would.

"Have you spoken to Tracy?" Heller asked him.

"Fuck, him! Bitch-ass nigga's workin' wit' the enemy!"

"I spoke with his mother. She said he lost his voice in the car accident he was in. They say he might not be able to speak again."

"Hold up, what?! How's he gonna rap?"

"By the sounds of it, there won't be any more rapping in his future. He can still write, but it doesn't look like he'll be able to rap again."

Eazy started laughing. "Fuck 'im! Wish that'd happen to all them niggaz! Cube, Dre, all of 'em!"

The phone on Heller's desk started ringing right about then. Heller told Eazy to hold on while he put the receiver to his ear.

"Yeah... Okay. Put him on the line." Heller covered the mouthpiece and told Eazy, "It's Andre."

Eazy immediately hopped up and snatched the phone out of his hand. "Dre!"

Recognizing his voice, Dre said, "What up, E?"

"You tell me, nigga! You been wit' them slobs! You know what da fuck's goin' on!"

"Look, man, I didn't call for all'at. I don't know 'bout all'at. I'm hearin' this shit done boiled over into the streets."

"Them niggaz tried to kill Ren and ended up killin' a homegirl from the set. The whole hood is on one! The niggaz you and D.O.C. been kickin' it wit' ain't gonna be around for long."

"Man, you trippin'! You talkin' like I did somethin' wrong –"

"I'm trippin'?! You got me fucked up! I didn't start this shit. You the one trippin.' We been getting' money together. You was with me since the beginning. We started this shit! Now, you on some bullshit. Same shit Cube and that faggot-ass nigga Tracy on!"

"It ain't even like that."

"Then what is it? You wit' Suge and them? Or, you wit' me?"

"Us!" Heller cut in.

Dre heard both of them. There was a brief moment of silence over the phone. Then Dre continued, "I talked to a lawyer. He looked at the contract. E,

Ruthless was 'posed to be ours. I was 'posed to be a fifty percent owner. That's not what's on the paper. There's gotta be some changes if you want me to stay. For real! This nigga Jerry getting' paid twice! And it got me listed as your employee, E! How the fuck did that happen?"

"That shit don't mean nothin'!"

"I don't like this shit! None of it. Not the shit in the contracts or the shit that's going on in the streets! We need to fix this shit, E. We need to come to some sort of understanding."

"What're you sayin'?"

"We need to talk. I mean really talk. In person. No more of that bullshit where you put me off for another day. We need to renegotiate shit."

"I ain't been puttin' you off, nigga. I don't know 'bout the renegotiating part. We're all eatin' —"

"That's what I mean! We ain't all eatin'! The money's not getting' split right. Heller's getting' money he ain't 'posed to be getting'! What part of this don't you understand?"

Eazy looked at the man seated across from him. In his eyes, Heller was the driving force behind their careers catapulting the way it did. "What about now?" he asked Dre. "Why don't you come by the studio right now?"

"That's all I wanted to do, E. All we gotta do is talk. Come to some sort of understanding. The thing is, I'm over here at Solar recording a track. I got a few more sessions lined up. But what about you meet me here tonight? After I'm done."

Eazy had no idea Suge was connected to Dick Griffey and Solar Studio. If he did he would've never considered meeting with Dre there. Nevertheless, he thought about it for a moment. Dre was down-to-earth. Maybe he could talk him into cutting ties with Suge. If all he wanted was more money, he'd give it to him. He was more than willing to do that in order to secure his empire.

"A'ight. We can meet up. What time you gonna be ready?"

"Eleven is good. Come out here 'round then."

"Done."

After ending the call, Eazy looked at Heller. For a brief moment, he blamed the man in front of him for everything that was happening. His greed was ultimately the reason for all their problems.

It wasn't that Eazy didn't understand the way business went. The man with the master plan always got more than the others. Money always trickled from the top to the bottom. That part was understood. But Heller was greedy. He had known this from the beginning of their dealings. Nevertheless, he chose to make a deal with the devil. Which, undyingly made him a demon accomplice.

"You okay?" Heller asked Eazy.

"Yeah. Everything's all good. Me and Dre gonna talk things out. I'm gonna try my hardest to work all this out. But, first I'ma tell 'im to get that nigga Suge out our business. That's gonna be the first topic of discussion. Then we can go from there..."

$$$$$

Michel'le brought a tray full of drinks into Dre's home studio. Suge, Buntry, China Dogg, Silk and Co-Co were there with him. It felt as if she had just stepped into a war room.

Suge was the one speaking when she came in and started passing out glasses. She couldn't help but admire the way they all listened to him. Suge had an energy about him that commanded respect.

He was handsome too. When she handed him his cup, they locked eyes for a moment. For a split second she felt something. A spark of some sort. She couldn't quite place it, but there was something there.

"... You see how that faggot-ass nigga wouldn't even let you see your own contract before all this?"

"I know!" Dre replied. "He's full of shit."

"I got something for his ass, tho'!" Suge stated menacingly before addressing the others. "Blood ain't leavin' that building without signin' them papers. Onda set, blood got this comin'.'"

"We might as well take 'em to the desert and dispose of – "Silk started before Suge cut him off in mid-sentence.

"We can't kill him. I know he deserves to die. And he will when the time is right. For D.O.C. he's gotta die. But not yet. Not until we get all the contracts in order."

Dre started shaking his head, "I'm tellin' you... He's not gonna – "

"Dre!" Suge's voice roared. "On Mob Piru, I got this! I'm not leavin' that meeting till that crab-ass nigga releases y'all from your contracts! After that, we finna take over the rap game! You hear me?! We gonna start a label. Fuck around and buy a real studio! We gonna be even bigger than Ruthless! Watch!"

CHAPTER FIFTY-NINE

It was eight minutes after eleven p.m. when Eazy parked his '64 Impala in front of the Solar Studio entrance. He saw Dre's Cadillac there, too. Even though he knew Dre wasn't out to kill him Eazy still brought his .44. He couldn't wait to talk to him. Andre was right in what he was saying. Other than Suge Knight's involvement, he couldn't blame him for feeling slighted. It had taken him a little while to come to that conclusion, but in the end, he did. As he stepped out his car and headed to their meeting, he hoped they could finally end their discord once and for all.

They desperately needed to end this drama and get back to the music.

Together.

On the drive there, Eazy kept replaying the conversation he had with Heller after his talk with Dre. In a way, the conversation they had changed the way he viewed the older man.

"...My question," Heller had said, "is do you really wanna do this?"

"Yeah, man. My mind is made up."

"I'm just saying, you're talking about a lot of money here."

"So what! On some real shit, I'm not wit' getting' over on homies. Dre is the best at what he does. If it wasn't for his skills and all the work he put in, we probably wouldn't be here."

"You're wrong about that, Eric. You're playing yourself extremely short. No one comes to the shows to see him. The analytics tell us the fans come to see you. I told you all this in the beginning. The music industry is a business. A living, breathing business. And you're the main product here."

Eazy tilted his head slightly as he stared into Heller's eyes.

The man was dead serious. And Eazy believed him to a point. But, then there was the music. Eazy wasn't a rapper when it all started.

He never asked to be on anyone's stage. All he wanted to do was get paid. It was his niggaz who put him in the spotlight. If it wasn't for Dre, Cube, Tracy and them, he would've never started spitting in the first place.

"Man, fuck all'at! Dre was right! We came into this shit together. I'm splittin' everything with that nigga fifty-fifty. It's what's right. It'll squash all this bullshit and it'll keep the label together!"

That was the moment he saw the true greed in Heller's eyes. Yes, he'd gone along with everything he planned from the beginning of their introduction. Shit, he actually paid seven hundred and fifty dollars to get introduced to the man. That's how much he believed in his skills and connections. And, he couldn't deny the fact they started really eating afterwards. He had to admit all of that.

Yet, still, in his heart of hearts, Eazy knew two things: First, the fans loved that thug shit... that Compton shit. The swag he brought to the table was undeniable. His Crippin' spread like a wildfire. He even had suburban white kids rocking Raiders hats and Dickies. But, secondly, the music is what made them platinum-selling artists.

Dre brought the music. NWA brought their lifestyle out in their lyrics. The sound, the beats, the rhythm of the music was all Dre's. He deserved his due cut. And that was what he set out to give him that night.

Before he left the office, he made Heller draw him up a contract giving Dre fifty percent ownership of Ruthless Records. He knew he was losing equity, but he didn't mind. It was the righteous thing to do.

Even though it was late, the doors to Solar were still open.

The woman at the desk let him in and told him to take the elevator to the third floor. For some reason, he thought she looked familiar.

A dark-skinned sistah with a ghetto accent. He couldn't quite place where he knew her from, though. He ended up forgetting all about her by the time he stepped off the elevator on the floor he had been sent to.

When he reached the door, he was sent to, he knocked and was told to come in. That's when Eazy's whole world changed forever. The room had a soundboard with a soundproof recording booth in front of it. None of that was out of place. Neither was the weed smoke that lingered. What really fucked him up was that the room was crowded with a gang of niggaz dressed in red and black. He immediately felt out of place. But what made that even worse was how he found himself suddenly face-to-face with his arch enemy! Suge was seated right there in the center of the room.

Eazy heard the door slam shut behind him. Even if he had it in him to run, that option was gone.

"What da fuck is this?!" he growled at the crowd. "Where's Dre?"

Suge slowly got up. The cigar in his mouth made him look a little calmer than he should have been. Which was how he wanted it.

"Dre ain't here, homey," China Dogg hissed from the side.

Eazy looked at him until Suge commandeered his attention. "I already told you, Dre's my artist. If you got anything to say to 'im, you need to come to me about it.

Eazy was in the worst possible situation he could be in. He was locked in a room with twelve killers who had just signed a death decree on his whole set. Still, his Crippin' allowed no room for weakness. He held Suge's stare as if he was also 6'3", and they were the only two men in the room.

"Like I was sayin'," Suge continued, "this shit 'bout to end tonight. Dre and D.O.C. are my artists now –"

"Fuck what you talkin' 'bout!" Eazy snapped, as he reached for his pistol.

BAM!

China socked Eazy in the jaw. Blindsiding him with a haymaker that sent him and his gun stumbling onto the soundboard.

Before he had a chance to pick up his pistol, Suge kicked it across the carpet then ordered his dogs to take him into the sound booth. Still, there was no way he was going out without a fight. Eazy steadied himself and swung on Suge. Landing a solid punch to his eye! Suge immediately reacted with a two-piece before three of his niggaz started pummeling Eazy with a barrage of bruising blows to his face and head.

BOOM! SMACK! POW! PING!

They beat him till he lost his footing. When he hit the ground, they stomped him with no remorse.

"Don't kill the nigga!

"Take 'im into the booth!" Suge ordered.

Eazy fought hard, but he was no match for the parolees who dragged him into the soundproof recording booth. A whole different room connected to the engineering room. One that could be seen into, but not heard from unless the microphones were on.

They ended up dragging him into a corner where he still managed to hop up. The fight in him was authentic. His lip was busted, hair a mess, but his Crippin' was still intact.

Suge watched his Pirus whoop the smaller man for a while before he finally approached the wounded soldier. He knew he was dealing with a different beast than Vanilla Ice. Eazy-E was a Compton nigga. Which meant he was rugged. And that was precisely why Suge brought his braziest comrades. It took men cut from a certain cloth to break a demon. He knew he'd have to take Eazy to within an inch of his life to get him to do something he didn't wanna do

"Let 'im up!" Suge told his men.

Eazy struggled to get up. When he did, he still had defiance in his eyes. Defiance mixed with hate.

"I heard you was tryna have me killed? I'm right here, blood!"

"Fuck you!" Eazy spat defiantly behind a swollen mouth and broken teeth.

"You're gonna sign this contract I got. You're gonna release them niggaz, E. Straight up!"

"I ain't signing shit!"

BAM! BING! BOOM!

Suge took off on him. Eazy tried with all his might to fight back. But, again, the others jumped in. The blood-thirsty Pirus shot to the chance to put hands and feet on him. They pummeled him until he fell and couldn't get back up.

Eazy was fucked up! His left eye was completely shut. Both of his lips were swollen shut. His face was beginning to resemble a pumpkin.

Suge finally had him exactly where he wanted him. He could now take his time and be surgical about things. He re-lit his cigar as calmly as ever while his men backed off their mark. Eazy struggled harder than ever to climb back onto his feet. Suge wasn't worried about it. He took a long hit from his 'gar and blew out a large plume of smoke straight into Eazy's battered face.

"Look at yourself, E," Suge said. "It's over, bruh. I got this contract right here. All you gotta do is sign it and I'll let you go. I'm not even gonna kill yo' bitch-ass. I really should, tho'. For D.O.C." Suddenly, Suge 's demeanor became dark. The thought of what happened to Tracy angered him to his core.

"On Crip, I ain't signin' shit!" Eazy managed to say through the aching pain and swirling head he was experiencing.

SMACK!

Suge slapped him so hard, Eazy collapsed. This time, he wouldn't be getting back up.

CHAPTER SIXTY

"Hold that bitch-ass nigga down!"

Easy was still very much conscious even though the room was spinning like a tea cup.

"Hey, cuz! Cuz! Wake up, nigga!" Suge told him as he squatted down next to him. Eazy wasn't moving, so Suge told Buntry, "We need to wake 'im up."

"Hold up, blood!" Heron cut in. "I got this!" Before anyone knew what was happening, Heron kicked Eazy between the legs hard enough that his balls went into his stomach.

Easy screamed out in excruciating pain. He had never felt such agony in his whole life.

"Shut up, blood!" Suge growled. He then took his 'gar out his mouth and said, "You ready to sign?"

Eazy didn't reply. Yet, his defiant anger boiled over in the form of a single tear. Suge showed no mercy. The man lying there in front of him had tried to kill him. He took his cigar and stuck the cherry onto Eazy's swollen cheek.

"Ahhhh! Ahhhh!" Eazy yelled as his flesh burned. No one outside the soundproof booth could hear his blood-curdling screams. But the men in the booth felt his agony.

"Somebody bring me that contract," Suge called out over his shoulder. Then, to Eazy he calmly stated, "It's over, cuz!"

Eazy looked up at him. He was in the worst pain of his life. Yet, his Crippin' wouldn't let him submit. It was apparent in every fiber of his body. He would die before he gave his opps what they wanted.

"Look, man. I gotta admit, you're a soldier, E. Most niggaz would've tapped out by now. Something told me it'd be like this, tho'. So I made a few contingency plans. Your Jew... The homies snatched blood up about an hour ago. Yeah. We got your boy, Jerry. So, that's on you."

Suge knew he had Eazy's attention when he managed to open the eye that wasn't swollen shut. "Now, just in case you don't give a fuck about the honky as much as I think you do, I made another move. A little closer to home. Check this out."

Suge then took a crumpled piece of paper from his back pocket and unfolded it. He held it open for Eazy to see. "You see that, cuz? Onda set, I know you recognize yo' mamma's address, nigga."

That was it. He couldn't take any more of the torcher he was experiencing.

He couldn't let them kill Heller. And, the fact Suge had his mother's address in his hand sealed the deal.

"I'll sign," Eazy muttered. He was fucked up in the worst way. Still, he had to do whatever it took to leave that studio alive. But, at the same time, he also knew if he signed anything he'd lose everything.

Suge handed him the contract along with a pen to sign his name with. Then he pointed at the dotted line where his signature was supposed to go.

Eazy couldn't sit up. He could barely move his arms. He still managed to take the pen in his shaky hand. Then he scribbled on the paper and pushed it back towards his nemesis.

"Pleasure doin' business wit' you, homeboy!" Suge whispered in his ear before taking the contract and walking off.

Suge didn't take the time to study the signature. If he had, he would've seen the name Mickey Mouse signed where Eric Wright should've been...

$$$$$

Suge was in China Dogg's passenger seat on his way home. The contract to his future was in his hand and he was ecstatic. "On Piiiru, it's on!" he said over and over again, more to himself than anyone else. "It's on! We got it!"

"What's next?" China Dogg asked him.

"We 'bout to take over the game..."

EPILOGUE

The sun was high in the sky. The day couldn't have been more beautiful than it was at that very moment.

Suge, D.O.C. and Dr. Dre were all standing outside of Solar Studio about to make the biggest move of their careers.

Suge looked at his watch but didn't say anything. He couldn't wait to go inside and take care of business. He was a chess player about to checkmate the competition.

D.O.C. looked on patiently. Since his accident, he didn't say much. He could barely speak, so most of his communications were done in whispers. And, even that was so straining he usually stayed quiet.

Dre smiled from ear to ear, knowing what Suge was thinking. "She'll be here, dog. Sharitha's a rida!" he told his friend. He then looked at the building they were standing in front of and read the sign to himself. It said "Solar Records." Dre slapped his palms together and rubbed them against one another. He couldn't wait to take it down.

Suddenly, they all heard loud music playing from an approaching vehicle. A convertible Mercedes Benz with Sharitha behind the wheel turned into the parking lot and stopped right in front of them. When she got out, she went straight to Suge and handed him a cashier's check.

"Here you go, baby. Twenty-Five G's," she told him.

Suge could no longer hide his elation. He turned towards the others and asked, "Y'all ready?"

They all went inside to finalize the purchase of Solar's recording studio. It was officially the end of the beginning. The next chapter of their lives was just about to start...

THE CELL BLOCK

BOOK SUMMARIES

MIKE ENEMIGO is the new prison/street art sensation who has written and published several books. He is inspired by emotion; hope; pain; dreams and nightmares. He physically lives somewhere in a California prison cell where he works relentlessly creating his next piece. His mind and soul are elsewhere; seeing, studying, learning, and drawing inspiration to tear down suppressive walls and inspire the culture by pushing artistic boundaries.

THE CELL BLOCK is an independent multimedia company with the objective of accurately conveying the prison/street experience with the credibility and honesty that only one who has lived it can deliver, through literature and other arts, and to entertain and enlighten while doing so. Everything published by The Cell Block has been created by a prisoner, while in a prison cell.

THE BEST RESOURCE DIRECTORY FOR PRISONERS, $19.99 & $7.00 S/H: This book has over 1,450 resources for prisoners! Includes: Pen-Pal Companies! Non-Nude Photo Sellers! Free Books and Other Publications! Legal Assistance! Prisoner Advocates! Prisoner Assistants! Correspondence Education! Money-Making Opportunities! Resources

336

for Prison Writers, Poets, Artists! And much, much more! Anything you can think of doing from your prison cell, this book contains the resources to do it!

A GUIDE TO RELAPSE PREVENTION FOR PRISONERS, $15.00 & $5.00 S/H: This book provides the information and guidance that can make a real difference in the preparation of a comprehensive relapse prevention plan. Discover how to meet the parole board's expectation using these proven and practical principles. Included is a blank template and sample relapse prevention plan to assist in your preparation.

LOST ANGELS: $15.00 & $5.00: David Rodrigo was a child who belonged to no world; rejected for his mixed heritage by most of his family and raised by an outcast uncle in the mean streets of East L.A. Chance cast him into a far darker and more devious pit of intrigue that stretched from the barest gutters to the halls of power in the great city. Now, to survive the clash of lethal forces arrayed about him, and to protect those he loves, he has only two allies; his quick wits, and the flashing blade that earned young David the street name, Viper.

LOYALTY AND BETRAYAL DELUXE EDITION, $19.99 & $7.00 S/H: Chunky was an associate of and soldier for the notorious Mexican Mafia – La Eme. That is, of course, until he was betrayed by those, he was most loyal to. Then he vowed to become their worst enemy. And though they've attempted to kill him numerous times, he still to this day is running around making a mockery of their organization .... This is the story of how it all began.

MONEY IZ THE MOTIVE: SPECIAL 2-IN-1 EDITION, $19.99 & $7.00 S/H: Like most kids growing up in the hood, Kano has a dream of going from rags to riches. But when his plan to get fast money by robbing the local "mom and pop" shop goes wrong, he quickly finds himself sentenced to serious prison time.

Follow Kano as he is schooled to the ways of the game by some of the most respected OGs whoever did it; then is set free and given the resources to put his schooling into action and build the ultimate hood empire...

DEVILS & DEMONS: PART 1, $15.00 & $5.00 S/H: When Talton leaves the West Coast to set up shop in Florida he meets the female version of himself: A drug dealing murderess with psychological issues. A whirlwind of sex, money and murder inevitably ensues and Talton finds himself on the run from the law with nowhere to turn to. When his team from home finds out he's in trouble, they get on a plane heading south...

DEVILS & DEMONS: PART 2, $15.00 & $5.00 S/H: The Game is bitter-sweet for Talton, aka Gangsta. The same West Coast Clique who came to his aid ended up putting bullets into the chest of the woman he had fallen in love with. After leaving his ride or die in a puddle of her own blood, Talton finds himself on a flight back to Oak Park, the neighborhood where it all started...

DEVILS & DEMONS: PART 3, $15.00 & $5.00 S/H: Talton is on the road to retribution for the murder of the love of his life. Dante and his crew of killers are on a path of no return. This urban classic is based on real-life West Coast underworld politics. See what happens when a group of YG's find themselves in the midst of real underworld demons...

DEVILS & DEMONS: PART 4, $15.00 & $5.00 S/H: After waking up from a coma, Alize has locked herself away from the rest of the world. When her sister Brittany and their friend finally take her on a girl's night out, she meets Luck – a drug dealing womanizer.

FREAKY TALES, $15.00 & $5.00 S/H: *Freaky Tales* is the first book in a brand-new erotic series. King Guru, author of the *Devils & Demons* books, has put together a collection of sexy short stories and memoirs. In true TCB fashion, all of the erotic tales included in this book have been loosely based on true accounts told to, or experienced by the author.

THE ART & POWER OF LETTER WRITING FOR PRISONERS: DELUXE EDITION $19.99 & $7.00 S/H: When locked inside a prison cell, being able to write well is the most powerful skill you can have! Learn how to increase your power by writing high-quality personal and formal letters! Includes letter templates, pen-pal website strategies, punctuation guide and more!

THE PRISON MANUAL: $19.99 & $7.00 S/H: *The Prison Manual* is your all-in-one book on how to not only survive the rough terrain of the American prison system, but use it to your advantage so you can THRIVE from it! How to Use Your Prison Time to YOUR Advantage; How to Write Letters that Will Give You Maximum Effectiveness; Workout and Physical Health Secrets that Will Keep You as FIT as Possible; The Psychological impact of incarceration and How to Maintain Your MAXIMUM Level of Mental Health; Prison Art Techniques; Fulfilling Food Recipes; Parole Preparation Strategies and much, MUCH more!

GET OUT, STAY OUT!, $16.95 & $5.00 S/H: This book should be in the hands of everyone in a prison cell. It reveals a challenging but clear course for overcoming the obstacles that stand between prisoners and their freedom. For those behind bars, one goal outshines all others: GETTING OUT! After being released, that goal then shifts to STAYING OUT! This book will help prisoners do both. It has been masterfully constructed into five parts that will help prisoners maximize focus while they strive to accomplish whichever goal is at hand.

MOB$TAR MONEY, $12.00 & $4.00 S/H: After Trey's mother is sent to prison for 75 years to life, he and his little brother are moved from their home in Sacramento, California, to his grandmother's house in Stockton, California where he is forced to find his way in life and become a man on his own in the city's grimy streets. One day, on his way home from the local corner store, Trey has a rough encounter with the neighborhood bully. Luckily, that's when Tyson, a member of the MOBTAR, a local "get money" gang comes to his aid.

The two kids quickly become friends, and it doesn't take long before Trey is embraced into the notorious MOB$TAR money gang, which opens the door to an adventure full of sex, money, murder and mayhem that will change his life forever... You will never guess how this story ends!

BLOCK MONEY, $12.00 & $4.00 S/H: Beast, a young thug from the grimy streets of central Stockton, California lives The Block; breathes The Block; and has committed himself to bleed The Block for all it's worth until his very last breath. Then, one day, he meets Nadia; a stripper at the local club who piques his curiosity with her beauty, quick-witted intellect and rider qualities. The problem? She has a man – Esco – a local kingpin with money and power. It doesn't take long, however, before a devious plot is hatched to pull off a heist worth an indeterminable amount of money. Following the acts of treachery, deception and betrayal are twists and turns and a bloody war that will leave you speechless!

HOW TO HUSTLE AND WIN: SEX, MONEY, MURDER EDITION $15.00 & $5.00 S/H: *How To Hu$tle and Win: Sex, Money, Murder Edition* is the grittiest, underground self-help manual for the 21st century street entrepreneur in print. Never has there been such a book written for today's gangsters, goons and go-getters. This self-help handbook is an absolute must-have for anyone who is actively connected to the streets.

RAW LAW: YOUR RIGHTS, & HOW TO SUE WHEN THEY ARE VIOLATED! $15.00 & $5.00

S/H: *Raw Law For Prisoners* is a clear and concise guide for prisoners and their advocates to understanding civil rights laws guaranteed to prisoners under the US Constitution, and how to successfully file a lawsuit when those rights have been violated! From initial complaint to trial, this book will take you through the entire process, step by step, in simple, easy-to-understand terms. Also included are several examples where prisoners have sued prison officials successfully, resulting in changes of unjust rules and regulations and recourse for rights violations, oftentimes resulting in rewards of thousands, even millions of dollars in damages! If you feel your rights have been violated, don't lash out at guards, which is usually ineffective and only makes matters worse. Instead, defend yourself successfully by using the legal system, and getting the power of the courts on your side!

HOW TO WRITE URBAN BOOKS FOR MONEY & FAME: $16.95 & $5.00 S/H: Inside this book you will learn the true story of how Mike Enemigo and King Guru have received money and fame from inside their prison cells by writing urban books; the secrets to writing hood classics so you, too, can be caked up and famous; proper punctuation using hood examples; and resources you can use to achieve your money motivated ambitions! If you're a prisoner who want to write urban novels for money and fame, this must-have manual will give you all the game!

PRETTY GIRLS LOVE BAD BOYS: AN INMATE'S GUIDE TO GETTING GIRLS: $15.00 & $5.00 S/H: Tired of the same, boring, cliché pen pal books that don't tell you what you really need to know? If so, this book is for you! Anything you need to know on the art of long and short distance seduction is included within these pages! Not only does it give you the science of attracting pen pals from websites, it also includes psychological profiles and instructions on how to seduce any woman you set your sights on! Includes interviews of women who have fallen in love with prisoners, bios for pen pal ads, pre-written love letters, romantic poems, love-song lyrics, jokes and much, much more! This book is the ultimate guide – a must-have for any prisoner who refuses to let prison walls affect their MAC'n.

THE LADIES WHO LOVE PRISONERS, $15.00 & $5.00 S/H: New Special Report reveals the secrets of real women who have fallen in love with prisoners, regardless of crime, sentence, or location. This info will give you a HUGE advantage in getting girls from prison.

THE MILLIONAIRE PRISONER: PART 1, $16.95 & $5.00 S/H

THE MILLIONAIRE PRISONER: PART 2, $16.95 & $5.00 S/H

THE MILLIONAIRE PRISONER: SPECIAL 2-IN-1 EDITION, $24.99 & $7.00 S/H: Why wait until you get out of prison to achieve your dreams? Here's a blueprint that you can use to become successful! *The Millionaire Prisoner* is your complete reference to overcoming any obstacle in prison. You won't be able to put it down! With this book you will discover the secrets to: Making money from your cell! Obtain

FREE money for correspondence courses! Become an expert on any topic! Develop the habits of the rich! Network with celebrities! Set up your own website! Market your products, ideas and services! Successfully use prison pen pal websites! All of this and much, much more! This book has enabled thousands of prisoners to succeed and it will show you the way also!

THE MILLIONAIRE PRISONER 3: SUCCESS UNIVERSITY, $16.95 & $5.00 S/H: Why wait until you get out of prison to achieve your dreams? Here's a new-look blueprint that you can use to be successful! *The Millionaire Prisoner 3* contains advanced strategies to overcoming any obstacle in prison. You won't be able to put it down!

THE MILLIONAIRE PRISONER 4: PEN PAL MASTERY, $16.95 & $5.00 S/H: Tired of subpar results? Here's a master blueprint that you can use to get tons of pen pals! *TMP 4: Pen Pal Mastery* is your complete roadmap to finding your one true love. You won't be able to put it down! With this book you'll DISCOVER the SECRETS to: Get FREE pen pals & which sites are best to use; successful tactics female prisoners can win with; use astrology to find love, friendship & more, build a winning social media presence. All of this and much more!

THE MILLIONAIRE PRISONER 5: FREE MONEY, $24.95 & $7.00 S/H: Wish you could find more FREE MONEY like your stimulus? Seeking an end to your money problems? Look no further! Here's a master blueprint that reveals all that's available! *Tmp*

5: Free Money is your complete roadmap to finding all the FREE MONEY options out there for convicts. You won't be able to put it down!

GET OUT, GET RICH: HOW TO GET PAID LEGALLY WHEN YOU GET OUT OF PRISON!, $16.95 & $5.00 S/H: Many of you are incarcerated for a money-motivated crime. But w/ today's tech & opportunities, not only is the crime-for-money risk/reward ratio not strategically wise, it's not even necessary. You can earn much more money by partaking in any one of the easy, legal hustles explained in this book, regardless of your record. Help yourself earn an honest income so you can not only make a lot of money, but say good-bye to penitentiary chances and prison forever! (Note: Many things in this book can even he done from inside prison.) (ALSO PUBLISHED AS *HOOD MILLIONAIRE: HOW TO HUSTLE AND WIN LEGALLY!*)

THE CEO MANUAL: HOW TO START A BUSINESS WHEN YOU GET OUT OF PRISON, $16.95 & $5.00 S/H: $16.95 & $5.00 S/H: This new book will teach you the simplest way to start your own business when you get out of prison. Includes: Start-up Steps! The Secrets to Pulling Money from Investors! How to Manage People Effectively! How To Legally Protect Your Assets from "them"! Hundreds of resources to get you started, including a list of "loan friendly" banks! (ALSO PUBLISHED AS *CEO MANUAL: START A BUSINESS, BE A BOSS!*)

THE MONEY MANUAL: UNDERGROUND CASH SECRETS EXPOSED! 16.95 & $5.00 S/H:

Becoming a millionaire is equal parts what you make, and what you don't spend – AKA save. All Millionaires and Billionaires have mastered the art of not only making money, but keeping the money they make (remember Donald Trump's tax maneuvers?), as well as establishing credit so that they are loaned money by banks and trusted with money from investors: AKA OPM – other people's money. And did you know there are millionaires and billionaires just waiting to GIVE money away? It's true! These are all very-little known secrets "they" don't want YOU to know about, but that I'm exposing in my new book!

THINK & GROW RICH: $16.95 & $5.00 S/H. Unlock the secrets of building wealth and achieving your wildest dreams with *Think and Grow Rich*, a timeless classic that has transformed the lives of countless entrepreneurs, business tycoons, and even some of hip-hop's biggest stars.

In this powerful guide, which has created more millionaires than any other book, Napoleon Hill distills the wisdom of the world's richest men into a step-by-step formula for financial success, teaching you how to harness the power of your mind, develop unshakable confidence, and turn your burning desire into a lavish reality.

HOOD MILLIONAIRE: HOW TO HUSTLE & WIN LEGALLY, $16.95 & $5.00 S/H: Hustlin' is a way of life in the hood. We all have money motivated ambitions, not only because we gotta eat, but because status is oftentimes deter-mined by one's own salary. To achieve what we consider financial success, we often invest our efforts into illicit activities – we take penitentiary chances. This leads to a life in and out of prison, sometimes death – both of which are counterproductive to gettin' money. But there's a solution to this, and I have it...

CEO MANUAL: START A BUSINESS BE A BOSS, $16.95 & $5.00 S/H: After the success of the urban-entrepreneur classic *Hood Millionaire: How To Hustle & Win Legally!*, self-made millionaires Mike Enemigo and Sav Hustle team back up to bring you the latest edition of the Hood Millionaire series – *CEO Manual: Start A Business, Be A Boss!* In this latest collection of game laying down the art of "hoodpreneurship", you will learn such things as: 5 Core Steps to Starting Your Own Business! 5 Common Launch Errors You Must Avoid! How To Write a Business Plan! How To Legally Protect Your Assets From "Them"! How To Make Your Business Fundable, Where to Get Money for Your Start-up Business, and even How to Start a Business With No Money! You will learn How to Drive Customers to Your Website, How to Maximize Marketing Dollars, Contract Secrets for the savvy boss, and much, much more! And as an added bonus, we have included over 200 Business Resources, from government agencies and small business development centers, to a secret list of small-business friendly banks that will help you get started!

PAID IN FULL: WELCOME TO DA GAME, $15.00 & $5.00 S/H: In 1983, the movie *Scarface* inspired many kids growing up in America's inner cities to turn their rags into riches by becoming cocaine kingpins. Harlem's Azie Faison was one of them. Faison would ultimately connect with Harlem's Rich Porter and Alpo Martinez, and the trio would go on to become certified street legends of the '80s and early '90s. Years later, Dame Dash and Roc-A-Fella Films would tell their story in the based-on-actual-events movie, *Paid in Full*.

But now, we are telling the story our way – The Cell Block way – where you will get a perspective of the story that the movie did not show, ultimately learning an outcome that you did not expect.

Book one of our series, *Paid in Full: Welcome to da Game*, will give you an inside look at a key player in this story, one that is not often talked about – Lulu, the Columbian cocaine kingpin with direct ties to Pablo Escobar, who plugged Azie in with an unlimited amount of top-tier cocaine at dirt-cheap prices that helped boost the trio to neighborhood superstars and certified kingpin status... until greed, betrayal, and murder destroyed everything....(ALSO PUBLISHED AS *CITY OF GODS*.)

OJ'S LIFE BEHIND BARS, $15.00 & $5 S/H: In 1994, Heisman Trophy winner and NFL superstar OJ Simpson was arrested for the brutal murder of his ex-wife Nicole Brown-Simpson and her friend Ron Goldman. In 1995, after the "trial of the century," he was acquitted of both murders, though most of the world believes he did it. In 2007 OJ was again arrested, but this time in Las Vegas, for armed robbery and kidnapping. On October 3, 2008 he was found guilty sentenced to 33 years and was sent to Lovelock Correctional Facility, in Lovelock, Nevada. There he met inmate-author Vernon Nelson. Vernon was granted a true, insider's perspective into the mind and life of one of the country's most notorious men; one that has never been provided...until now.

THE PRINCE, $14.98 & $5.00 S/H. Written in the early 16th century by the astute diplomat and philosopher Niccolo Machiavelli, *The Prince* remains the definitive guide to the ruthless pursuit of power. Penned during a time of political turmoil, Machiavelli's work offers a raw and unflinching look at the tactics necessary for a ruler to seize and maintain control. With incisive strategies and a pragmatic approach to governance, this book delves into the often-treacherous reality of leadership and political maneuvering.

This edition of *The Prince,* certified by incarcerated author and publisher Mike Enemigo, is not only a timeless classic but also a masterclass in the art of power. Whether you're a student of politics or simply seeking insight into the dynamics of authority, Machiavelli's lessons are as relevant today as ever. Dive in immediately and discover why this essential work continues to captivate and educate those who dare to wield influence and power in the modern world.

THE MOB, $16.99 & $5.00 S/H: PaperBoy is a Bay Area boss who has invested blood, sweat, and years into building The Mob – a network of Bay Area street legends, block bleeders, and underground rappers who collaborate nationwide in the interest of pushing a multi-million-dollar criminal enterprise of sex, drugs, and murder.

Based on actual events, little has been known about PaperBoy, the mastermind behind The Mob, and intricate details of its operation, until now.

Follow this story to learn about some of the Bay Area underworld's most glamorous figures and famous events...

THE LIFE & TIMES OF MAC DRE: $16.95 & $5.00 S/H. *The Life and Times of Mac Dre* is an urban novel told in the voice of the Bay Area hip-hop legend as he describes his early years growing up in a California ghetto called Crest Side, in the city of Vallejo. Along the way, he encounters challenges and obstacles, leading to a thrilling journey that takes place during the crack epidemic. This memoir-styled tale depicts rapper Mac Dre's true-life experiences as he entered the music industry, became a bank robber and ultimately landed in the Federal Bureau of Prisons. With its compelling storyline and unforgettable characters, *The Life and Times of Mac Dre* is an urban masterpiece that will keep readers captivated from start to finish.

MOB TALES: $16.95 & $5.00 S/H. In 1992, Suge 'The Mobfather' Knight launched Death Row Records with a rumored 1.5-million-dollar investment from then-incarcerated drug kingpin Michael 'Harry O' Harris. Under Suge Knight's leadership, Death Row would go on to boast a roster consisting of some of the greatest names in hip-hop history, such as Dr. Dre, Snoop Dogg, and Tupac Shakur. Suge ultimately generated well over 250 million dollars selling records that detailed life in the streets.

Now, from his prison cell, Suge Knight has partnered up with incarcerated publishing boss Mike Enemigo and longtime Suge associate O.G. Silk, to create Death Row Publishing and drop a new series, *Mob Tales*, as a platform to shed light on some of the hottest incarcerated street-lit authors in the game today. Each book in this series will be a collection of stories written by those who have lived that of which they write, and who are surely to be among the next generation of street-lit legends.

THE MOBFATHER: STAIGHT OUTTA BOMPTON, $16.95 & $5.00 S/H: Suge Knight was raised in one of the deadliest neighborhoods in Compton, California. In the culture he was molded in, joining a gang and putting his life on the line for his set was a rite of passage. His inner circle was made up of killers, hustlers, and conmen – all of which had a part in creating the paradigm in which he muscled his way through life.

When Suge entered the music industry in his quest for money and power, he operated the only way he knew how – through intimidation and violence. He ignored the traditional ways of doing business and brought a new meaning to the term "hostile takeover."

But it all came at a price!

The behind-the-scenes feud between Suge and fellow Compton native Ruthless Records boss Eazy-E triggered one of the bloodiest wars the streets of Compton had ever seen. At the same time, jealousy and envy within Suge's own circle triggered a chain of events that created a civil war within his own clique. And in an environment where your closest friend can be the person who pulls the trigger that ends your life, only the deadliest manipulators are meant to survive....

The Mobfather: Straight Outta Bompton is the latest masterpiece from publishing boss Mike Enemigo and bestselling author King Guru. Based on the true story of Suge Knight and Death Row Records, and certified by Suge Knight himself, this series will have you turning pages until your fingers bleed!

COCAINE QUEEN (PREQUEL), $12.00 & $4.00 S/H. She was a loving mother.
She was also a ruthless and treacherous drug lord who's suspected of murdering more than one husband.

Who was she?

Griselda Blanco, the Queen of Cocaine, aka The Godmother.

From the streets of New York, to the ghettoes of Columbia, to the mansions of Miami, *Cocaine Queen: The Reign of Griselda Blanco*, is a based-on-actual-events story that takes you on a dangerous ride along the bloody rise to power of the most notorious female drug lord in history, as she kills anyone who gets in her way of complete dominance of the American cocaine market....

COCAINE QUEEN (BOOK ONE), $17.95 & $5.00 S/H.

COCAINE QUEEN (BOOK TWO), $17.95 & $5.00 S/H.

SOSA: KILLING TONY MONTANA (PREQUEL), $12.00 & $4.00 S/H. Cuban refuge, Tony "Scarface" Montana, had one thing on his mind when he got to America: To turn his rags into riches!

With the help of his best friend, Manny, he created one of the biggest, bloodiest, most vicious cocaine organizations in American history. But Tony made a grave mistake when he failed to carry out the hit on Orlando Gutierrez, a reporter who threatened the empire of Tony's boss, Bolivian drug lord Alejandro Sosa.

The consequence?

Death.

Sosa: Killing Tony Montana is the prequel to the upcoming, highly-anticipated Sosa saga. It details aspects of Sosa's brutal attack on Tony that the movie didn't show, such as Sosa contracting the violent hit squad of the Cocaine Queen herself, Griselda Blanco, to assist his most dangerous assassin carry out the murder, while Sosa tries to make right with his cocaine colleagues, such as Pablo Escobar, El Chapo Guzman, and the world's biggest cocaine cartel: The CIA.

SOSA: THE PRICE OF POWER (BOOK ONE), $19.95 & $5.00 S/H: The 1983 classic gangster film *Scarface* wooed over a billion fans worldwide, but it ended in the abrupt, violent massacre of Tony and his squad at the behest of ruthless Bolivian crime boss, Alejandro Sosa.

Since then, *Scarface* has birthed a nation of diehards who have been waiting decades for a Hollywood response. The wait is now over. Tony is dead, but his legacy lives inside of Elvira, who has resurfaced in the riveting masterpiece saga entitled: *Sosa: The Price of Power*. First, Sosa must scramble to pick up the pieces which were left shattered by the betrayal of Tony.

The true *Scarface* fan will be glued to the coldblooded cunning, the bigger-than-life characters who Sosa surrounds himself with, and the skilled moves he makes on an international scale. For the blonde bombshell, the game becomes life or death. Who can't remember Tony's enemies: Gaspar Gomez, the Diaz brothers and others? They are the Miami Cuban Mafia and are hunting Elvira down for the huge nine-figure fortune her husband left behind....

SOSA: THE REIGN (BOOK TWO), $19.95 & $5.00 S/H: In book one of this mega-hit series, *Sosa: The Price of Power*, Elvira appealed to Sosa to protect her from the Miami Cuban Mafia (MCM), who were trying to force her to hand over millions of dollars left by her dead husband. Surprised but eager, Sosa sent a couple of his best assassins to Miami to neutralize the MCM and muscle them into backing off the pregnant bombshell. Now Elvira (who may or may not know Sosa had Tony Montana hit) has made a new ally and friend, but with her husband out of the picture, Sosa finds himself in need of a solid business contact inside of the USA.

With Dr. Orlando Gutierrez assassinated, Sosa and his powerful crime syndicate literally has brand-new life and partners: The CIA. Sosa was expressly requested by the Americans to assist them with helping the Nicaraguan Contra Army stay afloat in the fight against the Sandinista Government. In return, Sosa demands that U.S. Marine Colonel Oliver North allow his organization – La Corporacion Mafia Cruenza – be allowed to fly fifty jets several times per week into the United States.

While Sosa, his Mafia, the CIA and President Ronald Reagan's National Security Advisor were involved in one of the most blatant and unethical conspiracies in American history, Elvira focuses on her pregnancy... and learns what real power feels like. As she absorbs that feeling, she learns also that she can't outrun demons buried in her past. To deal with them, she writes a book entitled *Dark Flight*.

It was a can of worms best kept closed....

MOB TALES, $16.95 & $5.00 S/H: In 1992, Suge 'The Mobfather' Knight launched Death Row Records with a rumored 1.5-million-dollar investment from then-incarcerated drug kingpin Michael 'Harry O' Harris. Under Suge Knight's leadership, Death Row would go on to boast a roster consisting of some of the greatest names in hip-hop history, such as Dr. Dre, Snoop Dogg, and Tupac Shakur. Suge ultimately generated well over 200 million dollars selling records that detailed life in the streets.

Now, from his prison cell, Suge Knight has partnered up with incarcerated publishing boss Mike Enemigo, and longtime Mob affiliate O.G. Silk, to create Death Row Publishing, and drop a new series, *Mob Tales*, as a platform to shed light on some of the hottest incarcerated street-lit authors in the game today. Each book in this series will be a collection of stories written by those who have lived that of which they write, and who are surely to be among the next generation of street-lit legends.

AOB, $15.00 & $5.00 S/H. Growing up in the Bay Area, Manny Fresh the Best had a front-row seat to some of the coldest players to ever do it. And you already know, A.O.B. is the name of the Game! So, When Manny Fresh slides through Stockton one day and sees Rosa, a stupid-bad Mexican chick with a whole lotta 'talent' behind her walking down the street tryna get some money, he knew immediately what he had to do: Put it In My Pocket!

AOB 2, $15.00 & $5.00 S/H.

AOB 3, $15.00 & $5.00 S/H.

PIMPOLOGY: THE 7 ISMS OF THE GAME, $15.00 & $5.00 S/H: It's been said that if you knew better, you'd do better. So, in the spirit of dropping jewels upon the rare few who truly want to know how to win, this collection of exclusive Game has been compiled. And though a lot of so-called players claim to know how the Pimp Game is supposed to go, none have revealed the real. . . Until now!

JAILHOUSE PUBLISHING FOR MONEY, POWER & FAME: $19.99 & $7.00 S/H: In 2010, after flirting with the idea for two years, Mike Enemigo started writing his first book. In 2014, he officially launched his publishing company, The Cell Block, with the release of five books. Of course, with no mentor(s), how-to guides, or any real resources, he was met with failure after failure as he tried to navigate the treacherous goal of publishing books from his prison cell. However, he was determined to make it. He was determined to figure it out and he refused to quit. In Mike's new book, *Jailhouse Publishing for Money, Power, and Fame*, he breaks down all his jailhouse publishing secrets and strategies, so you can do all he's done, but without the trials and tribulations he's had to go through...

All books are available on thecellblock.net website.

You can also order by sending a money order or institutional check to:

The Cell Block
PO Box 1025
Rancho Cordova, CA 95741